Sidetrack

To Kathy—
Marilyn DeMars
12/6/03

Sidetrack

Marilyn DeMars

NPI

Northwest Publishing, Inc.
Salt Lake City, Utah

Sidetrack

For information address: Northwest Publishing, Inc.
6906 South 300 West, Salt Lake City, Utah 84047
JC 2.7.95
Edited by S.J. Davis

PRINTING HISTORY
First Printing 1995

ISBN: 1-56901-190-7

NPI books are published by Northwest Publishing, Incorporated,
6906 South 300 West, Salt Lake City, Utah 84047.
The name "NPI" and the "NPI" logo are trademarks belonging to
Northwest Publishing, Incorporated.

PRINTED IN THE UNITED STATES OF AMERICA.
10 9 8 7 6 5 4 3 2 1

To Terry, Dennis, Brian and Mom…
who have known the real me all along.

One

A young woman in faded jeans, a white sweatshirt and sneakers ran out of Laurel Park, across Halloren Avenue and down the sidewalk toward the Halloren Towers. The wind whipped her long blonde hair into her eyes each time she tried looking back. There was a man in a business suit and sunglasses chasing her, though lacking her speed.

Megan Delany reached the tall elegant apartment building and tore inside. She hit the service button for the lobby elevators several times, saying, "Open, open." Breathing rapidly, she stepped forward and back, side to side, forward and back.

When the bell dinged and the heavy scrolled door on the left rolled open, two women and a toddler followed her into the car. The child's dawdling over the track caused a delay to the door closure. Finally they were on their way up, with Megan's floor coming first.

She got off on twelve and hurried down the hall, key ready in hand. Inside 12D she crossed the spacious beige-furnished living room, heading directly for the bedroom. It didn't take her long to empty two dresser drawers into a suitcase and pull a group of hangered clothes off the closet rod.

She heard the apartment door in the living room open, then slam shut. It was the man in the suit.

"Megan." He came charging into the bedroom.

She looked up from her packing. Lewis Sheldon, the impressive forty-two-year-old owner of Sheldon Electronics and this luxurious apartment, no longer impressed *her*.

He removed his dark glasses and shook them at her. "What the hell are you doing?"

"That's a dumb question, considering what just happened," she fired back at him.

"Come on—Megan." He was still panting from the run. "You knew about Dana."

"I do now." She pressed down hard on the pile of things in her suitcase to make room for more.

"You *knew* I was married."

"As of five minutes ago."

"From the beginning."

"You think there would have *been* a beginning for us if I'd have known?"

"Everyone knew."

"Everyone but me. How could you have kept something like that from me?"

"Megan, I just assumed—"

"That's not something you *assume*. I thought we had a real relationship."

"I thought it was an *adult* relationship."

"What does that mean? No, please, I don't think I want to know."

"Megan, listen." Lewis stepped in her way as she started

for the closet. "Just stop what you're doing and listen to me."

"There's more?" She went around him to fetch two sweaters off the shelf. "You tell me you're working late. I go to the park for a walk and there you are with this other woman. You stop and make introductions—'Megan, this is Dana, my wife. Dana, this is Megan, one of my employees.' None of that set very well with me, Lewis. Not when our living together for three months ends up with you referring to me as one of your employees while you spring a *wife* on me. There can't be more, Lewis, because that's it. The end."

"Dana and I have been separated for over a year." He started to reach for Megan, but the phone on the nightstand rang and he went for it instead.

"Yes, what is it?" he answered sharply. He sat down on the edge of the bed. "Beckermyer, that new account, yes."

As if his having a wife wasn't enough, there were always those endless business interruptions to contend with. Megan closed her suitcase, settling for the limited belongings she was able to squeeze into it. She started to leave the room, but something held her a moment more. Lewis's special ring atop the bureau next to the door. An expensive gold ring with a series of diamonds in the shape of a lightning bolt. A self-bought indulgence of his from a few years ago, symbolizing the success of Sheldon Electronics. A prized possession he wore only on choice occasions. She took it as if it were owed her. Lewis didn't see, as his back was toward her and he was reading numbers out of a little notebook to the caller.

She slipped out of the bedroom and out of the apartment, quickly, quietly, unnoticed. Not waiting for an elevator, she hurried to the exit door at the end of the hall and used the stairs. Twelve flights down, down, down.

The Halloren Towers, and picturesque Laurel Park right across from it with a pond and weeping willows, were in a wealthy area close to downtown's center of skyscrapers, stores, people and traffic. Megan went the opposite, less crowded direction by way of Ashwood Avenue. Her eyes blurred with tears and her heartbeat raced against her footsteps. She made frequent glances back to make sure Lewis wasn't after her. He wasn't.

A cold spring drizzle started to fall. Night was coming. She had nowhere to go. Though she'd lived in Minneapolis her entire twenty-six years, it suddenly seemed unfamiliar and strange.

Leon. She would call Leon. He was always there for her, a good friend. Someone she could count on to help pick up the pieces whenever her life fell apart.

She found a phone booth on the corner of a gas station lot and dialed his number from memory. "Be home, Leon...please be home," she said at the sixth ring.

"Hello?" a girl's voice answered.

Everything Megan had planned to say went blank.

"Hello?" the girl repeated. "Is anyone there?"

Megan was about to hang up. But then she heard Leon's voice coming through some shuffling sounds. "Yeah...got it...hello."

"Leon, it's me."

"Meggie?" he verified.

Her story surged forth all in one breath. "I walked out on Lewis because I just learned he's married and now I'm walking the streets with my suitcase with nowhere to go and I thought maybe I could come stay with you for a while till I get myself together."

"Married? The jerk is *married*?"

"Yeah."

There was a pause before Leon said, "Meggie, I've got someone living with me now."

"The girl that answered?"

"Yeah."

"Oh. That's okay. I mean, I'm happy for you." She shifted the receiver to her other ear and looked at the gray wet weather.

"Sorry," her friend apologized.

"Hey, you're entitled to a life."

"I hope so. So are you, Meggie."

"The one I have keeps turning upside-down."

"I know. Meggie, I wish I could—"

"I'll be fine, Leon. Except...could you maybe lend me some money?"

"I thought Lewis Sheldon of Sheldon Electronics was loaded."

"Come on, Leon...I might not have been paying rent, but you know I've been paying every cent I earn on all those bills of mine. Right now I've only got about five dollars to my name and next payday isn't until a week from today and—"

"Sure, Meggie, I can lend you some."

"Thanks."

"Meggie, are you okay?"

"I will be."

"Look, meet me at the Rusty Door later and—"

"Where?" She didn't know the place.

"The Rusty Door. It's a night club on Thirty-sixth and Langdon Road. Think you can get there?"

"I guess so. Yes."

"I'll bring you some money and we'll talk."

"The Rusty Door," she said.

"Right. It's where I hang out now. The house band is terrific. Lead singer is Ann's brother."

"I wouldn't be imposing?"

"No."

"Sure?"

"Meggie, come on—Rusty Door, later."

"Okay. See you there. Thanks, Leon."

She walked three blocks to an MTC line, caught a bus, and eventually transferred to a second one. By the time she reached Plymouth, a western suburb of Minneapolis, it was eight thirty.

The Rusty Door was easy enough to spot, with its bright blue flickering sign. She had only to go across the street and down some from where the last bus let her off. The club was a large one-level place with a boardwalk and spindle railing across the front, widespread parking to the sides and rear. Megan found its crossbuck door in good condition and only artistically painted to look old and rusty for its namesake.

She went inside, shivering with dampness and lugging her suitcase. The atmosphere was dark and smoky and already full of Friday night action—mostly young people, laughing, funning, darting about. She wandered among them. No band was playing yet, but their instruments were set up and ready on the small stage in back.

The bartender, who'd been observing her from the very moment she'd walked in, called over. "This ain't a hotel, miss."

He had gray hair and a teasing smile. She smiled back and went to take a stool before him. "I'm meeting someone here."

"I remember faces real well. Don't think I've ever seen your pretty one in here before. My name's Joe." He offered his hand to her across the bar counter.

"Megan." She shook with him.

"What'll you have, Megan?"

"Have?" She hadn't thought about having anything, only about finding Leon.

"Drink—eat—we serve good hamburgers."

She suddenly realized she hadn't eaten since breakfast. Things had been hectic at the office and she'd worked straight through her lunch hour to stay on top of it. Then when Lewis said he'd be late that evening, she'd held up dinner to wait for him, but they'd never eaten. "Hamburger," she told Joe.

"One hamburger basket coming up. I'll order it from the kitchen. Like a beer to go with it?"

"Yes. No, wait. How much is the hamburger?"

"Three eight-five. Comes with coleslaw and fries."

"No beer," Megan said. After the pay phone and bus fare she barely had enough for the hamburger, and who knew when exactly Leon would show up with her loan. He hadn't said a precise time.

The bartender signaled the waitress. Then he asked Megan, "Want me to stash your bag down here behind the bar?"

"Would you? Thanks." She heaved her suitcase up onto the counter and he took it from there. Then she got out her money and paid him.

He rang it on the register and was soon back with her fifteen cents change plus a glass of beer. "The beer's on me, Megan."

"Thanks."

"You're welcome."

When four guys, all wearing boots, jeans and western-style shirts, came striding into the club together, Megan figured they had to be the band. They greeted Joe as they passed the bar, and checked her out. She wondered which one was the lead singer, the brother of Leon's new girlfriend. She guessed she would soon find out. She wondered when Leon would get there, hoping he wouldn't keep her waiting alone too long.

• • •

Will Westin followed his fellow band members through the club toward the stage in back. The cute blonde sitting by herself at the bar really took his eye. Looking more at her than where he was going, he walked directly into a chair and fell most of the way over it.

At the chair scuffling, along with his sudden gasp of surprise, the other guys turned, laughed and heckled him. He hoped he didn't look like a complete idiot to that girl. He smiled, gave her a howdy nod, restraightened the chair and walked around it.

Before the music got under way he had to go use the pay phone in the back hall. It was a narrow area with rest rooms on one side, an exit door on the end, the kitchen door plus the wall phone on the other side. "Mom, hi," he said to the woman who answered.

"Will. Where are you? Are you all right?"

"I'm fine. I tried calling you earlier, but your line was busy. I'm just about to go on stage, but—"

"I haven't seen or heard from you in weeks."

"I know. I'm sorry. I don't know where the time goes.

Mom, I...I really hate to ask you this, but—"

"You're short for your rent again?"

"Yeah."

"Oh, Will," she said in that way she had of sounding sympathetic and disapproving both at once. "How much this time?"

He shifted his weight from one foot to the other. "A couple hundred."

"A couple hundred?" she repeated.

"Yeah."

"When do you need it?"

"How about this weekend?"

"Fine."

"I'll get over to your place Sunday, okay?"

"All right, Will. I'll have it for you."

"Thanks, Mom." He hung up but remained standing there before the phone with some shamed afterthoughts. He didn't like having to use his mother for a money tap. Except that he did. And every time he did, he hoped it would be the last. Only it wasn't.

• • •

Megan was amazed. The Rusty Door crowd seemed to have doubled in size just since she'd gotten there. Uproarious cheers and applause broke out as the band stepped up onto the wooden platform. The four members took their places among a conglomeration of instruments, microphone stands, speakers and cables. Their shirts were alike but for color. The drummer, a husky guy with shoulder-length hair, wore blue. The guitarist on the left, tall, thin and bearded, wore purple. The bass guitarist on the right, very young and wearing glasses, wore aqua.

The musician front and center, the one who had run into a chair a few minutes ago, wore black. Strapping on his guitar and approaching his mike with an air of confidence and a wide, friendly grin, he announced, "Hi, everybody! We're the Sidetracks and ready to kick it loose!"

A spotlight shone into the group. Their music began.

Loud. Driving. Instantly setting Megan's feet to tapping and head to bobbing, luring her so profoundly into the rhythm that she herself seemed to become the music.

"Wanna dance?" some guy asked her.

Before she could answer him, the waitress delivered her hamburger basket and set it before her onto the bar.

"Oh, okay…maybe later." The young man left, allowing her to eat.

Joe the bartender scurried down the inner side of the bar like a protective father. "If anyone bothers you, Megan, just let me know."

She nodded and started in hungrily on her meal.

As she ate she stayed turned toward the stage. Though her view of the band was not clear, she was able to catch broken glimpses of it through the ever-stirring audience.

The front and center musician was soon singing the song to its fullest. As his whole body rocked and twitched in time to the beat, and his fingers strummed forcefully fast against his guitar strings, his sexy voice ranged from bellows to wails,

"Why don't we say hello, hello again
Don't want to know where you are going or been
Just put reflection and direction on now
Hello, hello, just want to be your friend…"

He was definitely the lead singer, which meant he was the brother of Leon's Ann.

Ann. Megan hated that Leon was involved with some Ann. He had always been there for *her* to turn to when she needed him. Always *her* ready available old friend. Now he was taken up, seized, occupied. Even though he was coming to meet with her, talk with her and lend her some money, surely their special feeling for one another was bound to have changed, lessened. Yet she knew that she herself risked as much a while back when he'd first warned her about Lewis and she hadn't listened.

Lewis. She wondered what he was doing at that very

moment, if he was desperately missing her or if he'd already returned to his wife. It didn't matter. She didn't care. She only wondered. She never imagined anyone could fall out of love as rapidly as she had after that surprise meeting in the park. Everything she'd felt for Lewis had stopped and vanished right then and there on the spot. As if maybe she'd never really loved him in the first place. As if maybe she'd only been fooling herself all along. She wasn't sure. About that; about anything.

"Hi, Joey." It was Leon's voice speaking to the bartender behind her.

Megan swiveled her stool. Her dear friend pulled her to standing and hugged her. Though a lot had happened since they'd last seen each other, the reunion was full of warmth.

When they broke apart, he drew the girlfriend closer. "Megan, this is Ann. Ann, Megan."

There was a familiar ring to the introduction. Megan thought it felt a lot like the earlier one had between her and Dana, Lewis's wife. A lot like being out-ranked twice in one day.

Ann spoke first. "I'm happy to meet you, Megan. I hope we can be good friends, because my life is crap and I'm in real need of good friends right now."

Megan dropped her resentment of the dark-haired, petite woman, finding her humor and directness immediately likable. "Yeah, I know what you mean."

Ann kept her arm linked through Leon's. "So, Megan, what do you think of the band?"

Megan nodded. "They're good."

"The lead's my brother Will."

"So I've been told."

Leon ordered three bottles of Miller Lite from Joe. Handing Ann hers, he motioned to a table that had just opened up. "Why don't you grab it. I want to talk to Meggie a minute and then we'll be right there."

Megan sat back onto her stool and Leon stood close to her, staring, smiling, full of things to say. "So, Meggie, didn't I warn you not to get involved with that Lewie jerk? Didn't I tell you right from the start it would be a mistake?"

She deserved an I-told-you-so, but hated hearing it. "You never said he was *married.*"

"I didn't *know* he was married. Only that there was something wrong there. Something sneaky about the guy. That I did know."

"How? How could you have known?"

"I just did."

"I guess I should have listened to you."

"You should have." He gave a serious nod.

"Such foolproof intuition must predict clear sailing ahead for you and Ann."

Leon laughed. He had a cute boyish laugh that fit his cute boyish looks, making him seem younger than his actual age. "Annie's just a friend."

"*We're* just friends."

"Yeah," he agreed.

"But *we* never slept together."

"What makes you think Annie and I—"

"Come on, Leon, you were in the middle of something when I phoned earlier."

"You could tell?"

"Without a doubt."

"I'm embarrassed."

"*That* I doubt. Leon, I've missed you."

Sensitivity glistened in his eyes. "Meggie, I'd give anything to have been wrong about Lewie. Please believe that."

"I do."

"You know, I've always called him a jerk, but he turned out to be an even bigger jerk than I thought. Married—how could he do that to you?"

"I don't know." Her own eyes began to water.

"Meggie, I'm just so sorry you got burned."

"I'll never get burned again," she said as a promise.

He raised his beer to her. "Whoa—big statement."

"I mean it."

He dipped his head. "Acquired wisdom."

"I suppose so, behind the pain."

"Give it some time, you'll be okay."

"I know."

"Really."

"I know."

He motioned to the stage. "So you like the band?"

"They're great. Especially the lead."

"I've gotten to know him and the rest of the guys pretty well, I've been in here so much in the last few months. Then lately Annie started coming here, we met, we danced, and she moved in with me."

"You look happy, Leon."

"I am. And now that you're free of Lewie, we've got to get *you* happy again." He took out his wallet and gave her some money. "Will a hundred and fifty get you started?"

"Thanks, Leon."

"And when that runs out, maybe we can—"

"I really can't think ahead too far right now."

"Okay. Come on." He coaxed her away from the bar. "Let's go join Annie at the table. I want you to relax, forget your troubles, have some fun the rest of the night."

It seemed like a tall order. But with a beer in hand, motel money in her purse and a friend at her side, maybe she could try.

When the Sidetracks broke from their first set at nine forty-five, the lead singer came directly out to Leon and the girls.

"Hey, Willie," Leon welcomed him, putting the *ee* sound to his name, as he did to most everybody's most always. "Want you to meet someone—Megan Delany. Meggie, Will Westin."

An easy smile accentuated the singer's good looks. With his dark hair across his perspiring brow, and black shirt opened midway down his lean chest, he made a gentlemanly bow to her. "Hi, Megan."

She'd never met a singer before, and a stupid shyness

flushed through her. "Hi. I really like your music."

"Thanks. Leon here is our number one fan. He's at the club every single night we play."

"I thought *I* was your number one fan," Ann cooed to her brother.

Will gave her a look and shook his head. "You only started hanging out here since your divorce two weeks ago, which gives Leon a much longer standing."

Two weeks? Ann had just been divorced *two weeks ago* and was already living with Leon? It bothered Megan that he would involve himself so hastily with someone so newly divorced. It seemed like an obvious set-up for getting hurt. Didn't he know? Couldn't he see? He who was supposedly so intuitive? She passed him a concerned look, but his own look was nonchalant.

Will confiscated a chair from another table, then straddled it backward, close to her. "So, Megan...are you going with anyone?"

This guy moved fast. In fact there seemed to be something about the Rusty Door that made *everyone* move rather fast. Megan wasn't sure she was up to the pace. She had hoped to maintain what frail stability she still had left.

Will Westin awaited her answer, sincerely expecting one. Though she tried looking everywhere else besides at him, her eyes were helplessly drawn back to his. "No, no one," she answered.

Two

"Another quarter, please." Megan's holding an open hand out to Leon had become routine by late Friday night.

"Another quarter?" As puzzled as he seemed, he dug one out of his pocket just the same. "This is the fourth quarter, Meggie, on top of the hundred and fifty dollars I lent you. Not to mention all the beers I've been buying you. What's going on?"

"Maybe she's out to take you for every cent you've got," Ann jokingly warned him.

"Well, that won't take much longer." He gave Megan the coin.

She got up from the table, grinning, saying nothing. Then she walked off, sorting through the Rusty Door crowd, heading for the pay phone in the back hall.

It was after midnight. The Sidetracks were still going strong. As Megan cut across an edge of the dance floor in front of the stage, she waved to Will. He was unable to wave back, playing his guitar, but smiled and nodded. The rest of the band also nodded and smiled to her, each having been introduced to her earlier.

It was a kick, knowing an entire band. She'd come to know the long-haired drummer as Randy, the tall thin lead guitarist as Vince, and the youngest member, the bass guitarist, as Jeff. Of course the flirtatious rhythm guitarist and lead singer was Will. For all the hanging around her he'd done on each of his break times, Megan had finally begun feeling less threatened by it and much more carefree. Carefree toward him, toward the night, toward life in general. She supposed that feeling was coming from all the beer she was downing and wasn't used to, but it was wonderful to feel so wonderful.

She dropped quarter number four into the slot in the pay phone. She dialed Lewis's number, just as she had three times before. He answered, just as he had three times before. Then she slammed the receiver down hard, just as she had three times before. With a grand sense of personal satisfaction, she tossed her head and started back through the club. She passed the stage, making finger twiddling waves at the band again.

Though neither Leon nor Ann questioned her as she sat back down with them, Leon had developed a worried look. But it was too difficult trying to talk much over the music. And anyway, Megan thought her Lewis-hassling seemed like something best kept to herself. However, occasional giggles escaped her that no one else understood.

Throughout the evening she danced now and then with Leon and also with the guy who had asked her earlier and since come asking again. Sidetracks music was in her head, her feet and her soul, possessing her. She wriggled, rocked and bopped as if she would never get enough.

Megan was so wound up by one o'clock that it was hard for her to accept closing time. She was in a partying mood and felt she was only just getting started. But eventually nearly everyone cleared out and the place became cotton quiet. Even the band left, except for Will, who stayed with his attentive interest in her.

The club's simmering eventually worked to calm her as well, though she found standing still in one spot required much more effort than dancing. As her balance wavered, she took hold of Leon's arm.

"I think we should see about finding you a motel room," he said.

"I'm not tired," she whined like a child pleading to stay up longer. "I'm really not tired yet."

"It's not a matter of being tired, Meggie…it's a matter of getting you situated somewhere."

"Tell you what," Will volunteered, "I'll take her out for coffee then get her checked into a nice motel."

Leon gave him a slanted look. "I don't think so."

"Why not?" Will questioned.

"No."

"Why?"

"You're not a good choice, Willie."

"Maybe the choice is hers."

"She's had a lot to drink."

"I'll look out for her, Leon."

"No, Willie."

"So what are you, her *keeper*?"

"Yeah, sort of."

Will rolled his eyes and shifted his weight from foot to foot. "It's late. Give it up. Let me help. You can trust me."

"Don't trust him," Ann advised Leon.

"Shut up, Ann," Will told his sister.

"Meggie's coming with us," Leon decided.

Megan had had it with everyone arguing over her welfare. She flagged her hands in the air. "Hey! Stop! I'll go with Will."

As the musician went on ahead to get her suitcase from Joe, she gave good-bye hugs to both Leon and Ann. "I'm fine," she assured Leon. "Thanks for everything." And to

Ann, whom she'd really gotten to accept and like, she said, "Nice meeting you, Ann. I hope we'll be seeing lots more of each other."

Will took Megan and her suitcase out to a black Mustang in the parking lot. It was still drizzling, but Megan thought it felt invigorating and drew deep breaths of the cool moist air. "So, where are we going?" she asked.

As they drove off he said, "There's a motel not far from here with an all-night coffee shop. I think you could use six or seven cups."

The whole evening from beginning to end started running through Megan's mind like a fast-forward video tape. Hurt mixing into anguish, mixing into anger, mixing into frustration, mixing into music, dancing, laughing, drinking.

Suddenly, she didn't feel as well as she had back at the Rusty Door. She was dizzy and her stomach seemed to be rising up into her throat. "I think I'm going to be sick."

Will turned off Langdon and pulled to a stop. Megan opened her door, leaned out, and threw up along the curb. Will grabbed some Kleenexes from the glove compartment and handed them to her.

She wiped her mouth, then leaned back into her seat, embarrassed. "I'm sorry. I never drank that much in my whole life."

"I kind of figured. I also kind of figured there was a particular cause behind tonight."

She nodded, but didn't explain.

For a long while they stayed parked on the dark and desolate side street, waiting to see if she got better or worse. Megan hated that her high had crashed so soon, so ugly. She moaned and closed her eyes.

The stranger beside her decided, "I'm not going to drop you at a motel in your condition. I'm taking you home with me." He started the engine and drove off again.

Megan felt no resistance, no fear that anything worse could happen to her. Her head went down and to the side. All she cared about was sleeping.

• • •

It wasn't easy for Will to wake Megan, once they'd arrived at his place in north Minneapolis. He shook her and called her name. But she was so comfortably nested, so over-indulged and out of it, she barely budged. He stooped down beside her, on the passenger side of the car, looking at her and wondering what she was all about. Why didn't she have a home to go to? Why had she never been to the Door before tonight? How the heck many beers had she actually drunk?

When he finally got her awake, she looked thoroughly confused, as if this was the very first time she'd ever seen him.

"Will Westin—Leon's friend from the Rusty Door," he reminded her.

Nodding and muttering to herself, she got out of the car.

He carried her suitcase in one hand and led her along with the other. They climbed the inside stairs to third floor. His apartment was at the far end of the long dimly-lit hall. As soon as he unlocked the door and pushed it open he clasped his free hand around the girl's waist because she looked close to fainting.

"I'm okay," she said. "How much farther?"

"We're here. This is it."

They entered the tiny apartment, where the living room and kitchen were combined with no partition wall. A bachelor's clutter and mess gave a homey lived-in sort of look to the place...though maybe a little to the extreme.

As soon as Megan started focusing on her whereabouts she covered her mouth and said in a muffled voice, "Where's the bathroom?"

"Through the bedroom," Will pointed.

She ran off to be sick all over again.

He felt really sorry for this rookie drinker. And sympathetic to whatever underlying cause had provoked her into it. Likely a guy, he figured. He went to the kitchen area to make her a cup of tea.

When Megan came back out to the living room half of the apartment, patting a wet wash cloth to her face, she was looking and walking much better. There was some color in her cheeks again. And though her eyes were still pitifully sad, they looked bluer than they had all evening.

"I'm making you some tea," Will told her. "I think tea will help you much more than coffee. Are you okay?"

"Yeah," she replied, though her voice was thin and unsure. She pushed some rumpled newspapers aside, clearing herself a place to sit on one end of the couch.

When Will took her the steaming hot mug with a tea-bag string hanging over its rim, she managed a smile and said, "Thanks."

He smiled as well, and put himself into a frayed chair with parts of stuffing oozing out of it. "Leon never mentioned you. Of course we only talk on my breaks; that's really all we know each other from."

Megan took a couple sips of tea, then set the mug onto the end table beside her. "He's crazy about your music."

"He's a good guy."

"Yeah, he is. He's special to me. He and I go back a long way."

"You and Leon go back a long way?"

"Friends. Just very good friends."

"Friends." Will felt a surprising relief. "So, where are you from?"

"From?"

"What town? You're obviously coming from somewhere else, having a suitcase and nowhere to stay."

The cute, mysterious, blonde girl yawned. Talk seemed an effort for her and her eyes kept shutting. She curled her legs beneath her and little by little snuggled her head and shoulder down into the lumpy arm of the couch.

"Oh, no you don't," Will went to pull her up by the hands. "Come on."

"W-where…?" she weakly protested.

"Bed."

"No. No, really…I…"

He brought her to her feet. "You're taking the bed, I'm taking the couch, that's that."

• • •

Megan jumped, startled. Something had awakened her, she wasn't sure what. Her eyes scanned the darkness then fell closed again. She was comfortable. Amazingly comfortable. She wasn't sure what she'd heard or even where she was, only that she felt so comfortable she didn't care.

Another sound. Like a thud. Then some shuffling and scuffling sounds. Another thud. Voices. She sat up amidst a billowy comforter in a strange bed. Her eyes adapted enough to make out the door. There was a line of light at the bottom. The sounds she were hearing were coming from the other side. Will. She was at Will Westin's place. And that was his voice intermingled with two others. Words were unclear but argumentative. More scuffling, more thuds. Then a moan she was sure belonged to Will. Fighting. There was fighting.

Megan left the bedroom, only catching a glimpse of two guys fleeing the apartment. Bleeding from the mouth and clutching his stomach, Will was doubled over and going down. As he hit the floor, she knocked the door to the hall shut and locked it. Then she dropped to her knees beside him. "Are you all right? What happened?"

He lay motionless except for his heavy breathing. His eyes stared at the ceiling. "It's okay...go back to bed."

It was far from okay to her and there was no way she was going back to bed. She ran off to the bathroom for a washcloth. She knew where they were, having found one for her own use earlier. She wet it with cold water.

When she returned, Will was trying to sit up. She eased him back down, sticking a couch cushion beneath his head and placing the wet cloth on the cut at the side of his mouth.

He winced at the first contact, then brought his own hand up to hold the cloth in place. "Thanks. It's okay. I'm okay. Go back to sleep, Megan."

She stayed. "I want to know what just happened here. Were you robbed? Should I call the police?"

"No. Nothing. I knew the guys. I let them in."

"You knew them?" Megan gasped.

"Yes."

"*You knew them*?" she repeated.

"They came to collect the money I owe them."

"Obviously you didn't have it."

"Obviously."

"It's the middle of the night. Why would they come here in the middle of the night to collect money?"

"Go to bed, Megan." Will massaged his stomach, which had evidently been punched in addition to his mouth.

"How is it?" she asked.

"Terrific."

"How bad? Will, tell me how bad."

"I'll live."

"What can I do?"

"You can go back to bed. Look, I don't feel like talking about this right now, okay?"

She rose reluctantly. "Why don't you at least take the bed?"

"No."

"But, Will, you—"

"No. Just go. I'm fine."

She slowly backed to the bedroom, feeling extremely insecure about everything. She was not the only one with problems. Will had his own, which were far worse than hers.

She crawled back into bed, pulling up the comforter like a form of protection. She'd left the door to the living room open, to be ready for any further disturbance or if Will should need her. But things stayed calm, and Megan's weariness eventually drew her back to sleep.

The next time she awoke it was daylight. She was on her side, still hugging the comforter for all it was worth.

She rolled onto her back, and from that position took a groggy-eyed look around the unfamiliar room. There was a tall antique dresser with no mirror, a wooden cabinet, holding a stereo set, two speakers and a large collection of cassettes. A guitar stood in the corner. Clothes were everywhere, either hanging on the edges of things or in heaps on the floor, questionable as to being dirty or clean.

The sun, through the partially open mini blinds, laid bright stripes across the blue comforter. Megan wondered what time it was. What day. She had never in her life felt as foggy as she did now. Saturday. Okay, she determined it was Saturday. Probably late afternoon. Yes, late afternoon. And this was Will Westin's apartment, a musician she'd only just met last night. Suddenly she sat bolt upright, remembering what had happened in the wee hours of morning.

Still in the sweatshirt and jeans she'd slept in all night, she hurried out of the bedroom to go check on Will. He was in the kitchen, having a cup of coffee at the small table behind the couch. "Hi," he said, still wearing his black western shirt from last night, one pocket ripped and hanging down.

"Hi." She went toward him.

"Sorry about last night. "

"Are you all right?" she asked.

"Yeah, fine—shit." The grin he gave her gave him a painful reminder of his cut mouth. He touched it and became somber. He got up from his chair and went to the counter. "I'll get you some coffee. I made a pot."

She sat at the table that was laden with dirty dishes, empty beer cans, empty plastic bread bags and an unrinsed empty soup can. "I don't think I've ever slept this late before."

He brought her a filled mug. "Guess it was a rough night for both of us. How *you* feeling?" He took away the cans and bags and dropped them into the trash basket near the sink.

Though her head ached horrendously, she said, "I'm probably feeling better than you are. Will, I know it's none of my business, but I'd really like to know why those guys came and beat you up during the night."

He sat in his chair again, and drank some coffee. He gave her a long look. "I'll make you a deal. I'll tell you about my situation if you tell me about yours."

She drank some coffee. It tasted good. Much better than the tea last night. "Okay, deal. There's this guy named Lewis Sheldon, a rich guy with his own business, Sheldon Electronics. I worked in the office there. He asked me out. We began seeing each other regularly. He asked me to move in with him. I did. We were a happy couple for three months. Until yesterday…when I found out that he's married. And I split. Left him. Just like that. And I looked up my old friend Leon. Who happens to be very occupied with your sister."

Will's eyes stayed fixed on hers, as if deeply absorbing something much more than just her words.

"So what's your story?" she asked him.

"Ever hear of loan sharks?"

"They loan money to people."

He nodded. "They loaned some to me. And I haven't exactly been able to pay them back."

"And…" she prompted.

"That's it. That's where I'm at right now." He left the table and went to the living room window. He opened the blinds, looking outward and down.

Megan went beside him. The building parking lot was three floors below and two guys were leaning against the black Mustang. "That's them?"

"Yeah—Henry and Stan."

Megan shuddered. "They stayed? They're waiting for you?"

"Like vultures."

"How much do you owe them?"

"Lots."

"A totally impossible amount?"

"Totally." Will turned his face to hers. "Twelve hundred."

"Wow. Will, what if you don't pay them?"

"You saw a preview."

"Then you've got to get the money for them."

He moaned, leaving the window.

"Maybe I can help," she said.

He gave a weak laugh.

"Really, I mean it. Just a minute." She rushed off to the bedroom for her purse and returned, rummaging through it.

"Here." She gave him the lightning-bolt ring. "This should do it. Diamonds and gold. It's worth far more than your debt."

Will examined the ring, as though he'd never before seen anything like it, and as though he couldn't for one second believe Megan's offer. "I can't take this. Megan, where'd you even get it? Where'd you—" He stopped asking, and guessed. "It's hot off that Lewis guy, right?"

When she nodded, he gave the ring back to her.

"Will, wait—listen." She followed his pace in and about the furniture-congested room. "I want to do this for you. Lewis loved this ring. And now I hate him. What better way for me to get even with him for doing what he did to me? I want revenge."

"Revenge?" he said skeptically.

"Yes."

He shook his head. No, no, no.

"Please, Will." She stepped over an empty pizza box lying in the middle of the floor. "Let me put the ring to good use. I want to do something useful with it. Something good. Like helping you. Let me do that. Please."

Will walked and walked, around and around, thinking, contemplating. Finally he stopped between the easy chair and the TV. "Anyway I don't think Henry and Stan want a ring. I think they probably only want cash."

Megan scooted in front of him. "A pawn shop. Just take me to a pawn shop. Come on—before they close for the weekend. Do you know where one is?"

He went back to the window to peer down again at the four-fisted alternative by his car.

"Please, Will," she urged him. "You've got to do this. Maybe it's your only chance. Maybe it's mine. Do it for both our sakes."

"Megan, you *stole* the ring."

"I didn't steal it…I just took it."

"So what if this Lewis guy—"

"He won't. Don't worry about him. Just worry about getting these guys off your back right now."

"I don't know."

"Do it."

"Megan, I don't know."

"You need help and I'm giving it."

After what seemed like forever, Will gave a sigh and a nod and left the apartment to go down and plea bargain with the sharks.

Megan watched from the window, just long enough to see that the two guys straightened from his car and appeared to be listening to him.

Then she turned back, tightening her hand over the ring. Lewis's ring. This had to be the right thing to do, this exchange idea of turning a wrong into a right, a revenge into a lifesaver. It had to be good. She needed something good.

While waiting for Will to come back, she picked up a newspaper from the end table for something to look at. It was yesterday's, and folded open to the Horse Racing Section. Some of the entries were highlighted with a yellow marker. There was another paper with a different look. She picked it up, finding it was a Racing Form. "So this is what the money thing is about?" she said aloud to her discovery. "He's into gambling. And does this mean I am now too?"

Three

"Hi, everybody," Will greeted the Saturday night crowd at the Rusty Door. "We're the Sidetracks and ready to kick it loose!"

Megan sat at a table with Leon and Ann easily, as if the Rusty Door had become as much her hangout as it was theirs. Except that she wasn't drinking anything more than a club soda this night. Maybe she would never drink anything more than that ever again. Anyway, she wanted to keep a clear head to see how Will's meeting with Henry and Stan turned out. He said they had given him more time, but only a few hours, and would be coming by the Door later that night.

Megan hoped the loan sharks would accept the ring in place of cash, since she and Will hadn't gotten to a pawnshop before closing that afternoon. They had tried, but had run all over town to no avail. Will said not to worry, that it would work out all right, but Megan was scared. Before going back to the apartment to shower and change for the evening, he'd talked her into stopping at McDonald's for hamburgers, his treat.

Prior to stage time, Will had tried the ring on to see how it looked and felt. He liked it, admired it. Megan encouraged him to leave it on for a while, to wear it into set one. He had, and it sparkled spectacularly in the spotlight as he played his guitar and sang.

Though she wasn't sure she would even know Henry and Stan when they arrived, she kept a continual watch out for them. Neither her look at them as they'd fled Will's apartment last night nor her view of them from the third floor window that afternoon was much to go on. All she recalled was that one's hair receded far back on top of his head and hung stringly long in the back, and the other one was of a solid muscular build.

"You're doing a lot of scanning around," Leon said, leaning close to her to make himself heard over the music. "I really don't think you need to worry that Lewie might show up here."

It had been Henry and Stan on her mind, not Lewis. But now that Leon had brought up his name, thoughts of Lewis took over. She supposed by now the highfalutin business man knew her leaving was permanent. Good. She hoped so. Because she had values and limits that kept her from having anything further to do with him. Though she would have to go back for her remaining clothes and to drop her key, she never wanted to lay eyes on Lewis Sheldon again. Ever.

Ann was leaning across the table shouting to her, "So did my brother behave himself last night?"

Megan resented the question, the assumption, but gave it a nod.

"What motel did he check you into?" Ann asked.

"He didn't," Megan replied.

"What do you mean, he didn't?"

"I stayed at his place."

"I knew it!" Ann screeched.

"I'll kill him!" Leon hit the table with the heel of his hand.

"It's not like you think," Megan told them. "It's not like you *think!*" she repeated still louder. "I had too much to drink last night and got really sick after leaving here and Will took care of me."

"Took care of you?" Ann exclaimed. "Megan, Will's hardly able to take care of *himself*. Don't let him fool you. Just don't let him fool you."

Megan turned herself away from Leon and Ann, and gave up looking for Henry and Stan. She directed all her attention to the band. The Sidetracks were *great*. She felt cheated for having never heard them before last night. Listening attentively to them now seemed her only means of making up for lost time.

Will's eyes kept meeting hers as he sang,

"I saw you yesterday
You were walking my way
You smiled that smile
Hey, hey, hey..."

Randy, Vince and Jeff joined in on chorus,

"I knew you were right for me
The evidence was clear to see
Evidence, evidence
I knew you were right for me..."

When the Sidetracks took their first break of the evening, and Will came to take the chair next to Megan, his sister anxiously demanded of him, "Where on earth did you get that ring?"

He held out his hand, smiling as he looked at it. "I only wish it was mine."

"Well, whose is it?"

"It's...borrowed."

"From who?"

Will grinned, not saying.

The look on Leon's face denoted that *he* recognized the ring and knew precisely where it came from. Of course. Megan realized he'd seen Lewis wear it on at least a couple occasions, and it was hardly an item to forget.

"What's going on here?" he asked.

Will ignored the question, trying to signal down the waitress. But since she was extremely busy and unlikely to reach their table for a while, Megan slid her half a glass of club soda over to the thirsty musician. He accepted it gratefully and drank it quickly.

Leon started in again. "I know that ring and I want to know what's going on here."

Henry and Stan appeared along the right wall and motioned for Will to come join them outside. He excused himself from the table and started through the crowd. Megan tagged after him. He tried to make her stay, but she wouldn't.

Together they exited the club into the rear parking lot and met with the loan sharks midway down an aisle of cars.

"Bring your bodyguard along?" the one with the slid-back hairline asked Will.

"No," he answered easily. "But it looks like *you* did, Henry."

"You got the money?"

"Not exactly."

The guy with the muscles, who had to be Stan, grasped the front of Will's checkered shirt. "What'd you say?"

"Relax," Will pulled free. "I've got something better than money for you guys."

Henry leered at Megan. "She's a sweet little thing all right, but I'm not sure she's worth twelve hundred."

Megan closed up tight to Will's side, already regretting that she'd come along.

Will worked the gold and diamond ring off his finger. "Taking this rather than the money will set you way ahead on value. Here."

Henry refused it at first. But staring at the ring in Will's open hand made him curious enough to eventually pick it up and examine it.

"It's worth fifteen hundred," Megan stated.

Henry lifted his eyes briefly to look at her.

Will pressed his arm back against her, as a warning to keep still.

Tension slowed the passage of time. There was a steady coming and going of people throughout the parking lot—laughing talking voices a world apart from the heavy transaction occurring between Megan and Will, Henry and Stan.

Megan wondered if Will went through this sort of thing very often. Though she hardly knew the guy, she was worried about him...and right now for herself as well.

Henry finally asked, "This is the best you can do?"

Will's temper flared. "Give me a break here, guys. You think it's easy for me to part with this ring? Hey, I'd much rather part with money, but this is all I've got."

Henry and Stan held off into a private whispered discussion. Henry's thin hair rippled in the night breeze. Stan's broadness stood as a wall against any possible misdoing. After several long minutes Henry said, "We'll take the ring."

"Good," Will responded quickly.

"However," Henry added, "we'll have it appraised, and if it comes up short you'll both be very sorry."

"Both?" Will put his arm around Megan. "She's got nothing to do with this."

"Right," Henry said, leering at her again. "Not unless you're shitting us about this ring. We'll just have to take a whole lot more into account if we find out you were shitting us about this ring, Westin."

The sharks left with Lewis's ring, going for their car at the far end of the lot.

Will rubbed his head and turned a circle. "Megan, I know that ring looks valuable, but—"

"It is," she assured him.

He seemed more distracted and troubled now that things

were settled than he had before they were settled.

Megan decided to reveal what she'd found out on her own earlier. "Will, it's the track, isn't it?"

"What?" His worry changed to surprise.

"Horses. That's what this is all about, right?"

He didn't answer. He only took long hard strides ahead of her back into the club.

• • •

Gloria Westin made her very first entrance ever into the Rusty Door. She found the place crowded, smoky and vibrating with live music.

The attractive blonde woman of fifty-eight immediately felt out of place there. Wearing a red dress didn't help any. The color was too bright, too showy; everyone else was wearing tee shirts and jeans. She had come straight from her co-worker Connie's retirement party at the LaGreesha Restaurant, down Langdon Road, and had been especially dressed up for that.

The bartender was trying to wave her over—at least that *seemed* to be what he was doing. Eyes directly upon her, left hand rolling toward himself in the air. But why? Surely this greeting wasn't routine. Was it? It had to be the dress. It was drawing a kind of attention she didn't want. She was so embarrassed.

Young people circulated closely around her, making her feel all the more awkward and intimidated. She shouldn't have come here. She knew that now, except that it was too late. Blank as to which way to turn or advance with this silly notion of hers, Gloria began to take the bartender's signals more seriously.

The man welcomed her approach to his bar. "Hi. My name is Joe. Is there something I can help you with? You seem a little lost."

"Gloria." She offered her own name, as well as a half smile and an unexpected trust in this gray-haired man. "I'm looking for my kids."

"Kids?" he questioned.

"Big kids, adult kids." She made searching glances in all directions. The band was near, but she couldn't see it through the crowd of people. "That's my son singing and—"

"Will?" the bartender exclaimed. "You're Will's mother?"

"Well, yes," Gloria said with as much surprise. "You didn't think he had one?"

"*Not like you.*"

She didn't allow herself to even try and imagine what that might mean. "I guess I know where Will is, but I'm also looking for my daughter Ann. Short dark hair, brown eyes. I...I'm not real sure if she would even be here, but—"

"Right over there," the bartender pointed out a precise location. "The table near the post."

"Thank you." Gloria took his directions and left. Though she was still unable to see the stage, she listened to Will's music while weaving her way through the audience. The music was rowdy, very rowdy. And so loud that her ears ached. Though she didn't appreciate his type of music, it did make her feel amazingly hyped up. And she understood why everybody in the entire place seemed to be jiggling. There—there was Ann.

"Mother!" the girl squealed as if seeing a ghost. "What is it? What's wrong? What are you doing here?"

Gloria had been better welcomed by the bartender.

Her daughter, in tight jeans, a knit shirt and too much make-up, made introductions among her friends. "Mom, this is Leon and Megan. Guys, my mom, Gloria."

Everyone said hello to one another and then the cute young man named Leon pulled out an empty chair for her. "Can I get you a drink, Glory?" His offer was polite, in spite of his getting the name wrong.

He looked so young that Gloria wondered why *his* mother wasn't there checking up on *him*. "No, thanks. I'm not staying. I just stopped in for a minute."

"You've never done this before," Ann said, still with that startled look on her pixy face.

"No," Gloria admitted, feeling as though she were committing some sort of crime. It was obvious that Ann wasn't happy with her being there. But then Ann hadn't been happy with much of anything Gloria had or hadn't done in a long while. "I'm here to see Will about something."

Ann was no further pleased.

"And," Gloria said, extending her reason, "since I'd heard this had also become *your* latest spot, I thought I'd try tracking you down and saying hi to you as well."

Embarrassed as Ann seemed to be, Gloria felt she had the right to keep reasonable tabs on her children, no matter what their ages. And if they would no longer come to her, then she would go to them, wherever that happened to be. Anyway, hadn't Ann distressed *her* enough over the years? Eloping on a whirlwind marriage, which Gloria knew nothing about but wouldn't have approved of if she had. Then divorcing the guy after six months, without even giving the marriage a fair try, only to start running around doing bars and who knew what all.

With a good view of the stage from the table, Gloria turned her complete focus over to the Sidetracks. She'd never seen Will sing professionally before. She guessed it was about time. She was impressed with how he looked and sounded. There seemed to be such emotional drive to his music. Everyone in the entire club seemed in tune with one another, as if there were a significant energy exchange going on between the crowd and the band, the band and the crowd. The only thing Gloria didn't get was, "Don't they ever play anything *decent?*"

"Mother!" Ann raved. "Rock 'n roll is the only decent thing you *can* play in a place like this."

Though Gloria caught snickers coming from both Leon and Megan, she asked, "Don't they ever play *slow* songs? I really prefer slow songs."

"Me, too," someone standing beside her said. She looked up. It was Joe, the bartender. He handed her a glass of beer, saying, "It's on the house."

Gloria didn't like beer. But it pleased her to know that

someone else in the place might be on the same music level as she. "Thank you," she told him.

"You're welcome." His eyes narrowed into a warm, friendly smile, then he turned to go back to his station behind the bar.

"That was Joe." Ann thought she was telling her mother something.

"I know," Gloria said, and took a brave sip of the amber beverage. She made a face at its taste, causing her daughter to burst into laughter.

It sounded good to hear Ann laugh, despite the reason. But it made Gloria wonder all the more about the real balance of her daughter's happiness.

When the band took a break, Will came out to the table to greet the newcomer. "Mom—I can't believe you're here."

"Neither can I." Her surprise equaled his.

"How do you like the music?"

Gloria adored Will, even though she'd never understood his career choice and felt he was giving up too much self-worth as a musician. He was good looking, almost the spitting image of his father when he'd been that age. The age at which John Westin had walked out on her and the kids many long years ago. And these days it pretty much seemed that both Will and Ann had walked out on her too, with their busy, grownup, indifferent lives. She smiled softly, overlooking and forgiving as a mother always could. "Your music is lovely, dear."

"Lovely?" he grimaced.

"Hot," Ann stated. "It's what you call hot!"

Gloria noticed the cut by Will's mouth. "My goodness—what happened to you?"

"It's nothing," he claimed.

It was more than nothing to a mother.

Ann and Leon both sprang forth to take closer looks at Will's mouth. But Megan's staying back made Gloria wonder if Megan had been the one who smacked him.

"I don't believe this," Will said of the drink sitting before his mother. "A beer? You're actually drinking a beer?"

"Joe himself paid for it and brought it over to her." Ann's eyebrows arched playfully, telling her brother.

"He seems quite nice," Gloria said.

"Mom, he's a *bartender,"* Ann reminded her.

"Well, I'm not marrying him, for pete's sake…not that marriage seems to mean anything these days."

"So you've met everybody?" Will asked.

"Yes." Gloria thought Megan and Leon made a suitable couple.

But when Will squatted down close to Megan's chair and draped an arm around the girl, the whole picture changed. As for couples—it now appeared to be *he and Megan* and *Ann and Leon.* It felt like a double whammy shock to Gloria.

She was glad when Will whisked her away from the table saying, "Come on, let's find a place to talk."

They went a short distance to stand along a side wall, as if that were a good place for a mother-son talk.

Will's eyes looked away from her more than at her. "Mom, I really didn't expect you to come here like this."

"You're embarrassed."

"No, that's not it."

"Ann's embarrassed too."

"No, I think we're both just surprised to see you here, that's all. Because it's definitely not your thing."

"Like I'm not allowed to do something different?"

"I thought we planned that I would come to your place tomorrow. You could've waited."

"You *are* embarrassed."

"No, I'm not."

"You wanted me to wait."

"I just said you *could* have. You didn't have to come into a bar alone like this. You're the one who seems embarrassed about it."

"I am…a little. It's just that I was so nearby I thought I might as well stop in with your money. I came directly from Connie's retirement party at the LaGreesha. You remember

Connie. It was a very nice party…I mean, if one needs to face retirement. I dread the coming of mine."

"Mom, you've got a while yet."

"A while. Anyway, you asked for a loan and I just thought it would be handy for me to bring it by. I thought I could *do* that."

"Well, *I* wouldn't have thought so," he said laughingly.

"Will, I didn't know you had a new girlfriend already since Chris."

"Julie," he corrected her. "Julie was the last one, Mom. Chris was before her. And Megan is not a girlfriend."

Gloria saw what she saw. "Megan happened rather fast to you, didn't she? Like all the others."

"She's not like the others."

"How long have you known her?"

"You're not listening. I'm telling you she's not a girlfriend."

"You had your arm around her."

"It meant nothing."

"Exactly my point."

"What?" He squinted his eyes at her.

"Honey, I wish you'd settle down…slow down. Build a serious life for yourself. Find a nice decent girl. A *dark-haired* girl. The kind you can really trust and—"

"Mom, *you're* blonde."

"Well, uh…not basically," it pained her to say. "Dear, you have to watch out for—"

"I certainly don't have to watch out for the color of a girl's *hair*. And anyway, Megan's more Leon's friend than mine."

Gloria brightened. Maybe she'd had it right to begin with. "Oh…then she's *Leon's* girlfriend?"

"No, not *girl*friend. Just friend. *Ann* is Leon's girlfriend."

"Oh." Gloria's enlightenment dimmed. She dug into her purse for the money. Two hundred dollars this time. This time…this time…she always hoped it would be the last. That Will would finally be able to start managing his finances without her help. But his needy times were frequent, and she worried about him, and was always there to hand it out.

"Thanks, Mom." He didn't even count it before sticking it away into his pocket. "I hated asking you, but—"

"But it seems you're always coming up short for your rent."

He dropped eye contact with her and spoke to the floor. "Yeah, seems so."

"You're a smart boy, Will. You could get yourself a much better job than playing music in some bar."

His look returned, in that quick defensive way he always had over his music. "This is more than just some bar, Mom. It's a club."

"Whatever."

"And we're the house band here which means we no longer need to scrounge up new gigs every week. It's a set thing. A status-building thing."

She wasn't so sure. "It doesn't mean you're getting stuck in some kind of rut?"

"It's not a rut. It's what I like doing, you know that."

"I do know it's not paying your rent regularly."

"I'll make it up to you, Mom."

Gloria laid her hand on his arm. "Just make it up to *yourself*, Will. That's all I want. For you to want better for yourself, and then to obtain it and hold it."

She loved him so much. It felt good seeing him, talking to him. When his head went down again she wanted to brush his hair off his forehead, put her arms around him, and hold him. But they were in public, and he was twenty-eight years old, and this wasn't the time or place to be that motherly. "I've got to go, dear. You take care."

"Yeah. You, too, Mom."

As Gloria passed the bar, leaving the front way, Joe the bartender smiled and waved good-night.

• • •

Vince and Jeff came from the band over to Will almost the moment after his mother had left.

"Hiding out?" Vince asked accusingly.

"No," Will said.

"So why are you standing way over here?" Jeff charged him equally.

"Is there a law against it?" Will snapped.

"Might be." Vince had a slight smirk on his face.

Will owed him money. From the all-night poker game last week that ran him way over his bankroll. What timing. The guys must have seen the money transaction between him and his mother and Vince wanted to collect.

He took out his wallet. The money in it had hardly cooled. It was for rent, only now part of it was going elsewhere. "Let's see...sixty, wasn't it?"

Vince nodded, looking surprised, as if maybe he *hadn't* been hedging for any money right then and there.

"Here." Will shoved three twenties at him.

Vince took it. "Thanks."

"Where's mine?" Jeff jokingly held out his own hand to Will.

The real joke was that Will wasn't really sure if it *was* a joke or not. "Do I owe you?"

Jeff laughed. "No. Kidding, just kidding. I'm not into this gambling stuff like you guys. Not me. I'm saving up for my future. I take my money seriously. It goes straight into the bank and stays there."

Will felt like telling Jeff the do-gooder *fine for you, you little wise-ass*. But he didn't. Maybe Jeff's discipline was to be envied and learned, not ridiculed.

Vince thanked Will again for the payoff, then he and Jeff walked off. Will leaned against the wall for a few moments before returning to the table. Maybe someday money wouldn't be such a hassle. Just maybe.

• • •

Megan's eyes had taken in the entire scene from where she'd sat. Will standing there talking with his mother and her passing him some money, then Vince and Jeff talking with him and Will paying Vince some money. It made her sure that Will's financial problems went a lot deeper than the loan sharks and the racetrack.

He returned in an elated mood she wouldn't have expected. "I'm buying a round of drinks," he said. "What does everybody want?"

"I want to know," Leon took the opportunity, "why Megan doesn't have a motel room yet. You said you were going to look out for her, Willie. I trusted you."

Before Will could say anything, Megan spoke. "Leon, I told you, we haven't had a chance yet."

"What do you mean, you haven't had a chance yet?" Leon's voice grew harsh.

"We've been busy," she said.

"Busy?" His look switched back and forth between her and Will. "I don't think I like what's going on here."

"Come on," Ann coaxed him to his feet and away from the table to go dance with her. A new disc had just started on the jukebox, which was temporarily replacing the band. "I *love* this song."

As the two left, Will laughed and asked Megan, "Are we in trouble here or what?"

She laughed about it, too. "Leon can act like a bratty brother sometimes."

"He cares about you."

"Yeah, like a bratty brother."

The waitress came with three beers and a club soda. Will paid her, along with a generous tip and a flirty smile.

"Your mom is real neat," Megan told him when they were alone again.

Making no comment, he took a drink from his bottle.

"I'm glad we got rid of those sharks," she said.

He nodded wordlessly. He seemed to have dipped into a low mood now.

"Will, are you mad that I found out about your playing the horses?"

"Mad?" he asked.

"I saw those marked racing papers in your apartment."

"Everybody knows I play the horses. It's no secret,

Megan. I'm just sorry for getting you mixed up with it."

Then what, she wondered, was so wrong? Something. Something else was consuming him. She gave it some time.

Eventually he came out with, "Megan, I've been thinking...you could just continue staying at my place if you'd want to."

That? That was what had been going on in his head? "No," she answered him firmly and precisely.

"Why?"

"*Live* with you?" she asked.

"Yeah."

"No." Her answer was the same.

"Why?" he asked again.

"Because that's not what I want, Will."

"Until you *get* what you want."

"I don't believe this." She shifted uncomfortably in her chair. She glanced away from him, then back. "Will, another involvement is the last thing I want right now."

"Hey, me too." He held his hands open in the air, insuring it would be a hands-off deal. "Look, I was just thinking financially for both of us, that's all. I'd been considering getting a roommate to help share the rent anyway—might as well be you. I mean, if you want. What do you say? You can have the bedroom."

"No."

"Why? You got any place better to go?"

"Will, I don't even have a job."

Randy, the drummer, came, searching Will out. "Hey, man—it's show time."

"Okay," Will told him, though he stayed seated with his eyes fixed on Megan.

Vince and Jeff, on stage, were strapping on their guitars. Feeling responsible for delaying the Sidetracks, Megan spoke in a nervous rush. "At least I *assume* I don't have a job anymore, and I wouldn't even consider going back to it if I did still have it."

"Sheldon Electronics?"

"Yes." Her statement made her face the fact that she was homeless, jobless and broke. "How *much* rent?"

He grinned in that way of his. "Half of five-fifty."

"That would be two seventy-five."

"Right." His grin continued working on her.

Randy was doing some light drumming on stage, while Will stayed at the table, waiting for Megan's answer.

"I don't know," she said, beginning to reconsider.

"It's a good deal, isn't it?"

"Not if I'm not even working."

His blue-gray eyes kept watching her. "You'll get another job, Megan. Till then your credit is good with me. Come on."

"I don't know."

"Say yes." He got up from the table. He had to go, the band was waiting. "You can have the bedroom, I'll take the couch."

"No. No, *I'd* take the couch."

"We'll take turns."

"Turns?"

"Week by week." He offered his hand to her.

She took it. They shook. The deal was made.

Will hurried onto stage, putting his usual energetic opener into the mike. "Hi, everybody! We're the Sidetracks and ready to kick it loose! Again!" The music exploded, igniting immediate life back into the Rusty Door.

Leon and Ann stayed on the floor for a couple more dances before returning to sit with Megan. When they came back, Megan told Ann. "Your mom is real pretty."

"Thanks." The girl seemed bored with it.

"Do you have a dad?"

Ann played with her napkin. "No. Yes. What I mean is that my mother is divorced. Will and I haven't seen our so-called dad since we were babies."

"I'm sorry." Megan could tell that Ann was sorry too, even though she tried acting cool about it. "That must have been hard."

"What about *your* family?" Ann asked back.

"None," Megan replied. "I have none...only Leon. He's the closest thing to family I have."

"Kind of like a brother?" Ann assumed.

Megan gave Leon a fond smile and a hard, but playful, jab. "Yeah—a brother."

Leon slung his arm around her with mutual admiration, but no jab.

All sweetness dissolved, however, the moment Ann left to go to the ladies room and Leon confronted Megan with, "What about the ring?"

She hated the topic. Following a sigh she claimed, "Nothing."

"You break up with Lewie, get instantly cozy with Willie, then suddenly Willie is wearing Lewie's ring. That's not nothing, Meggie, it's something."

"He's not wearing it now, is he?"

"No. All the more mystery. For which you owe me an explanation."

Leon was fine in his place, but sometimes, like now, he overstepped it. "First of all, Will and I are not *cozy.* And secondly, all I owe you, Leon, is a hundred and fifty dollars."

"Yeah, that too, but—"

She whipped out the unused money from her purse and forced it upon him. "Here, take it back."

He was all the more bewildered. "I don't understand. Not that I ever fully expect to with you, Meggie, but—"

"I won't need it after all," she said smugly. "I'm going to be living with Will."

"*What?*" Leon exclaimed.

"For a while."

"*What*?" he said again.

She got up and left him, heading across the club toward the bar. Joe was pleased to see her.

"What can I do for you, Megan?"

She pointed to the HELP WANTED sign posted behind him. "What *kind* of help?"

"Waitress. You interested?"

"Full time?"

"Forty hours."

"A week?"

"A week."

"I'll take it."

"Whoa, whoa," he laughed at her. "Maybe we're not so sure we'll take *you.* Any experience waitressing in a club?"

"No."

"In any place?"

"No."

"So why would you want this job?"

"Because."

"Oh, now there's a reason."

"I need a job."

"There are other jobs to be had."

"A change of pace."

"You like the *pace* here?"

Megan's patience snapped. "What kind of interview *is* this?"

"It's not. You'll have to talk to the manager for an official interview. His office is right over there." Joe pointed to a door on the side wall just beyond the bar.

"Thanks." Megan went to it.

The door fronted a sign reading MANAGER. She knocked and someone called to come in. She entered a small wood-paneled room.

A guy who looked about Lewis's age glanced up from his desk. He had a thick mustache and a cocky smile. He flicked his cigarette ashes into an ashtray, waiting for her to speak first.

"Are you the manager?" she asked

"That's me, Nick Gerard. And who might you be?"

"Megan Delany. I'd like to apply for that waitress job."

"Okay," he said. "You're hired."

Four

"Thanks for coming with me," Megan told her new friend Ann as they entered the Halloren Towers together Sunday afternoon.

"I'm glad you asked me." Ann turned circles observing the lobby's mauve-printed wallpaper, thick green carpeting, crystal chandeliers and large leafy floor plants. "I had no one supporting *me* when I left *Alan.*"

"Not even your mother?"

"Especially not my mother. Wow, you *lived* here? This place is awesome. How could you leave it?"

"Your mother seems so nice."

"She is, but she's too controlling. Her trying to control me and Will only tended to drive us away from her."

"Controlling?" Megan found it hard to understand, having no mother of her own.

The elevator on the right dinged and opened and the girls got on. Ann marveled at its interior of cream colored walls patterned with black velveteen piping.

Megan had her empty suitcase. It would hold the rest of her things. She'd phoned prior to coming and Lewis wasn't there, giving her the chance to get her belongings without hassle. But going down the twelfth floor hall to 12D, she began to feel nervous and was glad having Ann along.

"Wow!" Ann exclaimed at the spacious living room of plush beige furniture and coordinating accessories. Walking on tiptoe, she followed Megan into the bedroom.

Megan set her suitcase on the king-size bed.

Ann smoothed a hand over the satiny blue and green floral spread. "Wow! Not a wrinkle. It's so perfect...everything is so perfect. Whoops, sorry...I guess not everything."

Megan shook her head and smiled. "It's okay. I'm not hurting over this break-up like you'd think. I did at first, like I thought I'd die, but I'm okay now."

"Pretty fast recovery."

"Yeah, it was. The anger just sort of took over the pain. I...I just have all this anger toward Lewis now."

"Did you love him?"

Megan opened her suitcase and stared down into the emptiness of it. "No. I guess not. Otherwise I couldn't have gotten over him so fast."

"Are you? Over him?"

"Yes."

"Because he sprung a wife on you? Or because you didn't love him?"

"You know, Ann, I honestly don't think I really even know what love is. Do *you?*"

"Hey—I'm newly divorced—are you kidding? I'm probably more disillusioned about it than you are."

"What about Leon?"

Ann rolled her eyes and laughed. "I don't know about

Leon. I guess I, too, have become very cautious about what's to be considered love. So I'm settling for *like* right now. I do know I like Leon. How about you and Will?"

"Come on, Ann, we just met."

"But you're living together."

"Sharing the apartment, the rent, that's all."

"Well, as his sister I have to warn you, Megan, Will is a fast worker."

"At what?

"Do you think it would be okay for me to stretch out on this gorgeous bedspread? Just for a minute? To feel what it's like? If I smooth it right out again?"

Megan laughed. "Go ahead—a bedspread is *not* something you need to be cautious about."

"Unless, of course, there's a man on it." Ann lay across the satiny fabric, closing her eyes, sliding her arms about, enjoying every luxurious inch of it.

Megan emptied the last dresser drawer that had been hers, took her clothes from the closet, collected three remaining pairs of shoes, then checked the bathroom. There were still her curling iron, hair spray, hand lotion, and some head bands to clear out. Then there would be no trace left of her for Lewis. Nothing.

It wasn't long before she was closing her filled suitcase and sighing with relief. "That's it. Let's get out of here, Ann." She tossed her apartment key onto the center of the restraightened bed, and they left.

The girls waited at the elevators.

"Why am I feeling like a thief on the run here?" Rather than commenting on fine decors now, Ann was taking quick skittish looks up and down the hallway.

Though Megan herself felt edgy, she pretended otherwise, bouncing on her toes, swinging her suitcase casually. "It's my stuff and I have the right to come and get it."

"I know. But it just feels like we're going to get caught or something."

"We're not."

"I know, but it feels like it."

One of the elevators dinged and its heavy door rolled open. Just as Megan and Ann were about to step into it *Lewis stepped out,* nearly walking right into them. Both girls screamed.

Megan still tried to catch the car, but Lewis blocked her way until the door closed again. She punched the service button six times.

"Take it easy," he said, his appearance just as spiffy as ever in a navy blue pin-stripe, broomstick posture, and sunglasses. He tilted his glasses downward, concentrating his look over the top of them.

"Don't tell me to take it easy." Megan hit the service button another six times.

"I've been worried about you." He sounded almost sincere enough to believe.

But Megan stayed wise of the trap. "I'll bet."

"I want to talk to you."

"No."

"There are things I need to explain."

"There's no need."

Lewis set his look on Ann. "Aren't you going to introduce me to your friend here?"

"No," Megan said.

"You're being rude."

"Don't tell me about rude."

"There are also some things *you* need to explain, Megan. Like where's my ring?"

"What ring?"

"You took it."

"Did I?"

"I know you were upset, but stealing is criminal."

Megan thought she heard the hum of an elevator coming. She switched her suitcase from her left hand to her right hand and stood ready.

"I want it back, Megan." Lewis poked his shades back in place, staying resolute.

"What?" She played innocent.

"My ring."

"I don't have it."

"You know what it means to me."

"I don't have it." It was the truth, she didn't.

"We'll see about that, we'll just see about that."

The elevator dinged and opened. Megan and Ann hurried on.

As the door was shutting, Lewis shouted, "I knew it was you making those slam down phone calls the other night, Megan! I knew."

Neither of the girls spoke on their ride to first floor, nor as they rushed through the lobby. Only outside, going down Halloren Avenue, did Ann cut loose on Megan. "I'm really curious about the phone calls, but mostly I want to know about the ring. Is that the one that Will was wearing last night?"

Leon was waiting just down the block, standing against his gray beater car with his arms folded. He was glad to see Megan and Ann return. "Get everything?"

"Yes." Megan handed him her suitcase.

He put it in the back seat and she got in beside it. He and Ann sat in the front. "See Lewie?" he asked. "Because I thought it was him going into the Halloren a few minutes ago."

"Yes." Ann did the answering. "He scared the crap out of us."

"Well, I'm glad you're through with him, Meggie." Leon gave her a quick look over his shoulder before driving off.

They left downtown, taking Highway 55 west.

Ann turned as far around as her buckled seat belt enabled her, to see Megan as she spoke. "Okay, tell me about the ring now."

"*Lewie's* ring," Leon exclaimed, just as interested. "Yeah, Meggie, tell us about it."

Ann cut ahead of Megan with her own assumption. "You stole it from Lewis when you left him the other night, didn't you. Then gave it to Will."

Megan thought it was ironic, escaping Lewis's questions only to contend with this. "Sort of...but not exactly."

"Why don't you just tell us *exactly,*" Ann demanded. "Megan, Will is my brother and I think I have the right to know what you're involving him in here."

"It's no big deal."

"It sounded pretty big to Lewis just now. And what about Henry and Stan?"

"You *know* about Henry and Stan?" Megan had been so sure they were underground secrets.

"Yes, I know who they are," Ann spoke as if there was an unpleasant taste on her tongue. "They're loan sharks. And after Will came back from talking with them last night he was no longer wearing the ring."

"I can't believe you know Henry and Stan." Megan was still hung up on that much.

Ann's dark eyes sparked with knowing. "They're a couple of dirty rotten bums who prey on people like my brother. Will gambles. If he wins, he gambles more. If he loses, he borrows money to try and win it back. It's a vicious circle, and Henry and Stan are there to keep it going. God, Megan, how did you get sucked into this so fast?"

Megan closed her eyes, fearfully wondering the same thing. Had she lost such control that she knew absolutely nothing about what she was doing, where she was going? Had she only exchanged one mistake for another? Everything seemed to be spinning, spinning.

When she dared open her eyes again, it was to the tight noisy traffic encompassing the car. There was nothing calming to latch onto. At least not at that point. Except maybe that Leon was a good driver and this was his control.

She tried explaining. "When I left Lewis, I took his ring to get even for what he did to me. The whim hit me as I was leaving. Then I found out about Will's debt to Henry and Stan, when they knocked him around in the middle of the night. I made him take the ring to pay them off. I feared for his life and wanted to help him."

"Help him?" Ann raged. "That's like giving drugs to a junkie or booze to an alcoholic. Megan, that's not helping Will any."

Tears welled in Megan's eyes, for good intentions gone bad.

"I don't mean to come down on you," Ann softened, still straining against her seat belt to face Megan as squarely as possible. "I just want to make you understand something here. Other girlfriends of Will's have *left* him because of his gambling, but I think you're the first that's actually *contributed* to it."

"I'm not a girlfriend," Megan clarified.

"I know, you told me. But does *Will* know?"

"And I didn't know that I was contributing to a gambling addiction when I gave him that ring."

"Right. Like you thought maybe the guys who roughed him up were credit collectors against all that fine furniture he owns?"

"I didn't think who they might be, just that they were to be feared."

"Still...it sounds like a valuable ring, and you just forked it over to Will like nothing."

Megan's head was crowded and aching. "It's a done deal. Can we just forget about it?"

Leon glanced over his shoulder. "Meggie, is Lewie really going to let you get away with this?"

She hoped so. She only hoped so. "He has tons of money and tons of possessions. He'll forget about the ring just the same as he'll forget about me."

"Lewie doesn't strike me as a guy who forgets."

"Maybe I don't even care."

Leon glanced back at her again. "I don't think I know this side of you, Meggie."

She raised her chin and blinked her eyes. "It's new."

"Megan," Ann said in a warning tone, "you just detached yourself from a louse like Lewis...maybe you don't need to go right into an involvement with somebody like Will."

"You're saying your *brother* is a louse?"

"No, that's not what I'm saying. It's just that he—"

"Ann, there's nothing going on between Will and me. And there won't be. So I don't know why you even say things like this."

"You paid off his gambling debt. I'd say that's something."

Megan exhausted a long heavy sigh. "Maybe it was more like paying off *my* debt than Will's—where the ring is concerned."

"*Your* debt?" Leon questioned.

"My getting-back-at-Lewis debt."

"Megan," Ann's voice became more sympathetic than accusing, "just realize that Will's gambling is something beyond a hobby or a game. It's got a serious hold on him. Like a sickness. And he pulls others into it with him with his irresistible desperation. For instance, and I hate to admit this, he's into me for two thousand, Leon for several hundred and Mom for heaven only knows how much."

Megan felt overwhelmed—in over her head.

"It's true," Ann assured her.

"You're saying that you're all supporting his habit?"

"Not anymore. At least not Leon and me. We've drawn the line. I think Mom's still blind as to what exactly Will is doing, but don't you be, Megan. Be careful. That's all I'm saying."

Megan slid lower down in her seat, wishing she could disappear from all that seemed wrong.

Leon tried to cheer them up. "Let's do lunch at Taco Bell."

• • •

"Yes! Yes!" Will shouted, waving his winning ticket in the air and jumping up and down as he watched Wind-Donner cross the finish line first by a nose. Since the horse had not been a favorite, the payoffs would be good. Real good.

He headed for a mutual window to collect. He'd played

his hunch exactly right on this race, calculating the Racing Form statistics, going against the odds to stick with his belief in Wind-Donner.

The teller counted out four hundred and eighty-five dollars to him. "Nice going."

"Thanks," Will said, then handed part of the money directly back to him. "A hundred and fifty on Rex's Reason to win in the third."

With a good remainder of winnings still in his pocket and a hopeful ticket on the next race, Will stopped at a concession stand to purchase a thick bread-like pretzel knot. Then walking as he ate it, he went outside to take a bench seat and wait for post time.

His thoughts momentarily left the track to think about the girl he'd taken into his apartment to share the rent. He liked her. A lot. She was easily the kind he could fall for, and almost literally did, that first night he'd seen her. But no, he was in no position to get involved at this time. He'd had it with relationships for a while. Needed to be free for a while. This association with Megan was strictly financial. He had finances up to his neck to straighten out, and cutting the rent in half would really make a difference. Plus…it could expand his monthly gambling purse nicely.

He finished his pretzel, feeling confident as hell about everything. He was glad Megan Delany happened to him. Especially since she wasn't the kind who was looking for close ties or romance, but only a manageable living arrangement. She was his lucky break. Yes! Happening to him in good timing. Yes! She…with the long, loose-flowing blonde hair, clear blue eyes, sweet voice, giggly laugh, desirable body.

The horses paraded onto the track, going toward the starting gates. Rex's Reason looked good. He was about to go off at 9-2. Fair odds, a mid favorite. Will clutched his ticket tightly in his hand. Excitement swelled within him, directing all his faith and urgency into this moment.

•••

Megan entered Will's apartment alone. Before he'd gone to the racetrack and she to the Halloren earlier, he'd left her the key. He said he would be gone all afternoon and would go directly to the Door from the track that night, having put a fresh shirt in his car to change for the stage.

From what Megan knew about his gambling, she wasn't sure whether she should hope for him to have *good* luck at Canterbury Downs or *bad* luck. As Ann had pointed out, the hopeless fact was that either way only fed his addiction. Megan felt sorry. Sorry that Will had a gambling problem. Sorry that with the ring she'd probably done him more harm than good.

She put her new load of belongings away into the closet space and dresser drawers allotted to her. Then she put one of Will's CCR tapes into the stereo, laid down on the bed, and listened to the entire album. A transitional time was just what she needed. A respiriting for her soul.

Her Rusty Door waitress job started at four-thirty. She managed to scrounge up just enough change in the bottom of her purse for bus fare. It made her wish she'd kept at least part of Leon's loan rather than hastily dishing it all back to him last night. It would be tight going till pay day. But she could probably ride with Will the rest of the week, eat his groceries and maybe borrow a little money from him.

It was a weird day to start a job, Sunday. Especially since Sunday would actually be the last day of her work week. But it was mainly for introduction and training. Her hours would be four-thirty to one A.M., Wednesday through Sunday, the same nights the band played. Nick Gerard had explained that those were the club's busiest times, when they needed two waitresses on duty. Cheryl, the girl she was replacing, had left because she was pregnant. Nick asked Megan outright if *she* had any intention of soon becoming pregnant. She couldn't believe he'd asked such a thing, but gave him an instant no.

He was right there to greet her when she arrived at the club, smiling eagerly. Almost too eagerly. It jangled Megan, undoing the calm she'd tried so hard to achieve.

"Hi, Megan," he said beneath his mustache. "We've been waiting for you." The *we* was him and a waitress.

Feeling nervous and self-conscious caused Megan to do dumb little things like wringing her hands, chewing her bottom lip and rocking one foot from side to side. It wasn't the idea of a new job that freaked her out so much as it was the boss's eyes seeming to stare right through her. It was like—what did he want? Expect? And did she actually want to know?

"Hi, Megan," Joe called across the empty club to her. She hadn't noticed him when she'd first come in, but he was there, washing glasses behind the bar. His presence and hello lent her the warmth and support of a somewhat familiar friend. She smiled and waved back appreciatively.

Nick introduced the other waitress to her as Pam. They would be working the same shifts together. Megan remembered that she'd seen the girl working there both Friday and Saturday nights alone, and frantically busy. She had a long brown pony tail and looked to be in her mid-thirties.

Pam took Megan through the kitchen to a back room to get her uniform. It consisted of a black miniskirt and a black scooped neck silk blouse. Megan had been previously instructed to wear her own black panty hose and black flat-heeled shoes, which she did. She fit perfectly into the skirt and blouse.

Pam accredited it to, "Nick has an eye for figures. Not just his bookkeeping figures, but waitresses' figures as well. I'm sure the reason you were hired so fast was that you looked the right size to fit the available outfit."

Megan cringed hearing it, but tried to keep her focus. A job, quick and easy—pay the rent, pay the bills, buy some food, escape from Lewis. There were two extra outfits for her, so that one could always be kept laundered and ready. She would have preferred one skirt, more generous of material, to launder every day, rather than three so skimpy.

"Oh, yes…yes…fine." Nick fully approved her return to the outer club area.

Megan felt as exposed and shy as if she were about to do some exotic stage show rather than waitressing.

"You'll do just fine, Megan." Nick was so engrossed in watching her that he didn't notice his cigarette burning into the filter until it created a horrid odor. Then, moving fast, he crushed the remainder into an ashtray. "Pam will train you. There isn't much to catch onto. Sundays aren't bad at all. Good day to start. Club's officially open at five. Mostly dinner people come in first. I'll be in my office if you need me."

He left. Megan stood stiff and tense. She glanced over at Joe, catching his thumbs-up signal, which helped though was hardly enough.

"Come on," Pam said to her. "First thing we do is lift all the chairs down off the tables. The clean-up guy sets them up there to do the floor at night, then it's part of our job to take them down when we come in the next day. The *hardest* part, believe me," she laughed.

"I don't think it'll be the hardest part of the job for me," Megan said. "The hardest part for me will be dealing with customers. Plus this." She gave the hem of her very short skirt a tug down.

"Takes some getting used to, that's all," Pam's understanding was slanted with amusement. Her own legs were long and nice and at the moment much more lithe than Megan's. "Your section is from this row of tables over and mine's the other half." She pointed out the split.

"Do I get a pad?" Megan asked. "I mean, I don't have to try and remember everything, do I, without writing it down?"

"Yes...yes, you get a pad and a pen and just relax, you're going to do fine.

Office work. She'd only done office work before. What had she gone and gotten herself into, acting on a whim just to have a job? And did this really mean that she was *taking* control of her life, or *losing* control of it?

Later, when the first two customers of the evening came through the front door, both men, Megan gasped a quick shallow breath and felt like she was going to die. Then, as they wandered over and sat on Pam's side, she exhaled with relief. Okay, the initial shock was over. She was ready now. Ready for this new life beyond Lewis. New life, new job, new friends. A sense of pride and independence raised her courage. If only her *skirt* wasn't so raised. She gave it another tug down.

• • •

Gloria sat on the patio beside her house, curled on the chaise lounge, magazine in hand but unlooked at, a glass of iced tea beside her but untouched. She was physically comfortable in her stretch pants, big shirt and bare feet, but not mentally content. Her thoughts were distant, restless, searching, searching...for something...something other than *this*. Something more than spending this evening home alone.

Thoughts of the Rusty Door kept entering her mind in bits and pieces, hesitant yet attractive. Thoughts of the probable excitement and energy there. Thoughts of her kids there, laughing, talking, having fun. Thoughts of Joe the bartender, the way he'd spoken to her, looked at her, treated her. She'd been so put out with the place at first, Saturday night, and then later, leaving it, she found she'd actually left a little part of herself behind. There had been a kind of strange enthrallment she couldn't forget.

She dropped her magazine to the brick floor. It was getting too dim out to read now anyway. She gave a sigh and stared upward at the darkening sky, as if hoping to find some mystical answers or directions there. But there were none. Only the loneliest, emptiest color gray she'd ever seen.

• • •

Megan was glad to see Leon and Ann enter the Door later that night.

"I can't believe you took this job, Meggie," Leon remarked, coming over to the new waitress. He looked her up and down, laughing boyishly and saying, "You're askin' for trouble dressed like that. You know that, don't you?"

Ann swatted him. "Women don't ask for trouble, and it

certainly has nothing to do with how they dress."

Leon wasn't so sure. "How about the motto *you are what you wear?*"

"If you're trying to scare me here," Megan whined, "you're doing a pretty good job."

"Sorry," he apologized.

She smiled. "I made ten bucks in tips so far and it's only nine o'clock and a slow night."

"Great, Megan," Ann said.

"It's the short skirt," Leon insisted.

Megan looked about with a sudden delightful thought. "So, Ann, do you think your mom will be by tonight?"

Ann blinked her eyes and spoke with an edge. "I can only hope not. Come on, Leon, let's get a table."

Megan was sorry that Ann was so cold and uncaring about her mother. She herself liked Gloria and would have appreciated having her for her own mother.

When members of the Sidetracks started wandering in, all wearing white western shirts, Megan found herself anxiously singling out Will. She'd missed him and wondered about him.

Just as anxious to see her, he rushed over bursting with smiles, sweeping her off her feet and around in a circle. "Eight hundred, Megan! I just won eight hundred out at the track."

"Really?" She hugged him back, though she supposed it was wrong of her to share in the excitement of his gambling success. Except...the spirit of him and of the moment was so immediately infectious.

Will allowed some space between them, giving her a more directed look, then a long low wolf whistle.

"Can't be anything new to you," she said, giving her skirt hem a tug. "You must be used to seeing waitresses in these outfits all the time."

"But not you. Besides," he laughed, "the waitress you're replacing was really pudging out at the seams before she left."

Megan nodded. "She was pregnant, I know. Nick told me."

"Guess who the father is?"

"You?"

"No."

"Who?"

"Guess."

"Not Nick."

"Yeah. Megan, he goes after the waitresses, so be careful."

"Hey, Will!" Vince called to him from the stage. "Come on."

Will held off for more time with Megan. "Let's go out somewhere and celebrate my winnings after closing. Me and you. I'll take you for a late dinner and—"

"I don't think so, Will."

"Why not?" He was like a disappointed child.

Randy was rapping his drums.

"No," Megan said, even though she felt like saying yes.

Will's disappointment turned to anger. "Why not? Look, I'm not asking you to go to bed with me or anything—just to dinner."

"I don't think so."

"Why?" he persisted.

She shook her head, staying with no. "Let's just have a sandwich at the apartment," she suggested.

Will shifted. And waited. "Megan," he said, his voice simmered to soft and appealing, "I did good and I feel good and I'd really like to share that with you by going somewhere special, you know?"

She could no longer look him straight in the eye. She said to the floor, "Will...it's just that—"

"Just what? What, Megan?"

"The idea of...your having gotten the money the way you did."

He gave a half laugh, as if to a joke he didn't quite get. "I won it fair and square. What's wrong with that?"

She wanted to say that it bothered her, his owing a lot of people a lot of money over and above what gambling flurries he may have won that day. But she didn't. Couldn't. Had no right. Wasn't justified to step into the depth of his problem. Not that she really wanted to anyway. She shook her head no. She looked at him, trying to soften her no with a smile.

Will took off for the stage. And Megan was left far sorrier than she cared to be for turning him down. The feeling confused her, upset her. What she had just heard about Nick also had its affect on her.

"You'll lose tips with that long face," Pam warned, passing her.

Megan supposed so. Knew so. Yet stood unchanged, unmoved, for a moment longer, watching the band open.

Will strapped on his guitar and leaned forth to his mike. "Hi, everybody! We're the Sidetracks and ready to kick it loose!"

Five

As Megan dressed Monday morning she made a serious assessment of her life, a good look at where she'd been, where she was going, where she was now. A serious but simple calculation indicated she'd been too gullible and dependent in the past, needed to be wiser and more self-sufficient in the future, and should value the present as a stepping stone from one to the other.

Leaving the bedroom to make coffee, she passed Will's sleeping body on the couch. He didn't stir. She was glad. It was nice having some private time to think. She thought about how fast he'd happened to her. How it had been just a matter of hours on Friday between her leaving Lewis and meeting him. Not intentional. Definitely not intentional. But okay. Maybe even fate. She'd needed a stepping stone...and Will happened.

When the coffee was done she stood in the tiny kitchen corner of the apartment, sipping from her mug and gazing over at him. His blanket was tangled and had slid half off of him. He was longer than the rickety tweed couch and his bare right foot stuck up over one end of it while his whole left leg, still in jeans, hung off the cushion, his foot touching the floor. Despite the conditions, he slept as soundly as a baby.

Megan rolled her shoulders back and around. They were still tense from last night's waitressing. Her left wrist was sore from balancing the tray, and her legs and feet ached as if she'd run a ten mile marathon. It was a rough job, a lot rougher than sitting behind a computer all day. Nevertheless, it was a job. Another fast happening, another fate, another stepping stone. She guessed it was at least good to be progressing on her own, to have already put so much distance between herself and the mistake of Lewis.

She sipped some more coffee and glanced around at Will's tiny apartment—cluttered, messy, dirty. She didn't understand how anyone could live like that. Ideas for improving it began accumulating in her mind. More coffee. More thoughts. The place needed a woman's touch. She accepted the challenge, thinking that maybe she was *Will's* fate as well.

Soon Will was moving and moaning and opening his eyes. He reacted happily upon seeing her nearby. "Hi..."

"Hi," she said back. "Did I wake you?"

"I think my nose woke me. It loves the smell of coffee."

She poured another mug and took it to him.

He sat up in his jeans and tee shirt and drank his coffee as if it were a fix to save him. "Megan, I'm sorry I sounded so demanding last night—about expecting you to go out with me after the Door."

"No personal involvement here, right?" she reminded him of their living agreement.

He drank some more coffee, his eyes looking over the mug at her. Then he reminded her, "You pretty much involved yourself when you gave me that ring to pay off the sharks."

"That was business. Besides, that was before we decided to live together."

He took some money out of his pants pocket. "Here—a payment on the ring, more to follow." He held it out to her.

She refused it. "You don't owe me anything for the ring, Will. I told you, I only wanted to get rid of it, to put it to good use."

"I know, but I still want to pay you back."

"I don't *want* to be paid back."

"Don't make me beg," he said, grinning and still holding the money out to her.

"Anyway," she insisted, "I'm the one who owes *you*. A half a month's rent."

Though he put the money away, he didn't give up. "Okay, Megan, okay, so how about if we make an exchange—the rent for the ring."

"Forget the ring, Will. Please. It's not to be counted into this at all. It's separate. It's—well, we'll just take it from there. And when I get my final paycheck from Sheldon Electronics I'll pay you my share of the rent. It's reasonable. And I appreciate reasonable because...see, I...I'm kind of really in debt."

"Then why don't you just—"

"No. I can manage, but I just wanted to explain my appreciation for staying here because...I've been trying to catch up on a lot of bills for the past year now. Medical bills. I had my appendix out a while back."

"Appendix—wow. So you lived with a rich guy and he didn't help you with that?"

She shook her head. "I wouldn't have expected him to, wanted him to. My emergency surgery was before Lewis, before my job at Sheldon. And unfortunately before having any medical insurance. I...I was a typist in a small office, without any benefits. I didn't think about taking out any insurance because it cost me so much just to put myself through computer training classes. I thought I'd hold off till

I got better established. Two days after completing the course I got sick and wound up having surgery."

"That must have been rough."

"I got through it."

"No family? No one to help you?"

"Leon. Not financially, but—well, he was there for me. He fixed my meals, did my laundry, got me whatever I needed for a while. Then I landed a good job at Sheldon Electronics using my computer knowledge. And met Lewis."

"But he didn't help with your bills."

"He asked me to live with him rent free. That helped a lot."

"So you didn't live with him because you cared about him, you lived with him because he was free rent?"

"No, that was secondary."

"The caring? Or the free rent?"

"The rent. I *did* care about Lewis or I wouldn't have lived with him."

"Does that mean you care about me?"

"Will, we're not living together to live together—we're living together to share the rent."

"So your medical bills—they're a-ways from being paid up yet?"

"A-ways, yes."

"And Lewis? Where does he rank now?"

She shook her head and sighed. "It was an easy thing, moving in with him, because I hadn't much of my own anyway. My apartment had been a furnished room in an old house converted into apartments. Moving in with Lewis allowed me to put all my paychecks toward the hospital bill. Plus my job at Sheldon gave me medical coverage."

"So he was a good ticket for you?"

"More than that."

"You loved him?"

"That's enough about Lewis, okay?"

"So, Nick—you're working for Nick now. Does that mean—?"

"No."

"Sorry."

"I was real glad to know there's medical coverage with my waitress job at the Rusty Door. I would never be without it again. You never know what might happen. Do *you* have medical insurance, Will?"

The phone rang and he left the couch to answer it at the kitchen counter. "Hello? Yeah, right, this is him. Oh, really? That's weird. I sent the check last week. You should have gotten it by now. I know, but—Yeah...sure...okay, bye."

He hung up and turned back to Megan. "Mondays...they're always after you on Mondays." He laughed. "Speaking of coverage, yeah, my *car* has insurance coverage, except that was the agent saying the payment is past due. See, you're not the only one with bills."

Megan wiped a finger of dust off the end table next to the couch. "Will, where are your cleaning supplies?"

"Cleaning supplies?" He said it as though he didn't understand the term.

"If you don't mind, I'll do some cleaning around here."

The phone rang again before Will had even left it.

He answered with an overlap of irritation from the first call. "Hello!"

But this call turned out to be something more pleasant, as he was soon speaking in a much nicer tone. "Good timing, Frank. Yeah...yeah, I desperately do need a horse. Right."

Megan listened. When he didn't get out to the track he had someone call him and take his bets over the phone? He had a *bookie?* And could a bookie be just as dangerous as loan sharks? She didn't understand anyone having this type of lifestyle.

He hunched his shoulder to cradle the receiver against his ear, freeing both hands to get himself a refill of coffee. "From the form it looks like Iridescent in the sixth on Wednesday." He glanced briefly at Megan, as though he'd forgotten for a moment that she was there. He lowered his voice and spoke awkwardly into the phone. "No...I'm sure I won't get there.

Right. Yeah, two hundred. Right...okay...bye."

As soon as he'd hung up, Megan wanted to jump him with questions and warnings about the risks of serious gambling. But she didn't. Couldn't.

He headed for the bathroom. "Got to get a shower."

She had just begun to search the cupboard below the kitchen sink, hoping to find some cleaning supplies, when the phone rang again. She straightened up to reach for it. "Hello?"

"Oh," a woman's voice said hesitantly. Then asked, "Julie? Is this Julie?"

"No," Megan replied.

"Chris?" the woman guessed again.

By then Megan figured the caller to be Will's mother, going down a list of familiar girls. "Gloria?" she made a guess of her own.

"Yes. Yes, who's this?"

"Megan. We met at the Rusty Door the other night."

"Oh. Yes. The blonde."

"Will's in the shower. But I'll have him call you as soon as he's out."

"No. No, that's all right. I don't want to interrupt anything there. I mean...you two probably have some sort of plans together, seeing as you're over at his place as early as this."

Megan didn't know what to say. For sure not that she was Will's new roommate. "No...no, it's all right, he'll be able to call you back."

"It's nothing important," Gloria said. "But, well...okay. I'm at work. He can call me here if he wants to. Good-bye, Megan."

When Will returned to the kitchen, showered, shaved and dressed, Megan asked, "Who are Julie and Chris?"

"W-what...?" He stood in dismay.

"I just got this call that—"

"They called?"

"No, your mom did. She was trying to guess who I was and she started going down this list. I told her I was Megan. But I didn't tell her I was living here."

"Neither Julie nor Chris lived here—ever. They were just—"

"I wasn't prying," Megan assured him. She squatted down to the bottom cupboard again, resuming her search. "I don't really care who they were. Or where they lived. It doesn't matter."

"You asked."

"Who they were, that's all."

"Past girlfriends. But neither of them ever lived here."

She stood up, pleased to have found a rag serviceable enough to dust and a bottle of Mr. Clean and a sponge. "It's not my business. I'm sorry I asked. Your mother was calling from work. She said you could call her back there, but that it wasn't anything important."

"Then why did she call?"

"I don't know."

"Doesn't make sense," he said, shaking his head.

"She's your *mother*."

"Like there's automatic logic to whatever she does?"

Megan thought it began to feel like an argument. She watched him take his bedding off the couch and carry it to the bedroom. When he returned she asked, "Well, aren't you going to call her and see what she wanted?"

"No."

"Why?"

"Just no."

"But she's your mother."

"So?"

"Will, your *mother*."

"Look, you just claimed that Julie and Chris weren't your business. Well, neither is my mother."

"Excuse me." She raised her head and turned away.

"Just don't worry about it, okay?"

"Fine. Okay." It *was* an argument, and he had a horrid attitude. He snatched his car keys off the table and left the apartment.

As agitated as Megan was, she tried convincing herself

that she really ought not be concerned over any of Will's thoughts or doings. The guy had some very rough edges, of which she didn't understand or approve, but it really didn't matter. She shouldn't care one way or the other. Wouldn't. Didn't. What she *did* care about right then was cleaning the apartment. She needed a bucket. She began searching.

The phone rang and she grabbed for the receiver. Before she even spoke a single word into it, a man's voice belted over the line, "Two more weeks, Westin! Two weeks to catch up on rent or you're out."

• • •

Will drove to the Kenwood Advertising Agency on West Renner Boulevard. A building of multi-glass architecture, it sat on a hill with a long curved driveway leading up to it. He parked and entered. He asked at the front desk for Gloria Westin.

"Your name, sir?" the young receptionist with an upsweep of red hair asked him as she lifted her phone. She was new here. Yes, of course, replacing the retired Connie.

"Will."

"Thank you, sir." She pressed some buttons on her console. "Gloria, there's a Mr. Will here to see you." The girl hung up and said back to him, "She'll be out in just a moment. You may sit down if you like."

Will preferred standing and looking about. It'd been a while since he'd last been here. Its elegance still amazed him, intimidated him some. Leather furniture, tall lamps, valuable paintings, magazines arranged so neatly on a low glass-topped table they seemed not meant to be picked up and read.

Soon his mom came through a door behind the receptionist's desk, wearing a mint green suit and lots of jewelry. She was a very classy woman.

Will, in his tee shirt and jeans, was of a completely different world. "Hi, Mom. Working hard?"

"Will—darling—hi." She told the receptionist, "Brenda, this is my son Will."

The redhead looked embarrassed for having given his

first name as his last name.

"Come on." Gloria led Will out. "I'll buy you a cup of coffee in the cafeteria downstairs."

He hadn't intended to stay, only to pay back the money he owed her and leave again. Unable to say no, he followed her out the main door, down the long marble-floored corridor, and then down a fancy circular staircase leading directly into the very posh employee cafeteria.

"Hi, Joyce," Gloria said to the girl behind the counter. "Two black coffees and put it on my tab, please."

"Yes, Ms. Westin."

Another world, Will thought, a whole different world that his mother lived in, abided by. So separate from his that it was sometimes hard to believe they were related.

They sat down at a small corner table. The only other customers in the place were two business men across the room, working at a table full of papers, coffee cups and ashtrays.

"Well now," Gloria said in her cheery little way, "this is a rare surprise. A rare surprise indeed, seeing my son twice in three days. Let alone at my place of work."

"You came to *my* place of work," he reminded her. "So I thought I'd come to *yours*."

"It's been ages since you've been here, Will."

"Yeah, I know."

"There was a time you used to come sit in the lobby and wait for me to get through with work and then we'd go home together."

"When I was a kid," he reminded her.

"Yes. I miss those days."

"That was a long time ago, Mom."

"Yes," she said with a sigh.

"I understand you called me earlier."

"Yes. Just to talk, Will. I really didn't want anything."

"Talk about what?" He couldn't imagine.

She sipped some coffee then blotted her mouth with a napkin. "Do we have to have precise reasons?"

"No," he said, a smile escaping him.

"There." She smiled back, eyes twinkling on the verge of happy tears. "Now maybe *that's* all I wanted. A big smile from my son."

"Over the phone."

"Yes, you can *hear* a person's smile over the phone. You *can*. But this is still better, in person."

He nodded. "You're very tricky, you know?"

"It was hard to talk much the other night at the Rusty Door. Are you really okay, dear?" she asked as only a mother could.

"Yeah, really."

"And Ann...?"

"Ann's okay."

"She's living with that...that boy named Leon."

"Leon's all right."

"How *old* is he?"

"I don't know exactly. Mid-twenties, I guess."

"He looks eighteen."

"Mid-twenties at least, Mom."

"Ann's thirty-three."

"So?"

"Age difference."

"A few years is nothing, Mom. Don't worry about it."

"Mostly I worry that she just came out of a divorce and here she is involving herself with someone else right away. Leon...well, he wouldn't happen to be the reason she divorced Alan, would he?"

Will couldn't help but laugh. "Leon? No. No, Mom, he never came into the picture until after Ann was free and clear of Alan."

"I still don't like it."

"Like what?"

"Her being involved with...with that boy."

"She's happy."

"She was happy with Alan."

"At first, but not for long. She's trying to find herself and what might really make her happy now. Leave her alone. She'll be okay. She'll work this out."

"And you? You're happy with…with this Megan?"

To change the subject, Will took out the two hundred dollars he'd brought for her and handed it across the table.

"What's this?" She took it in a stunned reaction.

"Loan repayment."

"Already? You're paying me back already?"

"You don't want it?"

"I just gave it to you Saturday. How did you—?""

"Take it."

"Are you sure?"

"Mom, I know I still owe you a lot more from past times, but—"

"It's all right, Will."

"No, it's not."

"Well…*temporarily* all right. Because some day you'll have a good job and then we can straighten it all out."

He should have known their meeting would come to this, just as it did every time. "A good job? We sit down for two minutes together and you start right in on—"

"Will, Will." She grasped his arm. "Singing. A better *singing* job, of course."

He heard her say it but not mean it.

Still she went on, "I know how you like your music, dear, and I saw the other night just how good you are at it. I only meant some day you'll be playing at some nice place where the audience is quiet and appreciative of your talent and you get paid enough to live on."

He rolled his eyes, pained by the familiar dig. "You've got such confidence in me, haven't you?"

"Yes, of course, darling."

He slipped out of her hold and stood up. The few sips of coffee he'd drunk had no warming effect whatsoever on the chill of this meeting. He looked down at his mother, knowing it would never be any different. "It's too bad all that confidence you have in me isn't in what *I* want rather than in what you *think* I should want." He started to leave.

"Will. Will, wait," she said.

If Gloria couldn't reason with him on one matter, she had plenty of others to try. "Will, what's honestly going on with you and that Megan girl? I mean...she was there at your apartment so early this morning when I called you."

It didn't seem to matter that he'd told her Saturday night how he and Megan were no more than friends. His mom always preferred her own made-up versions of the truth. Okay. So be it. Then he might as well give her a juicy answer to satisfy what she already thought she knew. "I'm in love with her, that's what's going on. Bye, Mom. Have a nice day."

He paused with a last look back at her before going through the cafeteria door.

• • •

Megan was sitting on the couch, having just finished hand-sewing the ripped pocket of Will's black western shirt, when he returned to the apartment. She held the shirt up for him to see.

"Where did you get a needle and thread?" he asked.

"I have this little emergency mending kit in my purse."

He laughed. "Like you never know when you just might need to sew on a pocket."

"Exactly."

"Thanks." It was six-thirty. He made no explanation as to where he'd been the entire afternoon.

Megan guessed he didn't owe her one. "You're welcome."

Beyond looking at her and the shirt, he observed the clean, orderly appearance of his apartment.

"Look at this place! Wow...you did all this, Megan?"

"Yes."

"Looks great. Looks bigger."

"I know," she said with a giggle

"I...was getting kind of careless about things."

"Kind of?"

"A lot." When his eyes finished the inspection they

settled back on her. "Megan, I'm sorry about earlier."

"Earlier?" She stood up from the couch, handing him his shirt.

"It's just that Julie, Chris and my mom are all kind of sore subjects with me and—"

"You don't have to explain."

"See…they all think I'm somebody I'm not. And that really bugs me and I guess I just don't like getting into it."

Her interest sparked. "Somebody you're not? Who do they *think* you are?"

"Julie and Chris think because I'm a musician my life should be a lot more lavish than it is."

She grinned curiously.

"You know," he said, grinning some himself, "fancy car, fancy apartment, fancy parties every night, lots of fancy money to blow right and left. I'm just not a *fancy person*, Megan. You've probably already learned that about me."

"Surely that's not your mom's expectation of you."

"Mom…she thinks I should *quit* playing music and get a real job."

"No," Megan said. "Will, your music is wonderful. Don't let anybody throw you off track on that."

"Not even my mom."

"Nobody."

"Thanks." He seemed pleased, though slightly amused. Then after checking out his sewn pocket more closely, he added, "And thanks for this."

"You're welcome."

"Here." He gave her a key. "I had this made for you. You really should have your own key to the apartment."

She took it. Then she thought she'd better tell him, "Will, someone called about the rent."

He didn't seem shocked. Or worried. "Yeah, I'm a little behind."

But it had certainly shocked and worried *her*. "It sounded serious, Will. He said you had two weeks to catch up or you'd be put out."

Will laughed.

"How behind are you?" she asked.

"A little, I said."

"We're talking *eviction,* Will. How much?"

He went to the kitchen. "So…have you eaten yet?"

"No. In case you didn't know it, your cupboards and refrigerator are pretty bare."

His rummaging proved her right. "So…let me take you out somewhere. What are you hungry for?" He turned back, catching her surprise. "*What?*" he asked.

"Look," she began nervously. "A lot of stuff here bothers me, but is not my business."

"Except you still have this way of letting me know that you think it is. So why not just say it."

"Okay. Will, I'm thinking that you won at the track yesterday and…couldn't you just put *that* toward the rent?"

"No."

"Why?"

"Because I owe more than eight hundred, Megan. I owe two months, which is eleven hundred."

She was shocked, but hopeful. "Pay part of it and—"

"They don't want *part* of it. It's all or nothing at this point. I've got a horse for Wednesday and if he comes in I'll have more than enough for total catch-up."

"And what about your car insurance?" As soon as she'd said it she realized she'd gone too far and backed down by shaking her head and throwing up her hands.

"Megan." Will's voice turned soft and reassuring. "I'm going to handle it. I'm going to handle everything, believe me. *Everyone* is in debt these days. It's no big deal."

Following her day of rigorous cleaning, Megan had showered and changed into tan slacks and a crisp yellow blouse. From the way Will was looking at her now, it was almost as if he was taking her special priming as meant for him.

Wrong. She took her purse off the end table, her sweater from the back of the easy chair, and headed for the door.

"Good-bye, Will…I've got plans."

She walked out, haunted by his let-down look. But there was a responsibility to uphold here—keeping their living arrangement from becoming personal. Sometimes, like a moment ago, she felt a sway. But she didn't need that, want that. And a good protection seemed to be in fleeing from it.

She didn't know where she was going as she left the building, only that she had to go. She started down the street, with a feeling that Will might be watching from his third floor window. However, she didn't look back to see for sure. She had some tip money from last night. Maybe she would eat at McDonald's and go to a movie.

Clenched tightly in her hand was the apartment key he had given her. How ironic that she'd no sooner turned in her key to Lewis's apartment than she'd acquired one to Will's. But this was different. Different in that she hadn't paid rent at Lewis's, whereas she would at Will's. Different in that she'd been a lover or mistress or something to Lewis, but was nothing to Will. Nothing. She kept walking, distancing herself as proof.

Monday pretty well set the pace of the entire week between Megan and Will. Though they saw each other around the apartment days and then at the Door nights, from Wednesday on, they maintained only a light quiet politeness between them. No personal talk, no questions, no expectations—only cool, sparse exchanges of words fit to necessity.

Megan didn't even spend breaks with Will at the club. Her table-waiting kept her so busy that their break times got out of sync anyway. Plus it seemed that Will preferred to spend more and more of his breaks drinking and socializing with his entourage of eager fans.

Megan didn't care. She was glad he left her alone. It was easier that way. She was actually relieved, being ignored by him, even though he did take it almost to the point of rudeness. She spent most of her own spare time with Leon and Ann.

"So how are you doing?" Leon asked her on Friday night.

"Fine," she said.

"Getting Lewie out of your mind?"

"Lewie who?"

"Atta girl," he said with a laugh, and punched her arm lightly.

"Replaceable, right?" Ann commented on the matter.

"Hey—nothing's going on between Will and me." Megan flared up at the assumption.

Ann turned even more defensive than she. "I wasn't insinuating that there was."

"It sounded like it."

"Megan, I only meant that there are probably better guys than Lewis out there."

"Your brother isn't in the running."

"Did I *say* that? I'm talking guys in general, Megan. Don't be so touchy. Maybe it's just that your mind is locked into Will."

"My mind is not locked into Will. Or into anyone or anything. I'm *free-minded*."

"Is that the same as air-headed?"

"Girls, girls," Leon intervened.

"Well, she is *blonde*," Ann pitched the last word.

Megan got up and left the table. She'd had enough of Ann and Leon. The Sidetracks were playing "Roadway Run." It entered her blood, like a potent drug bound on making one feel either better or worse. She felt its effect, though she honestly wasn't sure which it was.

She looked at the stage, finding Will looking directly back out at her as he sang. His voice was equally directed,

"Roadway Run
A long time traveling without you
A long time gone, don't know what went wrong
Baby, baby, what can I do..."

"Enjoying the music, are you?" Nick was suddenly beside her.

"I...I just finished my break." She had only lingered

enough to feel the music—a transition between breaking and working.

"Good, then maybe you can see to the group that just came in and is seated at one of your tables."

She looked. And saw. She nodded to Nick, tugged her skirt hem down, slipped her pad and pen out of her pocket, and went back to her job.

Randy beat the drums powerfully. Vince's guitar entwined the melody. Jeff's bass throbbed the soul—ther-um, ther-um, ther-um.

The yearning in Will's voice reached and worked on Megan no matter where she went or what she did,

"Roadway…
Roadway Run
I need another chance
You can't tell me we're done…"

Six

Gloria was in one of her restless moods again, and not at all sure she understood it. It could have come from her churning concerns over Will and Ann, the balmy spring weather working its way into summer, or her lingering thoughts about Connie's retirement and the fact that she herself would be the next one to reach that stage at Kenwood. She seemed to be drawing upon and feeling everything in extremes.

It was Saturday night. One week since Connie's party. One week since Gloria had stopped in at the Rusty Door to lend Will the money he'd asked for and had wound up meeting his new girlfriend, Ann's new boyfriend, and the nice man tending bar named Joe. Okay, yes—thoughts of last

Saturday night at the Rusty Door, mainly of Joe, were a big part of this Saturday night's restlessness. But even though she admitted as much to herself, she still didn't know what to do about it.

Gloria's house, a modest colonial in the Brooklyn Park suburb of Minneapolis, felt more quiet and lonely than it had ever before. All day she'd roamed from room to room feeling like a secluded prisoner. She wasn't. All she had to do was walk out the door, jump into her car and go. It seemed easy enough, except for the catch that the real prison was her mind rather than her house.

Will. Maybe it wasn't so extreme of her to worry over his claiming to be in love with this Megan girl, whom he'd only just met, who only just followed right in line after Julie and Chris. And Ann—how could she not worry about a daughter who was involved with a boy several years younger than she, immediately after her divorce? Or maybe...no...it couldn't be. Could it? Was it more envy than worry she was feeling toward her kids? Maybe that was it. It made her stop and wonder and realize that she hadn't much of a social life herself.

Other than work, and the few gala events that were work related, such as promotion parties and retirement parties, she scarcely went anywhere, did anything, met anyone. Not that she never envisioned herself having more of a social life. She'd always just accepted it as a frightening venture beyond her capability.

It was hard for a woman her age to do much running around alone. Very hard. Still...she had gone to the Rusty Door on her own last week and it'd turned out fine. Hadn't it? Though it had seemed pretty threatening at first, she had gotten through. And the fact that she hadn't died from it made her begin to consider that maybe she should risk going there again. Tonight.

She went to change. This time she would don the proper attire of jeans. Or...no...though she had a pair she used for gardening, she really wasn't a jeans person. Navy Dockers with a tucked-in print shirt would be fine. She hurried, lest she lose her nerve again.

It was after nine when Gloria got to the club. Just as she reached the front crossbuck door from the right, a tall straight smart-looking man in a pin-striped suit and dark glasses reached it from the left. They collided slightly, laughing and apologizing to one another. Then the man held the door and allowed her to enter ahead of him. It surely seemed that someone as finely dressed and mannerly as he was even more out of place here than she was.

Though she felt she blended in a good deal more this time, her bravery was forced and hinged upon leaving soon. Her self-doubts told her she didn't *need* to give this a second chance, didn't *need* to do anything that scared her this much. Except...the friendly bartender saw her, called hello and waved her over.

She went, as if walking to a dentist's chair, and perched onto a stool before him. "Hi, Joe."

"Gloria, it's good seeing you again. What'll you have, beer?"

"White wine, please," she said.

He'd already gotten a clean beer glass off the shelf, but he set it back in exchange for a stemmed one. "So you're here to see your kids again?"

She tried to be cool and confident. "No, not really." She paid for the wine he brought and drank some right away. She needed to be calmer, much calmer. Hopefully the wine would do it. She sipped some more.

"Meeting someone?" Joe asked.

She wondered if he questioned all the customers this way. Anyway...she guessed she didn't mind. She smiled, telling him, "No."

He had on a blue and gray plaid shirt which complimented him well. His kindly eyes narrowed to slits as he smiled back at her. "Just out for a good time, huh?"

"The music," she said, as the Sidetracks went from one lively song into another. "I really do need to get more in tune with my son's music."

Joe nodded. "They're good. They really know how to rock 'n roll."

"I wonder if I could learn."

"Maybe we can get them to do a couple slow ones."

"I suppose we could try." Gloria laughed lightly and lifted her wine again. She couldn't believe she was sitting there on a bar stool, conversing with a bartender. "So, Joe, do you know Will and Ann very well?"

"Not really. Enough to say that I like them both very much and think they're nice kids."

"They're not exactly kids."

"No, I guess not—except in comparison to someone my age."

"Yes," Gloria related it to herself. "I know what you mean."

"No, you couldn't possibly. You must have had them when you were very young."

His flattery brought another smile from her. "Thank you. Do you have any kids, Joe?"

"A daughter, a son-in-law and four grandchildren in Colorado."

Gloria adored it, envied it. "I hope *I* have grandchildren some day."

"You're too young for grandchildren."

"I'll be too *old* for them if Will and Ann don't get their lives in gear pretty soon."

"So you'd like to see them married and settled down?"

"Yes, of course. I don't see any direction in either of their lives right now."

"I don't think marriage is especially a direction to young people these days."

"Maybe you're right. Joe, what do you know about Megan?"

"She just sort of wandered in one night and now she's working here as a waitress."

"Do you think something's going on between her and Will?"

"Whoa—I'm beginning to see your purpose for coming here."

"No," she said. "No, this isn't an inspection thing on my children. Really. It's a night for me, just me."

"Well, all right!" His narrowed eyes approved her.

When the couple who had been sitting next to her left, Joe took their empty glasses away and wiped that portion of the bar with a damp towel. As he did so, he asked Gloria casually, "You married?"

"Divorced."

"Ahh," he said, nodding. "I'm widowed. So is there a special direction in *your* life, Gloria?"

"I'm not sure." She held her glass of wine, smiling, swiveling on her stool, purposely creating a little mystery.

• • •

When out of the blue Megan saw Lewis shuffling his way through the crowd toward her, the tray she was carrying tipped off balance and sent its two glasses crashing to the floor. Liquid splattered and ice cubes tumbled among broken glass.

As if the accident had set off some sort of detector, Nick was there immediately. "What happened?"

Collecting splintered glass and ice cubes onto her tray, Megan glanced up nervously at him. "I'm sorry."

"I want to see you in my office," the boss said, taking off again before she could even begin to explain anything.

But minutes later, when she stepped into his office and shut the door, she blurted words fast and fervently, "I haven't done anything like this all week and I don't know how it happened tonight but I'm sorry and I'll really try to be more careful."

"Did you replace those two drinks for your customers before coming in here?"

"Yes. They were very understanding."

Smoking a cigarette, Nick backed up to sit on the front corner of his desk. "You know, Megan, Saturday is our biggest night here at the Rusty Door."

"I know."

"I do know you've been working very hard and that this sort of thing does happen. But it's just that...I'm wondering if...if there was a particular cause behind what happened just now."

"Cause?"

He acted as if he knew something about her that she herself didn't.

"The tray slipped," she said. "It just slipped."

Nick flicked his ashes into the ashtray and laughed a short low laugh. "Megan, I happened to be out there watching when that scene occurred. I saw a very disturbed look on your face right before you tipped your tray."

She lowered her gaze from his. Nick was something beyond a boss. He was more like the police—watching, sensing, accusing, trying to piece enough evidence together for a conviction.

"What was that look I saw out there?" he demanded.

Megan kept staring at the floor, thinking but not talking.

"Megan, share with me what happened out there," Nick worked at her. "You can, you know."

It seemed she was in for it no matter which way she did or didn't answer. Trouble if she told him about Lewis's presence, trouble if she didn't. When she lifted her eyes again, she felt herself weaken under Nick's pressure. "Someone I didn't expect came into the club and it just startled me, that's all."

"This person is some sort of threat to you?"

It almost seemed as if she ought to have a lawyer.

Nick kept drilling, "Something I, as your employer, might need to help you deal with?"

"No. It's okay."

"Sure?"

"Yes."

He took a deep drag from his cigarette. After exhaling, he stood and came so close to her that his sweater almost brushed her silk blouse. "I want you to know, Megan, that I'm here for you, whatever problems you may have."

She shrugged, shook her head slightly and took a half a step backwards. "None."

"I look out for my employees. Know what I mean, Megan?"

"Yes," she said, though she had no idea what he meant.

"Good. I'm glad you understand. I *want* you to understand."

"Yes, thank you." She backed herself toward the door.

"We'll talk again," he said.

She nodded, opened the door and hurried out of his office.

The Sidetracks were playing "Roadway Run," her favorite out of their regulars. Looking their way, she caught Will looking *her* way. He'd seen her come out of Nick's office. Now he would be wondering what was going on. She herself wondered, because Nick's questioning her about dropping that tray really seemed like more of a lead-in to something else. In fact...everything he did and said seemed like—

"Megan, we need to talk," someone beside her said. It was Lewis.

"I'm working," she told him and started away.

He followed. "Megan, wait."

"I already got into trouble because you're here." She flitted in and out among her tables. Just when she really wanted to concentrate on being a good waitress, none of her customers seemed to need anything. She looked again at Lewis. "Go away. How did you even find me?"

He adjusted his dark glasses, as if he needed them in such a dimly lit place as the Door. "That night you were phoning me and slamming the receiver down hard...well, on one of those calls you hesitated just a bit longer before slamming and I managed to hear something being said over the loud speaker in the background, an announcement or something about the Sidetracks. I asked around and found out it was the name of a local band. Then I did some research to find out where they were playing. The Rusty Door. So here I am. I thought I'd see if by chance I would run into you here. Which I did. But never in my wildest dreams, Megan, would I have imagined you to be *working* here."

"It's my new job."

"You act fast."

"Not as fast as you."

"Megan, you *have* a job."

"You know what you can do with that job, don't you?"

Leon came strolling up with the obvious intention of interrupting. "Lewie—"

"The name's *Lewis*." The business man was as annoyed as ever with him.

"Meggie," Leon next said to her, "is he bothering you?"

"Yes," she said, though she wondered what, if anything, Leon could do about it.

"Stay out of this, Leon," Lewis warned him.

"That's what I did before, Lewie…I stayed out of it, and look what happened to Meggie."

"Nothing happened to her," Lewis claimed.

"Maybe *you* consider it nothing." Leon raised his chin, as if it might raise his entire height up to Lewis's. It brought him nowhere near, but seemed to at least boost his morale enough to say, "Get the hell out of here, Lewie."

"The name's *Lewis*. But then you do have a problem getting things right, don't you. I'm not going anywhere until I talk with Megan."

Leon laughed. "Then may you grow old and die here."

"What's the problem?" Nick came, glaring at all three of them.

"No problem," Megan said.

"No problem," Leon added.

Lewis, however, said, "The problem is that this waitress will not wait on me."

"Because," Megan defended herself, "he keeps wandering around so much I haven't been able to determine whether he's on Pam's side or my side of the club."

"Assume it's yours and take his order," Nick told her, and left.

"Scotch on the rocks," Lewis said.

She flitted off to give Joe the order, surprised to find Gloria sitting at the bar. It cheered her. "Gloria...hi. Do Will and Ann know you're here?"

"I'm not sure," she said, almost sounding as if she didn't care. "How are you, Megan?"

"Fine." She stood waiting for Joe to make Lewis's drink.

"You work here?" Gloria asked.

"Yes, for a week now."

"Cute outfit."

"Sure." Megan grinned and self-consciously gave a security tug to the hem of her skirt.

"Will told me about the two of you." Gloria said, giving Megan an in-depth look.

Megan felt embarrassed and awkward, but supposed the truth was good. "Oh," she nodded, "you mean that we're living together?"

"You're *living together*?" Gloria gasped, looking at her in a whole new way.

Whoops. Megan shrugged with bewilderment. "Well, yeah...that's not what he told you? I thought that was what you meant when—"

"What Will told me is that *he's in love with you.*"

"*What*?" Megan couldn't believe her ears. Why on earth would Will tell his mother such a ridiculous stupid thing. "Gloria, what's going on?"

"That's what *I'd* like to know. Just because my son's a rock 'n roll singer girls think they can flaunt themselves at him and—"

"I haven't *flaunted* myself at him," Megan assured her.

Ann came over, discovered her mother was there, and greeted her with a crabby look on her otherwise cute face. "You're infringing on my territory lately, you know that? What's the reason tonight, Mom?"

Joe spoke up for Gloria, "She's having a drink and listening to the music."

"That's right," Gloria assured Ann. "And I do think this

place is big enough for the both of us."

"It may be big enough," Ann snipped, "but I'm not sure it's actually *right* for one of us." She spun around to Megan. "Do you know where Leon is?"

"Isn't he a bit *young* for you?" Gloria blurted at Ann's back, as if she'd been waiting to use that question ever since first meeting him the other night.

Ann turned enough to send an eye-blinking look around at her mom. "You mean—just like isn't it a bit out of character for you to be *sitting at a bar drinking*?"

Gloria raised her wine glass and said, "I don't think you know me well enough anymore to know *what* my character may or may not be."

"Touché," Ann said, and took off through the crowd to look for Leon.

"I bet you wouldn't treat *your* mother this way," Gloria said to Megan.

"I don't have one," she responded. "Excuse me, I need to take this drink over to an irate customer."

It was difficult locating the roving Lewis. When she did, it was along the far back wall. She went up to him and handed him his Scotch. He gave her a bill and said to keep the change.

It was a twenty. "I can't take this," she told him.

He refused to take it back, but wanted something else. "Megan, I want my ring."

How ironic that he should say he wanted his ring back but not her. It was also ironic that it should even matter one way or the other to her. But in a small surprising way she guessed it did.

"You know what that ring means to me," he raved.

"I don't have it."

He gave her an envelope. "Here—your last paycheck."

"Thanks." She took it, folded it and stuck it into her pocket.

"Why don't you quit this silly job and come back to Sheldon Electronics?"

"I like this job very much, thank you. Sheldon Electronics can go to hell."

"You liked it there."

"Did I?"

"You know you did."

"It was a bore."

"You never seemed bored to me."

"Probably because you were always thinking of Dana rather than of me."

"Megan, come on...you *know* how I felt about you."

"I thought I did. Until I found out it was all a lie.'"

"It wasn't a lie."

"You were married and didn't tell me. What do you call that?"

"Like I said, I thought you already knew."

"But you never thought to actually say it to me...or just talk about it with me."

• • •

Will went searching for Megan the very moment the Sidetracks took a break. He'd seen her talking to some well-dressed guy earlier and had been wondering ever since if that had been Sheldon. If it was, it was probably a scene she needed rescuing from.

"Will...Will, can I have your autograph?" some girl shoved a paper and pen at him.

He scribbled his name in haste for her. He had to find Megan. Time was limited, cause urgent.

There. He spied her near the back of the club, talking with that guy again. He rushed onward through the crowd. "Megan—are you okay?" he asked as he reached her.

"I'm fine." She looked strangely at him for showing up as he did.

He didn't understand how she could say fine. He *knew* she wasn't fine.

She made introductions. "Will, this is Lewis Sheldon. Lewis, Will Westin of the Sidetracks."

The two guys said cool, quick hi's to one another.

"Will and I are living together now," Megan added.

"Living together." Sheldon lowered his dark glasses to

make a clearer inspection on Will.

"That's right," Will added, slipping his arm around Megan.

Sheldon's face filled with silent rage. No more words came. He turned and left.

"Thanks for backing me up," Megan told Will.

"No problem. But it *is* the truth—we *are* living together."

"Living together, yes." Her blue eyes seemed to suddenly spark more at him than they had at Sheldon a moment ago. "But where do you get off telling your mom you're in *love* with me?"

She went to mingle her customers. Will tagged after her. He couldn't believe his mom was there again, let alone that she'd said such a thing to Megan. "I'm not in love with you," he pleaded to the flitting waitress. "Look, it was just something I threw at her because she was bugging me and—"

"Something you *threw* at her?" Megan stopped so abruptly that Will ran right into her. It seemed she was now more furious with him than she'd been with Sheldon.

"I'm sorry," he apologized. "I had no right to make up something like that and use it like a weapon in a fight."

"That's right, you didn't." Her look melted from anger to misty-eyed.

Will felt more sorry than he thought he could be. "Megan, I wasn't thinking at the time. She...she'd just made me so mad and—"

"You had no right," she repeated, almost crying.

"I know," he agreed guiltily. "Because I don't love you, Megan. I hardly even *know* you."

"Exactly," she said, then began circulating her tables again. A group of four flagged her attention and she stopped to take their drink order. Will followed her to the bar.

"Two lites, a screwdriver and a Door knocker," she told Joe.

"Hi, Will," Joe said, as he mixed the drinks. "Your mom's here."

"Yeah, I know."

"Off to the powder room right now."

"How many drinks has she had so far?"

Joe laughed, shaking his head as if it was nothing to count.

When Megan's tray was ready she started through the crowd to make deliveries.

Will kept after her, trying to break the cold shield between them. "I said I'm sorry, Megan."

"You *used* me." She glanced briefly back at him.

"*Used* you?"

"To get at your mom."

Okay, he'd had it with this guilt trip stuff. He turned it back on her. "Like you didn't use me? To get at Sheldon? Telling him you and I live together?"

"We do."

"Not like you insinuated to him. The *way* you said it to him was definitely using me."

Megan served her tray of drinks, collected the money along with a good tip, then started over to Pam's side of the club. Will gave up chasing and arguing and stayed in one place. For someone who didn't want to get involved, he sure didn't seem to be managing very well. There was something about her that had him going right from the start. He felt worn out from her.

In a moment she was coming back his way, smiling in a surprisingly friendly manner and taking him by the hand. A kind of weird, but nice, transformation. "I told Pam I'm taking my break now. Come on, let's go outside for some air. I think we could both use some."

He went with her, feeling high and hopeful all over again. "Still friends?"

"Friends," she said, pulling him along.

They went through the back hall and exited into the parking lot. The fresh air and quiet was a welcome relief. Megan leaned against a light post, closing her eyes and taking deep relishing breaths.

Will stood close, watching her, feeling much better about her and about everything than he had a few minutes ago. He was amazed at the zooming mood-altering effects this girl had on him. With his concern over Sheldon's visit still uppermost however, he had to ask, "So what was it really like, seeing him again?"

"Lewis?"

"Yeah."

"Difficult."

"Like maybe you still love him?"

"No...more a difficulty in realizing that what we had between each other never *was* love. Difficulty in realizing I don't really know what I ever thought I was doing with him."

"Regret," Will assumed.

"More like awareness."

Lewis, leaving in his white New Yorker, came cruising down through the lot past them. He drove slowly, staring at them from his window with rueful objection.

As he left the lot, turning out onto Langdon Road, Megan concluded, "From that look I'd say he really does believe there's something going on between you and me. And our being out here like this together now seemed to be added assurance of it."

"As good as poison," Will grinned agreeably.

"I think he'll leave me alone now."

"Good. If not, maybe we can think up even more assurance for him."

When both Will and Megan turned and looked off in the other direction, they saw Nick standing just outside the back door of the club, smoking a cigarette and observing them even more intently than Lewis had.

"Guess somebody else is considering us to be a couple," Will said.

"Good," Megan responded quickly and coolly.

"Like maybe you need me to ward him off too."

"No," she said.

But Will had already read enough into the matter to feel sure that Nick must have been putting some unwelcome moves on her. "Watch out for him, Megan."

"I know. You already told me that. But he—"

"No buts. If he gives you any kind of trouble at all, just let me know. Okay?"

"Okay."

"Good. And now Leon. Tell me what Leon thinks about us. Because I'm sure he thinks something."

"He doesn't approve of my staying at your place."

Will laughed. "Yet my sister is staying at his."

It brought an unexpected lightness to the moment, and helpless laughter from both of them.

As they stood there absorbing all the humor they could from the situation, Joe came rushing outside looking for them. "Will! Will!"

"Hey, Joe," Will greeted him, "what's up? And listen...go easy on my mom's drinks, okay?"

The bartender was out of breath. "Look, Will—how about a favor? When the band resumes—could you—maybe play a slow song?"

"It's *Saturday night,"* Will reminded him.

Megan joined Joe's plea. "Will, even on week nights you rarely play slow ones. A slow song would be nice now and then."

"Don't know many," he said.

"One," Joe stressed. "Just one, Will. For your mother and me."

"*My mother and you?*" Will gave him a curious look.

Megan had to get back to her tables and Joe to his bar. The Sidetracks regrouped and were soon playing uproariously again.

Following the reopening number, Will made a special announcement to the crowd. "We're going to slow the pace down some now, something we don't ordinarily do, but I guess maybe we'll give it a go. Because we had a request, and we do like to honor those requests that we can. So...here's a soft romantic...for all you soft romantics out there."

He gazed out over the audience during Vince's smooth guitar lead-in. Megan was standing off to one side, sweet-faced and attentive. Will gave her a nod and a smile. It was great having her out there, watching and listening. But then he had to catch himself and remember that this song was supposed to be mainly for his mother and Joe. Where were they? He searched the many faces and figures before him. There. They were together, coming onto the dance area.

His mom looked radiantly happy, and younger than ever. Joe, with his arm around her waist, almost too familiarly, seemed proudly responsible.

Will drew up close to his mike and began a tender vocal,

"The wind is moving my soul
My arms are out, feet off the ground
What a smooth ride, my eyes are closed
Drifting in circles, around and around..."

He watched Joe and his mom slow dance as he sang, wondering if they were paying half as much attention to his song as they were to the actual *effect* of it.

• • •

"I didn't think bartenders were allowed to do this during their work shift," Gloria said to her partner amidst their close wandering shuffle.

"You're a lady to break the rules for, Gloria," he responded charmingly.

They separated just far enough to exchange a smile.

"You dance like you get lots of practice," she commented.

"Not so much," he said.

As they passed in front of the stage, Gloria, in Joe's arms, smiled up at her son the singer. She was glad she had come to the Rusty Door that Saturday night. Glad for being somewhere, doing something, being with someone.

Seven

"I don't know how I let you talk me into this," Megan said to Will at the track Sunday afternoon.

"It was easy." He munched a hot dog and paged the program. "All I said was you've got to come with and see what it's like."

Canterbury Downs Racetrack was thirty some miles south of Minneapolis, just outside of Shakopee. It was Megan's first time there and she found it to be a beautiful place. The three-level grandstand was bright red and yellow, with a steepled roof, unique shaped windows, and several great observation landings. The outer grounds were velvety green grass, neat colorful flower beds and white rail fences. An immense parking lot was in the front, and down the road at the back were stables and workout areas.

Megan hadn't meant to be so manipulated that she wound up running off to do things she really had no intention of doing. Yet, though she had wanted to stay home and do laundry and clean the apartment, she was now at the track. And while she ought to be discouraging Will from gambling, she now was directly involved with it.

"Come on," he said, heading for what he called a mutual window to place a bet on the first race.

Megan followed.

The line moved quickly, and soon he was leaving the window waving a computerized ticket. "Totally Mine, Megan! Totally Mine."

Her own excitement was drenched with confusion. "You *won* already?"

He laughed. "No, the race hasn't even run yet. That's the name of the horse I just picked, Totally Mine. I put fifty across the board."

"Across the board?" She had no idea what that meant.

He explained, "Fifty to win, fifty to place, fifty to show. A total of a hundred and fifty."

"That's a lot of money."

"More if I win. Takes money to make money, Megan. You don't make anything on two dollar bets. Come on—let's go to the outside benches. It's almost post time."

"Post time...?" She hurried after him.

It was a nice day for being at the track. Cloudy enough that you didn't have to squint, cool enough for a light jacket. There was a good crowd, most people appearing to know exactly what they were doing and having a terrific time. Megan didn't see anyone who looked as befuddled as she felt.

She and Will took a bench just a few rows back from the track fence. A man wearing a red English riding outfit came out with a very long-necked sort of horn and played an introduction to the horses entering the track.

Jockeys in bright silks slowly rode their thoroughbreds back and forth before the audience in a warm-up and final showing. Totally Mine, number four, a shiny reddish brown, held his head high and drew eagerly on the reins with all the promise of a winner.

Actually, Megan thought every one of the horses was beautiful and had the look of winning. But she guessed the real judgment was to be gathered from the statistics in the Racing Form.

Soon all nine horses filed into the starting gates on the far side of the track. The bell rang, the doors sprung open and the commentator shouted over the loud speakers. "They're off!"

Will immediately jumped to his feet, yelling, shouting, waving his ticket. Everyone was crazily doing the same—except for Megan, who was unable to share the spirit. It was all too fast, too noisy, too confusing. Besides, she could hardly see anything.

Will pulled her up, which proved to be the only way to see, and pointed toward the horses. The race had only just begun, and they were already rounding the final bend and thundering down the home stretch toward the finish line.

Totally Mine got closed in by two other horses, one on each side of him. Still he was coming, coming, a head-length ahead. It looked like a sure win, a very sure win. But then he dropped back at the last and lost it.

Megan was sorry for Will. The build-up had been so intense, the let-down so sharp. Except...he wasn't really acting as if he'd lost. Rather he continued jumping and hooting and waving his ticket ecstatically.

In case for some reason he didn't actually know it, she tried breaking it to him gently. "Will...he didn't win, your horse didn't win. It was close, but Totally Mine didn't win. Didn't you see that?"

He laughed and nodded, not seeming to mind. "Right, he made third place and I can collect on show."

Megan had begun thinking she understood some things, but she realized now that it was far from enough.

Will explained, "See, I bet across the board. Which means I could collect on first, second or third place. Totally Mine only got third, but at least it's something and the odds were good."

They went inside the grandstand to a window. Megan peered over Will's shoulder to watch the teller count out his winnings to him. It looked like a *lot*.

"How much, Will?" she asked, as they came away. "How much did you get?" It was at that point, seeing so much cash being doled out to him, that she herself really started feeling drawn in.

"Two hundred, seven dollars and fifty cents." His face was full of grins, his hands full of spread-out bills to show her.

"Two hundred, seven dollars?" she exclaimed.

"And fifty cents," he added.

"Wow! I can't believe you won that much."

"Megan, my total bet was one fifty, remember? So I actually only cleared fifty-seven dollars and fifty cents."

"Oh," she said. It wasn't as great as she'd thought, and yet, "You made fifty-seven dollars on a horse that only came in third?"

"And fifty cents." He went into a fit of laughter over her. Then suddenly, in the fun of the moment, he was catching her up into his arms and hugging her.

Megan laughed and hugged him as well. It was definitely a laughing-hugging occasion. But when he tried to kiss her, she broke away from him in a fast retraction.

"Sorry," he apologized.

She pretended it didn't happen and grabbed the racing program out of his pocket. "So now what? Who do you like in the second?"

"*Who do I like in the second*?" He laughed all the more at the way she was getting into it.

Together they studied the list of entries for the next race. Will did some further reading in the Racing Form. When he'd put all the facts together, he concluded, "Coming Up Fast hasn't raced in a while, but his workouts were good and he has the top jockey."

"Okay," Megan said, rising up and down on her toes,

anxious to hit the mutual window. "Let's do him. How much you betting?"

"I think I'll hold off a while yet on this one and keep a watch on the changing tote board odds. Let's go get another hot dog."

She simmered, and settled for a trip to the concessions. "Will," she said earnestly as they walked. "I want to bet something on this one, too."

He paused with surprise. "You do?"

"Yes."

"How much?"

"Ten bucks. Lewis brought me my final check from Sheldon Electronics last night and Joe cashed it for me."

Will nodded. "A sound bet. Win, place or show?"

"What?" She was lost again. Though he'd already explained the terms to her, it was hard to remember. "Uh...across the board. Across the board like you did."

"Megan, ten across the board would cost you *thirty*."

"Oh." She blinked dumbfoundedly.

"Make it simple, okay. Like do you want to bet ten on the horse to come in first, second or third place?"

"I don't know. What do you think?"

They got their second hot dogs, loaded them with relish and mustard, then wandered the inner grandstand while eating.

Will watched the constantly changing numbers on the electronic tote board. Numbers that meant nothing to her were detrimental to him. "I'm going to do fifty to win," he finally decided.

"Ten to win," Megan said for herself.

They approached a betting window.

"Wait—" Megan slowed Will down and dug into her purse. "I also want to pay you at least a part of my part of the rent, now that I've got some money."

"Megan, you don't have to do this right now. You can wait until—"

"No. Here." She counted some bills out to him. "A

hundred and twenty-five. The other one fifty by the first."

"Sure?" he asked, taking it reluctantly.

"Yes."

Though he'd been slow to accept, a grin replaced his skepticism. As they proceeded to the window, he said, "Think I'll raise my bet from fifty to *a hundred and fifty*."

She hurried along beside him, not at all liking what had just happened. She regretted having given him the rent money. It seemed to burn in his hand. For as much trouble as he already was in with his rent, he was now going to use part of her part toward *betting*. "Will... Will, wait." She tugged at his arm, trying to stop him.

They got into line, he with a sudden need to rush. "It's minutes to post time, last chance to bet."

She tried letting go of her resentment toward his betting the rent money. Especially when her own turn with the teller came and she felt her own elated thrill. "Ten to win on number five, please," she told him.

Megan found the second race much more enthralling, having a bet of her own riding on it. She screamed and cheered and waved her computerized ticket along with everybody else. She and Will brushed sides with one another amidst their jumping up and down. It was scary that paying the rent lost momentary priority to this, for her now, as well as for him. How, in fact, the whole world seemed to fall into a backdrop during the race.

"Come on, Coming Up Fast!" Megan shouted with more voice than she ever knew she had.

Coming Up Fast came up very fast. From leaving the starting gate in fourth place, he passed and passed and passed and *won*. Megan and Will hugged and danced and whirled each other around. "How much did we win?" she screamed. "How much, Will? I'm going crazy! I can't stand this!"

Minutes later they walked away from a mutual window counting their collections. Will had five hundred and seventy dollars and Megan had thirty-eight.

"I can't believe I turned my ten dollars into thirty-eight

just like that," she squealed. "I can't believe it! And you cleared over four hundred."

Will tucked his thickened wallet away. "Nice, huh. Aren't you glad I talked you into coming here?"

"I'll buy you some popcorn," she offered. "Come on, let me buy you some popcorn, Will."

"With butter?"

"Of course."

They walked as they munched their popcorn, Will showing her every inch of Canterbury Downs, inside and out. She was impressed that he knew it like a second home. "How often do you come here anyway?" she asked.

"A lot. But not as much as I'd like. Why?"

"Just wondering."

"Sometimes I make bets without even coming out here. Through a—"

"I'm not sure I want to hear this." She stopped him from saying *bookie.*

Jockeys were mounting for race number three near the paddock. Megan watched Will more closely than she watched the horses. There was such intensity on his face, as if he were a world apart from the real world. She supposed she'd come to know that world to a degree herself, but nowhere near as much as he. "Will...what about losing?"

He shrugged. "Yeah...sure...it's a fact that sometimes you lose."

"Then what?"

He laughed, breaking his concentration on the horses that were circling the walking ring. "Megan, you can't possibly win 'em all."

She felt relieved that he at least knew as much and admitted as much, in spite of seeming so dependent on winning. "It's not always a sure thing, is it?" She guessed maybe *she* dreaded the down side of it more than he did.

His smile faded. "Is anything?"

"Jobs. Jobs are."

He leaned against the fence, balking at the idea. "Is this

going to be a lecture or something?"

"Will, why do you gamble?"

His gaze returned to the horses that were starting to head out for the track. "Because...my job's not enough. Also, because I *like* gambling. You like it now, too, don't you?"

"I...I really don't know that much about it."

"But you're learning fast."

"I'm also very scared of it. Why do I feel scared of it?"

"I guess..." His glance flitted back and forth between her and the horses. "I guess that's just a part of it. It's the uncertainty that makes it exciting. You have to let the ups compensate for the downs. Like a minute ago...your adrenaline was racing just as fast as those horses, right? You loved winning that thirty-eight dollars, right?"

"But it's so risky."

Will opened the program to the third race listing. "Megan, you know, everything in life is risky and scary. Look at what just happened to your relationship with Sheldon. We're only betting money here. What'd you wager on *him*? Your heart, right?"

Will the gambler, the winner, the philosopher. He'd certainly won this discussion. Except if it was supposed to have made her feel better, it hadn't.

"I'm sorry." He lowered the booklet as he apologized.

"It's okay."

"I shouldn't have brought Lewis Sheldon into this."

She smiled and shook her head that it was okay.

Will held the program before her, pointing. "My Sassy Girl looks good in the third. What do you say?"

"Ten to win."

"*All right!*" He laughed at her fast revival. "And two hundred for me."

"Two hundred?" Megan felt a rebounding fear.

He offered her his arm. "Shall we step up to the window?"

She took it and went along.

My Sassy Girl was a black maiden with white markings. Her head bobbed proudly as her long slim legs pranced before the audience in one last showing.

Then into the starting gate. The bell. The release. "They're off!"

Megan and Will jumped up and down, screaming, yelling. A *wonderful* high. My Sassy Girl held the lead, as if no other horse dared catching her. Coming, coming, around the track. Flying like the wind. The last turn. Long legs throwing out, kicking back. Downing the home stretch. A close contender moved up on her right. A challenge, though certainly no threat. No. No...and yet...the challenger suddenly took her by a nose at the finish.

Will dropped to the bench, tore up his losing ticket and threw it. He hung his head lifelessly.

Megan ripped up her own ticket and tossed it to the wind. She touched Will's arm as she sat down beside him. "Maybe we should leave now."

"Leave?" The idea seemed to enrage him more than losing. He opened the program and studied for the fourth race.

She wasn't sure, at that point, which disturbed her the most. Will's losing, or his compulsion to win. "You promised to get me back in time for my job," she reminded him.

"It's only two o'clock. We can stay for a lot more races than this and still get back in time."

"I'm not sure I want to stay."

"Hey, hey." He straightened his shoulders, regained his spirit. "We'll make it up. That's the way it works, Megan. You just hang in there and you make it up."

She no longer liked what she saw or heard—the proof that it was something much more than just a game to Will.

It was after six when he got Megan to the Rusty Door. They walked in together. Nick saw and signaled her into his office. She went, leaving Will at the bar ordering a beer from Joe.

"I know I'm late for work," she began before Nick said it, "and I'm sorry."

The boss stood beside his desk, smoking a cigarette, studying her. "You came in with Westin. Is he the reason?"

Megan had expected to catch it about being late, but not about being with Will. Her mouth dropped wordlessly.

Nick tapped his ashes into the ashtray without taking his eyes off her. "You're *dating* him now? The two of you? That's great, just great. Really makes for smooth work relations. No one knows that better than I do."

"I don't understand," Megan said of his sarcasm.

"Me neither."

"I mean, are you mad because I'm late for work or because I've been with Will?"

Nick drew from his cigarette, exhaled slowly. "I'm not mad, I'm concerned."

"About my being late or being with Will?" she repeated.

"I'm just not sure you realize what you may be getting yourself into with Westin."

"I'm not getting into *anything* with him. Except—"

"Except what?"

"I'm living with him, but only as a financial arrangement."

Nick shook his head. "Do you have any idea what that guy's like on finances?"

"We're both in a financial bind right now and—"

"All right, all right. Let's just stick to your being late. You were out with Will and—"

"You're bringing him into this again."

"Because I'm trying to make the point that while the two of you were out together, you seem to have forgotten that although *his* job doesn't start till nine, *yours* starts at four-thirty."

"Aren't I allowed to be late once?"

"Allowed?" He looked puzzled.

"To be late," she said, nodding. "I'm only human, you know."

Nick looked her up and down. "Mmm...yes, so you are."

Megan's patience thinned at the way he was handling this, whatever *this* was suppose to be. The final few hours at the track, with Will on a loosing streak and refusing to leave and drive her back, had really worn her down. And now Nick's attitude was the last straw. "So are you going to fire me?"

"Fire you?" It was hard to tell if he was angry or amused. "Is that what you're aiming for? Me to fire you?"

"No," she answered.

"Okay, Megan, okay." He paused to take a drag from his cigarette and give her situation some silent thought. Then, "How much will you compromise?"

"Excuse me?" She was extremely leery of him, of this.

"Compromise." He was doing that looking her up and down thing again. "Tell you what...go out with me after closing and we'll forget all about your being late."

She guessed she should have expected this moment to come sooner or later from all she'd heard about him. "This sounds like sexual harassment."

"Who mentioned sex?"

"You know what I mean. I've heard how you treat your waitresses. I could report you to someone and get you into a lot of trouble for saying what you just did to me."

Nick crushed his cigarette in the ashtray. He seemed to become more uncomfortable than she. "You're getting this wrong, Megan, all wrong."

"Do I still have my job?"

"Yes, of course."

"Then I need to change clothes and start working." Holding her head high, she made a quick exit from his office.

• • •

Will sat slumped over the bar, working his beer, staring at nothing. He'd lost hard at the track, several hundred dollars. It wasn't that he wasn't used to losing now and then, but he just didn't like doing it in front of Megan. It had scared her, pretty much took the fun out of the day for her, shattered what faith she might have otherwise started acquiring in the whole thing. She'd seen the down side of the game...and the ugly down side of him as well.

"You look like you lost your best friend." Joe came back

to him on the inner side of the bar, full of concerned attention.

Will glanced up, sad-eyed and feeling pitifully sorry for himself. "I don't *have* a best friend."

"Hey, sure you do. Everybody does."

"Not me."

"How about the other Sidetracks? I bet every one of them—"

"We work together, Joe. We're friends but not *best,* y' know."

"Okay then...Leon, how about Leon? You and he seem to hit it off."

"No. Hardly a best friend, Joe," He drank the rest of his beer and motioned for another.

Joe got him a new bottle, but served it hesitantly. "You've got a show to do at nine, Will."

"I know."

"This is your third fast beer."

"Megan."

"What?" Joe asked.

"I think Megan's my best friend."

Joe laughed. "Girls are for girlfriends, Will, not best friends."

"Hey, girls are people just like anybody else."

"Yeah, they are. I'm just not sure they can be a guy's best friend."

"Why?"

"Just doesn't work that way."

"What about you and my mom?"

"What about us?" Joe mixed a screwdriver for a customer two stools down.

"That dance last night."

"I thought we were talking about you and Megan."

"I want to know what's going on with you and my mom."

"Nothing."

"You don't usually dance with your customers, Joe."

Joe grinned with narrowed eyes. "Key word is customer."

"You said girls are for *girlfriends.*"

"I meant that if your feelings really start to grow for a girl it's usually in a romantic way rather than a best friend way."

Will gave that some thought. "Your feelings aren't growing for my mom?"

"I hardly *know* your mom."

"I hardly know *Megan.*"

"Then why does she bother you so much?"

It was a good question. Too good of a one for him to know the answer. "Give me twenty pull tabs, Joe." He slapped a twenty dollar bill on the counter.

"Like that's going to solve everything?" He counted them out for Will just the same.

"My heart belongs to gambling, you know that."

"Maybe the odds run better with girls."

Will tore down tab after tab after tab. Nothing, nothing.

Joe stayed near, watching. "I like Megan."

"Me too," Will said.

"I liked her the first moment I saw her."

"Me too," Will agreed.

"So what are you going to do about her, Will?"

The pull tab pile was done in a hurry. No winners. "What am I *supposed* to do?"

"Come on, Will—you know the basic steps, don't you?"

"I'm not a basic person, Joe. See, I have this gambling monkey on my back, and it gets me into a whole lot of trouble."

"You can knock it off, Will."

"I'm not so sure."

"If you want to, you can."

"Like an easy choice."

"I didn't say easy."

Will held his head, rubbed it and did some more thinking. "A girl like Megan makes me wish to hell my life was straightened out. Yeah. She also makes me realize how very much it *isn't*. I don't know, Joe...I don't know if I'll ever be able to leave gambling alone."

"Worse yet," Joe said softly, "can you leave Megan alone?"

"Why don't you give me twenty more pull tabs."

"Will, why don't you put twenty bucks into a savings account instead, and start saving up for a nice little family and home?"

Will wasn't sure he wanted to hear any more of Joe's advice. Yet now he wasn't even really sure that he wanted those pull tabs. He rubbed his head again. He hated himself, he really hated himself.

His thinking came to life, as Megan came over to the bar in her black skirt and blouse. She was the fix he needed. "Hi," he said. "So did you get yelled at from Nick for being late?"

"Yes."

"Sorry."

"Are you okay, Will?"

She was looking so deeply at him that he was sure she saw all and more than he cared for her to.

He shifted uncomfortably. "Yeah, I'm fine. You?"

"Fine," she said. "Except I didn't like what happened to you."

Here it comes, he thought. The sore spot.

"Megan, you win some, you lose some. It's all part of the game."

"It made me sad."

He took a drink of beer. He felt responsible for having *caused* her sadness, and over something that was a regular part of his life.

"Will," she said, touching his arm, "I didn't feel sad because you were losing. I got sad because of your serious belief that you'd win it all back in the next race or the next or the next. I felt sad because you seemed to really see it as a sure thing. I don't think it is, Will. But…then…maybe my perspective of it is a little too new to really know." She smiled, not in a forgiving way, but more in a pitying sort of way. "Got to tend my tables. See you later."

Off she went. And Will swiveled his stool to stare after her.

Joe was right there with his bartending service. "Still want those twenty pull tabs?"

"No," Will said, as a form of punishment to himself.

"Maybe I was wrong," Joe said. "Maybe she *is* your best friend."

Will felt lifted by the possibility. "Yeah…I think so, Joe."

• • •

As if it wasn't enough for Megan to worry about Will and where he was going with his life and Nick's meanings and intentions because of the importance of holding her job, Lewis came into the club, like a menace, to top it all.

He knew which side was hers and sat at one of the tables within it, looking smug as he waited for her to wait on him.

She made the dreaded approach. "What would you like? *To drink?*" she quickly added.

"Scotch. You know that."

His dark glasses were on, but Megan felt his eyes searing through them and through her. She jotted his order on her pad.

Lewis detained her by asking, "Can we please have a talk? Just a talk?"

"I don't have time," she said, quite nicely, compared with how she felt.

"You seemed to have plenty of time for one of the band members last night."

"We work together here, you know."

"And *live* together, it seems."

Lewis had the wrong impression, thanks to the way she'd purposely misled him. And she was glad.

"You go from me to him just like that," he analyzed the matter.

Megan's look warned Lewis not to question her behavior over his own.

"Okay, okay." He removed his sunglasses. His eyes, surprisingly, looked as sad as Will's had. "Ten minutes, Megan—your next break time. Just give me ten minutes to straighten out a few things with you."

"That's how it all began," she reminded him. "At Sheldon Electronics. You called me into your office for a talk and the next thing I knew we were lovers."

"Are you saying you're afraid to spend ten minutes talking to me now?"

"I'm not afraid. I just don't see any point. You're no longer my boss, no longer my lover."

"How about friend?"

"I don't think so." She caught a glimpse of Nick over near his office door, openly watching her and Lewis. To settle things in a hurry she met Lewis's demand with, "All right, my next break."

When Leon arrived at the Door later, he made a long serious observation of Will's singing, which eventually led to his asking Megan, "What's with him?"

So far she'd been trying to focus her attention *off* Will, not on him. She'd been trying to let the sound of the Sidetracks stay in the background of her waitress work. She shrugged, saying to Leon, "Sounds fine to me."

Still with an earnest watch on the band, he said, "No...I know Willie's music enough to know when something's off. And it is."

As Leon strolled through the club, Megan stood still, making her own close study of the Sidetracks. They were into a fast raw rock, Will doing lead. To her he was as good as always. Except...okay, yes, maybe there was a heaviness, a kind of aching, in his voice,

"Down the road, around the bend
Ain't gonna came back till who knows when
Yellow line taking me
Good-bye, the wind is my new friend..."

It chilled Megan's spine, burned at her heart. Will frustrated her as no other guy ever had. She didn't like it, need it.

When she finally turned her attention away from the band again, she spied Nick still keeping watch on her. She started re-rounds of her tables.

The boss caught up with her. "You're doing a lot of socializing tonight, Megan."

"I'm serving my customers just fine, Nick."

"You've been chatting with friends a lot. I don't like my waitresses becoming so social."

She was tired and emotionally drained. She'd had enough of Nick's hassling on top of her problems with Lewis and her concerns for Will.

She met him with a straight-on stern look. "You mean like the last waitress who worked here?"

Nick swelled with irritation of a new sort. "I'll see you in my office right now." He stormed off ahead of her.

But she didn't follow. Rather she went to sit with Lewis.

Lewis was more than surprised, and accepted her plunking down at his table as if he'd never actually expected her to come.

The table was far enough back that the Sidetracks weren't blaring directly at them and she thought maybe they could get their talk over with then and there. "Okay," she said, "talk."

He leaned toward her. "First of all, Megan, I thought you knew all along that I was married."

"No. I didn't."

"It wasn't a secret."

"I didn't know."

"People in my company knew. I would have surely thought the grapevine in the main office would—"

"I didn't know," she repeated.

"I thought you knew what you were getting into."

"You could have made sure. You could have been open and honest and made sure I knew everything there was to know. I had that right. You never respected it."

"I thought you were more sophisticated than this. I knew you were young, but I didn't think you were a child."

"I am not a child just because I don't like having an affair with a married man."

"Dana and I had been—"

"I don't want to talk about Dana."

"We have to, because she's part of this. Dana and I had been separated for some time. I really didn't think there was any chance of her and me reconciling when I asked you to live with me, Megan."

The conversation took a new, though not especially better, slant. "Well, I'm glad I could help fill your lonely needs."

"It was more than that, Megan. I was attracted to you in many ways. You were special."

"I was *temporary*."

Nick returned, searching her out and coming to stand beside their table. "Excuse me—what's going on here?"

Megan raised her look to him. "I'm on my break."

"You were told to come to my office."

"She's talking with me right now," Lewis stated.

"Oh yes," Nick acknowledged smartly. "The trouble-maker from the other night."

"I beg your pardon?" Lewis said.

"I certainly *hope* so," Nick wised back.

Lewis rose from his chair, as if ready to take him on.

"Perhaps *you'd* better step into my office," Nick suggested to him.

Suddenly a fourth party was on the scene. Leon. He took a gentle hold on Megan's arm. "Excuse me, Lewie...Nickie... but you're beginning to compete with the band. Besides, this waitress has some very impatient customers waiting for her." He escorted her away.

Giggling amidst their brisk departure, Megan asked Leon. *"What customers?"*

"Me and Annie, of course."

Eight

Megan took a mug of coffee out to Will late Monday morning while he was washing his car in the apartment parking lot. Her thoughtfulness surprised him, after yesterday's tiff over the racetrack, the tension that had built between them at the Door and the silent ride home last night.

"Here." She handed him the peace offering. He released the nozzle trigger and laid the hose down on the dirt.

"Thanks, I can really use this."

The Mustang looked wonderfully clean, its black sharp and shiny through the beaded rinse water on it.

"You kind of like this old car, don't you?" She was coming to realize that more and more.

"It wasn't so old when I first got it."

"You take good care of it."

Besides the notable pride he took in driving it, he tended to its upkeep far better than his apartment, had personalized license plates that read TRACK and a deluxe stereo system within.

"Ranks second to my music," he told her. Then after several swallows of coffee he lowered the mug with an "Ahh...and this ranks third."

"What does your gambling rank?"

"Let's not get into that."

"Sorry." She regretted the mention.

"It ranks pretty high," he admitted.

"Why," she asked. "Why does gambling have to be so important to you? I mean, where does it really get you?"

"Thought we were going to leave this alone."

"Sorry," she said again. She went up on the toes of her tennis shoes and back down again, stuck her hands into her jeans pockets, and shrugged her sweatered shoulders. "It's just that I...I can't understand your interest in it."

"Do you *have* to?"

"No."

"Sorry," he said it this time. "I guess I just have a passion for it."

"Passion?"

"Yeah."

"Even though it screws up your life?"

"There are a lot of passions that do that to your life, but you don't necessarily give them up."

He was looking at her in that confident, grinning way of his. He with his flannel shirt opened to a navy tee. He with wet pant legs and wet shoes. He with answers and charm and smooth easy takeovers.

"Don't be afraid of passion, Megan," he told her.

"No...I...I..." She was scared and he could see it. "I guess I'm just not much of a gambler."

"You're missing my point here," he said with a laugh. "While passion may be partly the fault of my track addiction, which causes me a lot of grief, I still consider passion, itself, to be a terrific thing. And if a person has any passion at all, it's usually in *many* areas, not just one."

"What are your other areas?" she asked.

"Music is one."

She nodded, knowing the passion he put to that.

"And freedom," he continued. "And my car. Come on, Megan, what are *your* passions?"

She shook her head. "I don't have any."

"Sure you do."

"I wish I did. But...I just don't think I'm a passionate person."

Will's smile widened. "Sure you are. Remember how you felt at the track yesterday when your horse came in first? There...see? That was a passionate high."

Her own smile carried minimum satisfaction. "So I, too, have a passion for gambling? How wonderful."

"It's a sign that you do have *passion*, which means it's also there for many other things."

"I don't think so, Will."

"Megan, *yes,*" he insisted. "You just have to open yourself up to it more. What about Sheldon? Didn't you feel passion with him?"

"No. More like *passive*."

"That must have been exciting."

"Maybe something's wrong with me."

"I don't think anything is wrong with you, Megan."

"There is if I don't feel passionate about anything."

"You've had some bad breaks in your life, that's all."

"So have you. But you still have *passion*. You do, Will. I can really see that. And I envy that."

"Feel, Megan. Just let yourself feel. Anything. Everything. Let go. Enjoy. There are so many things to enjoy. Open yourself to them."

"Like betting on the horses?" she had to say.

"More than that."

She shook her head, feeling hopeless.

"Megan, Megan." He laughed again. "I've got a lot to teach you. But right now I've got to finish my car." He handed her back his empty mug. "Thanks. You make great coffee."

"You're welcome. Maybe that's one of my passions."

As he picked up his chamois cloth and started wiping his Mustang, she headed back to the building.

Before she got to the door, a white car coming off the street into the lot took her attention. She stopped. It was a familiar car, a dreaded car. It was Lewis's.

Against her better judgment, she walked over to where he'd parked, just beyond Will. With his dark glasses in place, he was gloating out his driver's side window as though his coming there was some sort of achievement.

"What are you doing here?" she asked, nearing him.

"I could ask the same of you," he responded.

"I live here."

"How nice. How perfectly nice."

"How did you know where I live?"

"I followed you and your guitar man home last night. Watched where you went in."

"Why?"

"You actually *like* living here, Megan? In this dump of a place?"

"Leave me alone, Lewis. We're over."

"The parking lot's not even black-topped. How quaint for this day and age."

"The parking lot is fine. I don't want you coming around me anymore, Lewis. I want to forget my mistakes. I just want to get on with my life."

He nodded. "And me mine—as soon as I get my ring back."

"I don't have it."

"Does he?" He motioned to Will, just a few feet away.

"No. Go."

"Get it, Megan."

"I can't. You'll just have to do without it. Chalk it up as one of *your* mistakes, for getting involved with a thief."

"You're not a thief. I can't let this go by, for your benefit as well as mine."

"Oh please—don't worry about *my* benefit, Lewis."

Will came over beside Megan, pulling the hose along with him. He brought the nozzle up, aiming it at Lewis like a gun, threatening to squeeze the trigger. "Good-bye, Mr. Sheldon. Sorry you have to rush off right away, but I guess you probably want to try and beat the rain."

Lewis dipped his head to glance out and upward at the sky. The sun was shining. "Looks fine to me."

"Maybe you should take your shades off," Will suggested. "Then you'd see there's a big dark cloud right over you."

"Adolescent," Lewis shook his head at him. "Very adolescent, Westin."

Will further raised and aimed his weapon. "Good-bye. Come again on a brighter day."

"I'm talking to Megan."

"Sorry," Will said. "The talk has been called on account of rain." With that he squeezed the handle and shot a hard-forced spray of cold water directly into Lewis's face as well as the front interior of his New Yorker.

Gulping for his breath and convulsing at the shock of it, Lewis fumbled for the window closing button. Then he put his still running car into gear and spun the tires leaving.

In the same way that so many things affected her about Will, Megan wasn't quite sure whether she was happy or angry over what he'd just done. She guessed more than anything she was worried about crossing Lewis. "You might regret having done that to him," she warned.

Will laughed. "I would have regretted passing *up* that chance even more."

He went back to finish his Mustang and she went up to the apartment.

The phone was ringing as she entered 316, and she ran to grab it. "Hello?"

"Hello, is Will Westin there, please?"

"No. Would you like to leave a message?"

"Are you his wife?" the man asked.

Megan held the phone out and away from herself to look at it, *glare* at it. Will had a hidden wife also? No, no...she couldn't take it. It couldn't be. She closed the receiver back to her ear. "No, I'm not his wife. D-does he have one?"

"I don't know," the man said. "I just meant are you a relative or—"

"A friend." Megan breathed easier.

"Friend?"

"Yes."

"Then you will be so kind as to tell your good friend, Will Westin, that Eldridge Auto Insurance has still not received his payment and if it's not in our hands by the end of the week I'm afraid we'll have to cancel him. Now you can't be without car insurance, can you?"

"Thank you. I'll give him the message."

When Will came up to the apartment, he was still laughing about what he'd done to Lewis. "I can't forget the look on his face. He really didn't think I'd do it."

"It *was* pretty funny," Megan admitted, having to laugh some more over it herself.

He washed his hands at the kitchen sink. "So what did he want anyway? Does he want you to come back to him?"

"No, he just—"

"I'm sorry," Will glanced around at her. "I guess it's really none of my business. And I guess I really shouldn't have gotten rid of him that way either."

"He was annoying me. I'm glad you *did* get rid of him like that, Will."

The two of them started laughing all over again.

Will dried his hands on the towel. "Thanks again for bringing that coffee down to me."

"You're welcome."

"Hey—how about us taking a drive in my nice clean Mustang?"

"Where?"

"No place particular. Just a drive. Maybe out in the country aways."

She said okay. They left the apartment together, heading down the hall, down the stairs, out the main door.

They started through the parking lot, then stopped abruptly at the sight of Will's car. It was covered with dirt, as if someone had thrown it on by the handfuls. The hood and roof held scattered clumps of earth, the windows and sides were thick filmy dust.

"Sheldon?" Will seethed through clenched teeth.

Megan was right beside him as they reached the car. "He must have come back and done this right after you went inside," she said.

Will lightly and carefully brushed the worst of the dirt off his sadly dulled car. "I guess I asked for this, didn't I?"

"I'm sorry, Will."

He drew a couple of long deep breaths and stood several quiet minutes before saying, "Let's go."

She was glad he still wanted to go for the ride. She slipped into the passenger side and he behind the wheel.

As he started the engine, he snarled, "Tell me where to find his New Yorker. Home? Work? Where this time of day?"

"Will, no."

"I'm kidding." He laughed as he drove out of the lot.

Megan was relieved, and the next moment laughing as well.

"Okay now," Will simmered, "we're just out to have fun and forget all our—"

"Oh, Will—speaking of forgetting, I forgot to tell you there was a phone call for you before. A guy from Eldridge Auto Insurance. He said to tell you that you have till the end of the week to make your payment or else."

"Yeah, yeah…so what else is new?" Half kidding, half serious, he asked, "Megan, which do you consider most important to pay—apartment rent or car insurance?"

"Oh, Will…" Her worried feeling was back. "You shouldn't have to choose one or the other. You should be able to—"

"Stop. My fault. I said we were going to forget our problems. No more, okay? No more."

Circles. Her mind was going in such circles. She didn't seem to be able to turn it on and off like he did. She wrung her hands together in her lap.

"Come on, Megan," Will coaxed. "Relax."

How *did* he do it, she wondered, watching him. He seemed to free himself so easily and totally whenever he chose to.

"Megan," he said with a bubbling over sort of energy, "this is something to be *passionate* about. Freedom. Sunshine. The countryside we'll soon be in. Come on...you wanted to learn it, to acquire it. All you have to do is look around. Take it in—really deep within you."

So far she'd been watching him more than the passing scenery.

"Are you with me?" He gave her a sidelong glance.

"I guess I'm still a little bogged down."

"Cup your hands together under your mouth," he told her.

"What?"

"Just do it. Now blow into them."

"What?" she asked again.

"Blow all your bogs into your hands, Megan. *Do* it."

Silly as she felt, she blew and blew, hard into her hands.

"Okay," he instructed, "now throw them out the window."

Doing so made her burst into a hearty bog-less laugh.

They wove their way over to Highway 81 and headed north. Then after passing through Osseo, they turned off onto some old dirt roads. A massive dust cloud stirred behind them as they sped along.

"I feel less mad at what Sheldon did to my car now that I'm doing it to the car myself," Will said.

"I'll wash it for you later," Megan offered.

"You don't have to."

"I'd like to."

"Really?"

"Yes."

"Okay."

The roads were rough and bumpy. They passed bare farm fields not yet ready for planting, and endless unpainted rail fences. It was all so picturesque. Open. Serene. A nice diversion from the city hustle.

Megan began to feel farther and farther away from everything and everybody. Except from Will, that is. To him she was growing closer. To his beliefs, his ways, his irresistible appeal.

"What?" he asked, when he caught her studying him.

She was embarrassed by the trance she'd fallen into. "Have you always been into music?"

"Why?"

"Is that a difficult question?" she teased.

"I've been into music for as long as I can remember," he answered with feeling. "You seem to like music pretty much yourself."

"Yes, I do."

"It's passion to the soul, you know."

"There's that word again." She laughed.

"What say we put some soundtrack to this ride?" He reached forth to turn on the radio.

CCR's "Green River" had just started. Will let out an excited howl and cranked it up full blast. "All right! Now this is music! This is passion! Do you feel it, Megan? Do you?"

She answered yes, but didn't think he heard her. The car seemed to be going faster and faster, as though keeping up with the guitars, tambourines and drums. Will started singing the words right along with John Fogerty.

Megan joined in as best she could. It felt great. Nothing else in the whole world mattered, existed, right then. Only she, Will, and CCR. Sharing in the song. Giving...giving everything they had to it.

It was a let-down when the song ended and Will turned the radio volume back down. Yet, by then, they really needed some mellowing. Even Will's driving mellowed and eased back under forty. He gave Megan a look, as if checking her response.

"You're right," she told him, "I feel it now. I feel *passion.*"

"I know," he said, proudly taking credit. "I know."

The afternoon turned out to be an equal balance of quiet moments mixed with accelerated moments, depending on what radio music was playing. Slow, fast, hard, soft, noisy, dreamy. Megan and Will kept easily flexible to whatever.

Eventually Will got around to asking her. "Hungry?"

"Yes," she said. "Are you?"

"Yeah. I'm not exactly sure where we are, but—"

"You're not exactly sure?" She didn't know whether to laugh or cry.

"No. But the next restaurant we come to, we'll stop."

"*Next* one? I haven't seen *any* yet."

The sharing of a good laugh made up for the hunger in their stomachs. At least for a time longer.

When Van Morrison's "Brand New Day" came on the radio, Megan reached forth to turn up the volume. "I *love* this song."

"With passion?" Will asked.

"Yes, yes. Don't you?"

"Yeah, yeah, it's good," he agreed.

"A great one to slow dance to."

"You mean, unlike most of *my* songs."

"Do you dance, Will?"

"Hey, I'm a musician…with rhythm, remember?"

"But do you dance?" She waited. Got no answer. She teased him with, "You don't, do you? A musician with rhythm and you don't even dance."

"I dance."

"Sure."

"I do."

"Quiet, let's listen." Van Morrison's smoothness, dreaminess, captivated her.

Will pulled the car off the edge of the road, cutting partly into some tall brush and stopping. He left his side of the car and ran around to open the door on her side. He coaxed her out of it. "Come on—let's do it."

"Do what?" She gave him a startled look.

"Dance."

"Here? In a farm field?" She stepped out to him.

"Sure, why not." He leaned in to turn the car radio up to its max. Then he led Megan through the knee-high brush and on through to a lower-cut, dry bristly field. He took her into his arms, grinning and reminding her, "With passion..."

They slow-danced. Out in the middle of the open countryside. With Van Morrison's soulful voice and words reaching them, moving them.

Enhancing Morrison's voice was a strong bass and a heated sax. The music and its mood had taken over the field, belonging there as much as anything ever belonged anywhere.

Will's arms held Megan and guided her. Their bodies moved together easily, sensuously. It was a long song, seeming to grant a sense of eternity to whatever it was that was happening between the two of them.

There was a sureness that no other dance would ever compare. When it finally drew to an end the couple stayed close, staring deeply into each other's eyes, finding something else beyond the limit of the music, the dance.

"That was nice." Megan was first to speak.

"Yeah," Will smiled.

"You *do* know how."

He nodded. "Great exercise, dancing."

"*Slow* dancing?" She burst into a giggle.

"We were moving, weren't we?"

"Slow dancing is *not* what you call great exercise," she assured him. "You want *exercise*? Here." She shoved him hard enough to send him backwards and into a stumbling fall.

"Hey!" he yelled from his half sprawled position on the ground.

Megan took off running, expecting that Will would come

after her, *wanting* him to come after her. It was too great a location to waste on seriousness. It was time to feel a more *lively* form of passion. Besides, Chris Isaak's "Wild Love" had just begun blasting out of the car radio, making a perfect soundtrack for romping.

Running, running...all about the field. Megan with Will after her. Laughing, shouting, breathing in short gasps. She only managed to keep ahead of his exaggerated enragement for just so long. Soon he caught her and returned a playful rough push that landed *her* on the ground.

She didn't *mind* being pushed down. She deserved it. *Loved* it. It weakened her into more giggles and laughs, making it comically difficult to even get herself back onto her feet. But then it was *her* turn to chase *him* again. Fun, fun...silly child-like fun...all around the field.

It had grown dark by the time Megan and Will arrived back home to north Minneapolis. They were full from the Italian meal they'd had at a remote little place they'd found by luck. And tired from the drive, the field play and the fresh air.

They had watched the late afternoon sky grow more and more clouded. Distant rumbling thunder neared into loud crashes and booms, and a heavy rain opened and beat heavily on the dirty Mustang.

By the time Will parked the car back in the apartment lot beneath the light post, it showed a clean and gleaming wet shine that seemed to rectify all it'd endured that day. He and Megan were still on a fun and laughter jag as they ran through the cold wet weather to the building.

• • •

What was there to do as a follow-up to such a great afternoon? Will thought as they entered 316. What, when the mood was light and special and you didn't want to make a wrong move to possibly throw it off track? He didn't know. He wasn't sure what to do about Megan Delany. How fast to go with her. How far.

"Want to watch a movie?" he suggested.

"What?" she asked.

Was the look she was giving him that of not hearing? Or not believing? No girl had ever made him feel this awkward. Had she expected more? Was he coming across now as a cold turn-off following his lessons in passion? Was he making a mistake in saying, "Movie—in the VCR—I've got a good collection."

He was amazed that her interest in the idea went zooming way ahead of his. "I *love* movies. Let's see what you've got." She went to sort through the row of them on the shelf beneath the TV.

"Popcorn?" he asked.

"Yes." She was equally enthused with that.

Good. Great. He made a bag of Quick Pop in the microwave.

Soon they were sitting together on the couch, stocking feet over onto the hassock, popcorn between them, *Lethal Weapon* on the screen.

This was silly, Will thought within his hidden thoughts. Silly to be resisting the urge he had to ease Megan down, to kiss her madly, to caress the entirety of her, to have sex with her. Even more silly, he knew, to have these urges at all. They'd made an agreement about the conditions of their living together. He needed to respect that. Remember that. While his carefulness over Megan was making him crazy.

He settled instead for putting his left arm along the back of the couch behind her. An arm. Just an arm. Along the couch. Yes...okay...it seemed almost enough for now. He relaxed and accepted the casualness. She seemed relaxed and content as well, sitting there next to him with no further expectations.

They watched the movie. And ate popcorn. Lightning and thunder passed out of the area and the rain diminished to a soft patter outside the open living room window.

"So you really like this movie?" Will checked with Megan after Mel Gibson had been the center of attraction for a straight twenty minutes.

"I love it. You?"

"You chose my favorite."

"Really?" She turned her sparkly blue-eyed look on him, almost throwing him out of control again.

He wished she hadn't. God, that face, those eyes, that slightly parted mouth, her being so close to him. "Yeah... really," he answered about the movie. Then he dug his free hand greedily into the bowl of popcorn.

"So..." she said, taking a much daintier helping of popcorn herself, "you have a passion for *movies*, I'm finding out."

"And popcorn," he added before stuffing his mouth with it.

Nine

Monday through Friday had Megan believing she'd seen the last of Lewis, that he'd given up trying to make her understand him or give his ring back. The smoothness of the week also had her believing that somehow Will's rent would get paid, his car insurance would get taken care of and that he would swear off gambling by realizing what it was doing to his life. Everything seemed...hopeful.

Until Saturday night at the Rusty Door. When Will moped in directly from the racetrack with a three-hundred dollar loss and a bad disposition. And Lewis showed up to hound her the entire evening for a talk, just one serious private talk between them.

Megan felt the tormenting pressures mount. It affected

her work. It became more and more difficult for her to give smiles and good service to her customers when she was so worried about Will and annoyed with Lewis. Will went off broodingly by himself on his breaks, while Lewis kept after her every chance he got.

By midnight she'd given up expecting anything more from Will or anything less from Lewis. In a mental frazzle, she finally consented to leave the club and go for a ride with Lewis.

"You don't belong in that place," he told her as they drove off in his New Yorker.

"I belong where I belong," she said with an attitude.

"What the hell does that mean?"

"It means what it means."

"Fine." He took off his sunglasses and tossed them onto the dashboard, as if he'd needed them anyway in the dark of night.

"Why do you wear them all the time?" she snapped.

"Because I do," he said with an attitude matching hers.

Megan didn't know where they were going, only that it was somewhere to talk. She found it hard to believe she'd actually left with Lewis at all, let alone an hour before the Door closed.

She turned her head to look more directly at him. Beneath the short flashes of street lights she managed to see the set determination on his face. It meant this talk they were about to have was much more important to him than to her. As far as she was concerned, there were no loose ends to tie, no explanations other than Dana. Their relationship had been a regrettable mistake, and any talk of it now could only be another mistake.

They left the highway on Edgewood Parkway, a narrow, rustic, scarcely lit road, winding through a thick dark enclosure of trees. Megan became as uneasy, as if she were with some dangerous life-threatening stranger rather than the guy she'd lived with for three months. She started to worry about more than just a useless talk with him. She feared seeing a whole different side of Lewis Sheldon than she'd ever known. She was scared, sorry she'd left with him.

She was just about to ask where exactly they were headed when he pulled off into a rest stop on the right and parked at a low stone ledge. When Lewis cut the headlights, darkness fell so heavily it was as if a blanket had suddenly covered the entire car.

Quiet, quiet. Why wasn't he saying anything? The quiet forced Megan into speaking first. "Lewis, I've already told you several times that I don't have your ring, so please don't ask me for it again."

"I want my ring, Megan. I'm not asking you, I'm *telling* you."

She gave a sigh and tried looking out her window. But there was only a blackness she couldn't see through. "Why, Lewis? Why did you bring me to a place like this to talk?"

"Maybe so that I can get your full and undivided attention."

"How can I give you my full and undivided attention when it's focused on fear?"

"You don't have to be scared."

"Then why am I?"

"You took the ring to get even, didn't you?"

"That's all you care about, Lewis, your ring?"

"I'd hate to think that I turned you into a thief, that's all."

She laughed. "And whose conscience would we be trying to redeem here—mine or yours?"

"You've changed a lot, Megan. A real lot."

"Good."

"It's not flattering."

"Double good."

"It's not good trying to cover your feelings with a tough act."

"My feelings are no longer your concern. I'm not sure they ever were."

"Like I said before, Megan, I honestly thought all along that you knew I was married and separated."

"Like I said before, *I didn't*."

"I'm sorry."

"You should have made sure."

"I know."

"Did I *seem* like a girl who would go live with a married man?"

"Separated," he clarified.

"I guess we just had each other figured wrong, Lewis."

"Don't call it wrong, Megan." The dark silhouette of his right arm rose toward her. He started playing with her hair, stroking it, winding long sections of it around his fingers. "You've got the most beautiful hair, Megan."

She tried to ignore what he was doing, concentrating only on their discussion. "It was wrong because I…I know now that we never loved each other or—"

"*Of course* it wasn't love. Who ever said it was? Who ever said it had to be to live together? Do you love this *Will Westin*?"

"Leave him out of this."

"Well, well…maybe you do."

"So what was it, Lewis, that you and I had together those three months?"

He laughed, offering, "I'd be glad to review it with you."

Megan put her hands against him to try stopping him from coming any closer than he already had. "Lewis, no."

Her barrier meant nothing to him. His arms worked their way around her, clutching and pulling until he had her tightly in his hold.

"What's going on here?" She kept up her struggle. "You said you wanted to talk. If I'd thought you were going to try this I would never have left with you. Let me go, Lewis."

She'd never known he was so strong. But then she'd never tried fighting him off before either. Squirming, pushing—nothing seemed to be enough. The moment her own strength gave way to his he managed to get his mouth against hers. He was holding her and kissing her and she could do nothing. She hated it, hated him, though not so long ago his attentions had been the center of her life. Until Dana.

Maybe, she thought, in her misery, the best way to make this moment go away was to succumb, to let him kiss her a few times, get it over with. To not show any interest, but to not resist either.

But when Lewis started working a hand into the front opening of her blouse Megan started fighting again and managed to break away this time. She backed as far off to her side of the car as possible. "What do you think you're doing?" she shouted.

"Doing?" He laughed.

"Are you going to try and *rape* me? Is that why you brought me here?"

"No." His humor left him. "No, of course not, Megan. I'm sorry. I didn't mean to scare you. I just thought—"

"That you could take advantage of me."

"No. That's not it."

She'd moved so far over that the car door handle poked into her back. Yet its being there seemed more of a security than discomfort. She rebuttoned her blouse.

"Maybe I just wanted to prove something," he said.

Whatever it was, she didn't want to hear it.

But Lewis couldn't wait to explain. "That was it, you know—what we had together. A physical attraction."

"That's not enough."

"I know. I know that now. But I just wanted to see if it was still there. I could feel you giving in to it too, Megan."

"That's not what I was giving in to. My arms were hurting from trying to push you away."

"Don't tell me there's not just an ounce of you that isn't still attracted to me."

"You have a wife."

"Yes."

"Lewis, you have a *wife*."

"Which has nothing at all to do with this, us."

Suddenly Megan was more concerned about Dana's feelings than her own. "What are you talking about? How can you say that?"

"Megan, I'm just trying to show you that there's a difference between love and...well, what *we* had."

"What we had was very shallow, Lewis."

"Come on, Megan. See the light."

"If you wanted me to see the light, you shouldn't have brought me to such a dark place."

"You can't see what this is about?"

"I can barely see *anything.*"

"It was a test, a kind of proof. Megan...I love Dana. I do. I guess I truly didn't know that until just the other day. Now I realize I've always loved her and that I never really stopped. But loving Dana just doesn't mean that *you* weren't special to me in a different sort of way."

"Gee, thanks," she said smartly.

"I think maybe it even actually *took* you to make me more sure that I did want to and need to go back to her. To what she and I once had together. To what was really real. Therefore...I'm very thankful to you, Megan."

"And I'm confused."

"I have this sureness now. You know what I mean?"

She tried to consider it. "Well maybe if you're through running these tests now—"

"I don't know...maybe I don't deserve another chance with her," he claimed, "but we'd only just started walking and talking when you happened along and—"

"Well, excuse me for intruding. I mean, the park *is* right across the street from the Halloren."

"I know. Bad choice. Our running into each other like that was unfortunate for you and pretty much shot the hell out of Dana's and my meeting. But Dana is going to call me and set another time. Oh, Megan..." Lewis's voice softened, "I really love her. And...I'm really sorry if I misled you."

"If?" Megan repeated the word. Yet, strange as it was, she supposed she did feel Lewis's sincerity coming through. She guessed she believed him. And yet...she kept one hand behind her on the door handle. "Take me home now, Lewis."

"You *have* one?" His smartness returned. "You say that

like you actually do have a home."

"Please."

"Not yet. We're not through here."

Megan flexed her wrist, grasping the door handle tighter, ready to spring it down. She wasn't going to allow him another *test*, if that was what he had in mind.

"I want my ring back, Megan." He inched toward her again.

"Lewis, I told you—"

"If you don't have it then where *is* it? What the hell did you do with it?"

"I…I…"

"Get it, Megan, or…or I assure you I'll make life hellish for you."

"You mean like throwing dirt at Will's car?"

"My ring, Megan. Is that so much to ask?"

"You don't need that ring, Lewis. You don't need me and you don't need the ring."

He grabbed her arm, far more roughly than seductively this time. "Do I have to bring the police in on this? Because I will if I have to."

"Let go of me!" She tried pulling away.

"You had no right to take it."

"I don't think you know much about rights, Lewis." Her hand worked at the door handle behind her until she got it down. The door made a loud click as it released, distracting Lewis enough so that she was able to break clear of him and jump out of the car. She ran blindly into the dark.

"Megan!" he shouted after her.

She took off past the back of the car, heading toward where she could only estimate the parkway road to be.

The start of the New Yorker engine roared like a monster conjuring attack. As the car backed up and turned around, its headlights came flooding onto Megan.

There was no escape unless she fled off into the bushes and woods. But they were only a bad-for-worse alternative to Lewis.

Just as she reached the edge of the rest stop area, that met with the parkway road, Lewis braked behind her and jumped out of his car to pursue her on foot.

With good timing, another car came along the near-forsaken road just then, casting a second bright light upon the both of them and bringing them to a startled halt.

The car on the road stopped. Someone got out. Someone said, "Meggie!" It was Leon, dear sweet life-saving Leon.

"Leon!" Megan ran to meet him halfway.

He caught her into his arms. "Meggie...are you okay?"

"What are you doing out here?" she could only think to ask.

"Looking for you. I saw you leave with him, tried following, lost you, and was just now back-tracking."

Lewis came toward the hugging twosome. "Why don't you mind your own business."

Leon warned him, "Hold it right there, Lewie!"

"*Lewis*," the business man corrected him, fearlessly proceeding all the way.

"Get back into your car, *Lewie*, and stay the hell away from Meggie!" Leon let go of her and in one continuous motion threw his hands against Lewis, knocking him backwards. "I mean it, *Lewie*!"

Lewis regained his balance and plowed forth into the slight framed Leon. Their scuffle and tangle set them bouncing off the side of Leon's parked, but still running, car.

"Stop it!" Megan screamed.

They ignored her. More fighting. More scuffling.

"Stop it!" she cried.

Though Lewis was bigger and stronger than Leon, Leon was definitely more angry and feisty.

Lewis was first to make a sensible withdrawal, though not without some last breathless words. "I want my ring back. Stealing is a criminal offense. Are the two of you in this together? You probably are. I have a good lawyer I can call if necessary."

Though Megan felt safe driving away with Leon, she was

still shaking. He pulled his jacket off the back seat, gave it to her and told her to put it on. She slipped into it, finding the warmth soothing and settling.

He explained his arrival, "I couldn't believe my eyes, seeing you leave the Door with him. I ran out to my own car to at least try and tail you, but I got held up at a stoplight. Then I thought it looked like Lewie turned onto the parkway. I took it and drove quite a distance down, seeing nothing—no other tail lights, headlights, nothing. Then I wondered if maybe he could've pulled off into a rest stop and I turned around and was just heading back for a closer search when I saw you. Meggie I was so relieved to find you."

He turned his face, giving her a sidelong look. Though he finally began to slow his getaway driving, his concern was still going strong. "Did he hurt you. Did he? Tell me, Meggie—what'd he do to you?"

"He kissed me."

"*Kissed* you?" Leon gasped.

She might as well have said raped, he was so enraged.

"Damn!" he said. "Why did you even go off with him like that?"

"Mostly because I was tired...really tired of just everything, you know."

"Then you should have come to me. Usually you come to *me* when you get tired of things."

"Lewis convinced me that we needed to talk, to finish things off between us. I should have known better."

"Yeah, you should have."

"Leon, I can't believe you found me like that."

"Neither can I."

"You were wonderful."

"I was *lucky*. I don't know what I'd have done if I hadn't found you. Worse yet, what Lewie might have done."

"He wants his ring back. He just wants his ring back. That's really all he wants."

"Which you no longer have."

"No."

"I still don't get why you ever took it in the first place."

"I told you."

"I know, but I still don't get it."

Megan didn't want to go over it anymore that night. She couldn't. She was sick of the ring thing. "Where's Ann?"

"When I left, she said not to worry, she'd get a ride home from Becky and Paul. She *wanted* me to find you. She cares about you, too, Meggie. Look, why don't you come stay with us for the night? My couch is probably in a lot better shape than Willie's couch."

"I don't think so," she said, though it brought a smile from her.

"Are you really okay, Meggie?"

"Yes."

"Really?"

"I think so."

"How about if we go somewhere for a sandwich and coffee? If we just talk awhile before I drop you at Willie's?"

"Okay."

• • •

Will hated that he'd left the Rusty Door and come home without Megan. He hated that she'd disappeared earlier and no one knew anything about it. He paced his dark apartment, feeling sick with worry about her. He didn't know what to do. Waiting, just waiting, was driving him crazy.

He went to the kitchen phone to call Leon.

"Hello?" Ann answered.

"Ann, it's Will. Where's Megan? She disappeared from the club before closing and no one knew anything and I'm really worried and—"

"Whoa, slow down," his sister ordered him.

"Do you know anything, Ann? Do you?"

"Why would you think that I—"

"Come on, Ann. Don't play games. I'm worried and I'm looking for answers."

"I thought Megan was only sharing the *rent* there. Why are you acting like you own her?"

"I'd be worried about any girl who disappeared like that. I just...want to know if she's okay."

"She is," Ann said then, as if Will had finally earned the right to know as much.

Though he took a deep breath and exhaled it with grand relief, he still felt anxious and keyed up. "You're sure? You know that for sure? Is she there with you?"

"You said you only wanted to know if she was okay. Now you're asking fifty more things."

It wasn't easy trying to get anywhere with Ann. Once a big sister, always a big sister, Will concluded. How she loved dangling him and teasing him any chance she got. "I think I know what you're after," he said.

"So tell me," she said, "and then I'll tell *you.*"

"Okay...I *care* about Megan. Is that what you wanted to hear?"

"I knew it, I just knew it." Ann's voice was full of weird satisfaction.

"Tell me!" Will insisted.

"I could see it happening. I—"

"Ann, if you know where she is, *tell me.*"

"I *knew* you would fall for her and—"

"Tell me!"

"She's with Leon."

"Leon? Why? Why Leon? What's going on?"

"Jealous?"

"Megan's welfare," he reminded her. "That's what we're talking about here."

"Okay, okay, little brother. Lewis was at the club begging to talk to her. She broke down and went with him a while before closing."

"She left with *Lewis*?"

"Yeah. Leon happened to see it and took off after them. I got a ride home from Becky and Paul. Anyway...Leon did catch up to Megan and rescued her from Lewis. He called me just a while ago to say he and Megan were having a sandwich and coffee somewhere and everything was okay."

"Why didn't you call and tell *me* that?"

"I'm sorry. I guess I should have."

"Yeah." He hung up.

Will walked across his tiny living room to have a look out the window. His wait for Megan continued. And dragged. He was glad to know she was all right, but not so happy that he'd been kept out of this. The deep concern he felt for this girl caused twinging little pains throughout his chest, clamminess in his hands, and a dryness in his mouth.

He left the window to get a beer from the refrigerator. He hadn't meant to fall for Megan. He didn't *need* this in his life right now. The timing was wrong. He wasn't ready. His life was a mess. He had nothing to offer her. And yet...yet he felt he had so much to lose if he lost her.

It had been fast. Yes. His head was still spinning from how fast Megan had happened to him. Wondering what to do about her made it spin even faster. Or maybe it was the many beers he'd poured into himself since getting home. He sat down onto the couch. And stared at the door. Waiting for her. Waiting.

• • •

It was two A.M. when Megan let herself into the apartment with her key. It was dark. Before she could get her hand over to the light switch, Will's voice shot out at her. "What's going on?"

She jumped, then went again for the switch. When the light came on she saw Will sitting on the couch. The way he was looking at her bothered her far more than the tone of his voice. "I don't need this, Will," she warned him.

He rose to his feet. "Well, I don't either. But I couldn't help getting pretty worried about you."

"You don't need to worry about me."

"You mean like—go to bed, cover up my head and just completely disregard the fact that you disappeared from the club and nobody knew anything about it? Not Pam, not Joe, certainly not me."

She stood there shaking her head at the pressure he was

creating. "Will...we're roommates, not soulmates."

"I'd say either one deserves consideration. Come time to leave the Rusty Door and you're *nowhere.* I couldn't find you. No one could. No one knew anything."

"I left for a talk with Lewis."

"Why would you do that?"

"Isn't that *my* business?"

"You disappeared, Megan. You could have, *should* have, at least told someone you were going."

"Like you?"

"Yeah."

"Like I should have marched right up onto the stage and tapped you on the shoulder?" She went to the kitchen sink for a glass of water, wondering why any of this should have turned into an argument.

Will followed. "You thinking of going back to him? Is that what this is about?"

"No."

"Then why go off with him?"

"I don't know...I guess I'm asking myself the same question."

"He forced you? Did he force you, Megan?"

"Please, let's just drop this. I'm really tired." She went to the bedroom. Will followed. She made a quick attempt to shut the door against him, but in a move quicker than hers he managed to stick his foot in the way to block it.

"It's my turn for the bed," he said.

"Fine." She collected some of her things and went into the bathroom.

When she came back out in her nightshirt, she found the living room lights off again. The dark shadowy form of Will was sitting slumped and still by the window.

She arranged her sheet, pillow and blanket on the couch and lay down. Unable to ignore his being there, she eventually spoke to him through the darkness. "You wanted the bed, *so go to it.*"

"I will when I'm ready."

"Fine." She worked herself into a semi-comfortable position.

It stayed quiet until Will started on Lewis again. "You know…I really thought you were through with that guy."

"I am. I told you I am."

"Then maybe you could have given some thought to *my* feelings."

"Stop it, Will. Stop it. You have no right to do this. We're not a couple, you and me. Our living together is financial, that's all. Just financial."

"Financial." He repeated the word as though he disliked it.

"Yes. Don't you remember? It was your idea."

"I was worried about you tonight."

"Why? Why should you be worried about me?"

"You represent half the rent to me. Maybe I was just trying to protect my financial resources."

"I have a job, a key to the apartment, and a life of my own. You're just going to have to trust me, Will."

"Don't you understand, Megan?" his voice rose to a higher, more serious, level of desperation. "I was really worried about you—as in the hell with Sheldon and the hell with finances. *Worried*—as in caring about you."

She threw back her blanket in one fast sweep, got off the couch, and stomped across the room to him. "What *is* it with you, Will? Why are you doing this? We had an agreement, an understanding, didn't we?"

As he, too, stood up, they came face to face. The arguing stopped. Something else seemed to begin. Something in the looks they were giving each other. Something in the silence that came over them. Will's arms went around her. Gently. When she didn't complain, he kissed her.

She allowed him. Allowed what this moment was turning into. Enough that she was soon holding him and kissing him back. Enough that everything she'd raved about minutes ago no longer counted. He was very persuasive, in the tenderest of ways. And she was very tired.

"Will...?" she eventually managed to get a single word in.

"Mmm...?" came his own single word. His hands had started roving, over her breasts, down her hips, onto her bare thighs at the short edge of her nightshirt.

"Go to bed," she told him.

"Yeah, let's."

"*Separately*," she clarified, at the same time as her body was pressing and moving responsively against his.

He made a low moan. "Are you giving me mixed signals here, Megan? Because it really seems like you are."

"No. No signals. Just stop."

"Megan..." he coaxed.

"We can't do this."

"Yes, we can."

"No." She started pushing at him.

"Megan..." he said again, not believing her, not letting up. Out of the struggling match that began between the two of them, she finally got in a hard enough shove to send him backwards a step.

They stood apart, both quietly stunned. If she had led him on, she was sorry. If he had forced himself on her, she was even sorrier. Whichever way it was, he had the wrong idea now—about her, about everything. "Maybe I should leave," she said.

"Leave?" He seemed partly hurt, partly angry.

"I could call Leon and he—"

"Megan, don't call Leon."

"This wasn't suppose to happen."

"I know."

"It's exactly what I don't need in my life right now."

"Hey, it's pretty far from what I need right now, too. Okay, I'm sorry, Megan. I...I admit I started it...but you participated. You *did*. Look, it won't happen again. I promise. So stay. Just stay. You don't have to go."

"My staying here doesn't feel right anymore."

"It's right," he assured her, keeping his distance. "Trust

me. You can trust me, Megan."

"A familiar line all guys use. It doesn't mean a whole lot."

"I'm not other guys, Megan. Look, I don't know...I guess sometimes I come across as kind of fast and—"

"You do."

"But I'm really a nice guy. If you honestly want to keep things cool between us...you've got it."

He went to the bedroom and she to the couch. She felt confused, more now over Will than she'd ever felt over Lewis. She had to be careful. If Lewis was the frying pan, Will might very well be the fire. And no way was she making that leap. No way.

Megan was up long before Will Sunday morning. He'd slept soundly and was totally undisturbed by her running the shower then sneaking clothes out of the bedroom closet and dresser drawers.

She packed her suitcase. She was leaving. It was the only way she could be sure of handling this situation before it had a handle on her.

Tears welled in her eyes as she left the apartment. If she was so sure this was the right thing for her to do then why did it hurt so much? She didn't understand. She was afraid to even try. Three flights of stairs—down, down, down.

With her head hung low as she started out the front door of the building, she walked straight into someone. Surprised and apologetic, she looked up in starting to say, "I'm sorry, I—"

It was *Gloria,* equally surprised. "Megan! I was just taking a chance that Will would be home and brought this wonderful coffee cake over that he likes so well and—"

"He's still sleeping," Megan told her.

Gloria gave a calculating nod. "Sleeping...I see. While you're ducking out with your suitcase?"

Megan sniffled her nose.

"And crying besides," Gloria observed.

"It's not what you think."

"Come on...you're living with him and had a fight."

Megan said nothing, lowering her head again.

"It's okay..." Gloria's voice turned warm and caring. "These things happen."

Megan felt a sudden closeness to this woman. A need to share her problem with her. "It wasn't really a fight. More like a...a misunderstanding."

"A difference of opinion." Gloria nodded.

"Yes."

"Then probably you're wise to...to take some time away. But ducking out without his *knowing*?"

"I thought it was best." More tears were coming to Megan's eyes.

"Okay, okay..." Gloria took a hold of her arm. "So where are you going? I bet you're running away and don't even know to where."

Megan sniffled her nose again. Then wiped her wet eyes with the back of her hand.

Gloria put her arm around her shoulder and patted her. "Megan, you can come home with me if you'd like."

Megan found the offer unbelievably generous. "You?"

Gloria's concern seemed genuine. "Yes. Not to be imposing, you understand, but we could talk, or not talk, whichever you prefer. And you could have Ann's old room, or Will's. And later, when you feel better, you could choose to stay or not stay. Mainly it could just be a time and a place for you to start. To get yourself together. Maybe just a chance for you to make a decision as to what exactly you want or need to do next."

"You'd do this for me?" Megan asked.

"It's the mother-instinct in me, I suppose," Gloria said, with a smile.

"I don't have a mother of my own."

"I know, you told me. So maybe I could fill in a little."

"Why? Why should you?"

"Maybe because I don't feel much like I have a daughter of my *own* these days. But more because you just seem to need a friend."

Megan smiled back at her. "Thanks. I guess I do."

"Shall we go?" Gloria motioned to her car in the parking lot.

Megan nodded.

Gloria led the way. "You'll be fine, dear. A little change sometimes works wonders."

"Hey!" Will shouted down at them from his third floor window. "Hey!"

He'd awakened in time to catch Megan leaving with his mother and didn't like it one bit. He yelled furiously at them several more times.

But Gloria and Megan proceeded to drive away.

Ten

Gloria had no more than brought Megan into her home when the phone started ringing. "Isn't that the way it is," she spluttered, hurrying to the kitchen for it.

It was Will. "Let me talk to Megan."

Gloria glanced back through the dining room at her visitor, who was standing just inside the front door. "Oh, Will…I don't know."

"Let me talk to her, Mom." There was notable pain behind his insistence.

Having heard Gloria say Will's name, Megan was already shaking her head no.

Gloria told her son, "It's not a good time, dear. I'm sorry."

"What's going on?" he asked.

"What do you mean, what's going on?"

"I mean, *what's going on*? Why is she with you?"

"It's very simple, Will. Just calm down." Gloria twirled her free hand in the air as she spoke, in effort of helping her explain, "I was coming to see you, bringing you one of those almond coffee cakes you like so well. I picked it up from Markway's yesterday and—"

"Mom," he said impatiently.

"Well, Megan was leaving the apartment building and we ran into each other."

"It's the going to your house together I want to know about."

"It's a girl thing."

"Give it to me straight," he said.

"Well, I…" Gloria turned for another look at Megan, hoping she might help with this. But the girl was sad and quiet and near more tears. "Will, it's…it's kind of like a going-home-to-mother thing, except that Megan doesn't have one of her own."

"So you offered."

"Yes."

"You're playing *mother* to Megan?"

"Yes. Sort of."

"That's good, real good."

"Thank you."

"Except this isn't your business."

"It is now."

"Let me talk to her."

"No."

"If I could just—"

"Maybe you need to give this a little time, Will."

"Give *what* a little time?"

"Her…the situation…whatever. Meanwhile, she'll be fine here with me."

"I thought you didn't like her."

"I never said that."

"She's got blonde hair."

"We're...beyond that. I might have been wrong about that."

Will moaned. "I'm coming over."

Gloria rechecked Megan's whereabouts and saw that she had wandered out through the dining room French doors onto the patio. She told Will, "If you care anything at all about this girl, you'll respect her enough to leave her alone for a while. That seems to be what she wants, needs. So just cool your heels...or whatever else it is that needs cooling...and give this some time. I've got to go. Good-bye, Will."

She hung up on her son and went to join Megan. The girl was taking a slow stroll around the brick patio. Gloria had just last week brought out the wicker furniture from the garage and the setting was inviting and pretty. "Megan, whatever this is about, Will is not happy about your taking off like you did."

Megan kept walking and observing. "You've got a lovely house and yard, Gloria."

"Thank you." Gloria felt a pride beyond her home. The pride in trying to help someone. Somehow it had become very important to her to help Megan. "I'm glad to share it with you, dear. And...and we don't have to talk about Will if you don't want to."

"Thanks."

"Anyway, I think I got rid of him for now."

Megan laughed, causing Gloria to laugh also.

"Are you *really* his mother?" Megan asked teasingly.

"Yes. I am. I don't mean to cut him down; don't get me wrong. I'm just trying to understand *your* viewpoint for the moment."

"You don't even know me."

"I'm not sure how much I know Will, either." Gloria ran her hand over the tops of the green bushes edging one side of the patio. "These will soon be due for their first trim of the season."

"Who takes care of that?"

"Me. I do everything myself."

"The house? The yard?"

Gloria nodded. "Plus my job. *Everything*."

Megan smiled. "You even take in wayward girls."

"Well, not usually," Gloria had to say. "You're a special case. Meant to be, I think, from how we ran into each other."

"Like fate."

"Yes."

"*Will* sort of happened to me like fate."

"Did he?"

"Yes." Sadness returned to the girl and she started pacing the patio again.

"Megan—what can I do for you, dear?"

The girl shrugged and shook her head. "You've already done it. You caught me at a very low point and whisked me off to higher ground."

"You *were* pretty low," Gloria agreed. "I don't really know what you and Will are all about, but I hope he didn't—"

"No. Actually it's nothing Will did. I was just mostly trying to run away from myself."

Gloria touched the girl's arm, and looked deeply into her blue eyes. "Dear, I really don't think you can do that…run away from yourself. I mean, it may be just a bit impossible."

"Probably," Megan agreed with a smile.

"So you haven't run away from yourself, only to a different place. Maybe you only needed to get away in order to set something clear in your own mind. I hope this is precisely the place to do that. What do you think?"

Megan nodded hopefully, looking at the surroundings some more. "Yes, it feels like it to me."

"Good. Now…are you hungry?"

Megan shrugged.

Taking a shrug for a yes, Gloria took the girl's hand and led her inside to the kitchen.

They sat at the table by the sunshiny-bright bay window. Gloria made coffee and sliced up the coffee cake she'd brought back home with her.

"I don't know how to explain any of this to you, Gloria,"

Megan said after eating several bites of the almond streusel, drinking most of her cup of coffee and staring out the window at the back yard for at least ten minutes straight.

"You don't have to," Gloria told her gently.

"Will and I like each other, but as for a relationship the timing is very bad."

"You don't have to tell me anything about the two of you if you don't want to."

The girl gave Gloria an appreciative look. "I feel I can talk to you, Gloria."

"You don't know how nice that is to hear." Gloria was honored.

Megan ate another bite of coffee cake off her plate. Then she put her fork down and gave a long sigh. "I'm feeling restless and unsure about a lot of things right now and limited as to what I can handle. I've just come out of a broken relationship and the idea of rushing into another one scares me."

"Will is pressuring you?"

"In some ways yes, some ways no."

"Let me guess the ways…" Gloria grinned.

Megan shook her head. "No, he's been okay. Mostly it's just this problem within me, myself, right now. I guess that sounds funny."

"No. I understand. I am going through some problems within myself lately."

"You? But you seem like such a together person."

Gloria laughed. "Maybe I'm a little bit tired of being *together*. Maybe I want to burst apart, explode, tear loose."

Megan turned wide-eyed and wordless.

"I'm going through kind of a restless stage right now," Gloria stated.

"You?" Megan's surprise seemed to grow.

It was hard for Gloria to admit, but if there was ever a time for girl talk this was it. She had to tell *someone*, and Megan had happened like an answer out of the sky. Like fate. She nodded, looking across the table into those wonderful blue eyes that watched, waited, cared. "I guess it's my age. My...in between age. You know...well, maybe you don't. It's just that I'm too old to be young and too young to be old. And...and that, plus being alone so much, causes this restlessness in me. It's like I need something more, but I'm not sure what, and I'm searching, but I'm scared to death of finding. Oh, I don't know...I don't know..."

"But you...you seem like such a together person," Megan said again.

Gloria laughed. "An illusion. I give that illusion...yes, I suppose I do. Underneath I'm an innocent sixteen-year-old who has absolutely no idea what she's doing."

"In regards to—?" Megan questioned.

Gloria shrugged.

"In regards to Joe?" Megan asked.

"Why would you say that?" It surprised Gloria that the girl should suggest him that simply.

Megan smiled playfully but knowingly. "I've seen the two of you together. You have nothing to be nervous about. *Go for it.*"

"Go for it?" The term was not exactly the soothing advice Gloria sought.

"Look, these boy-girl situations are always a little scary at any age. So—"

"Megan, Will told me he's in love with you. Is that what *you're* so scared of?"

"No. Because it's not true. He only said that to you, Gloria, because he...he wanted to startle you, to get back at you because you'd made him angry."

"I don't understand."

"I know. It's crazy. Will does some crazy things."

"I guess I don't know when to believe him and when not to."

"Gloria, I know there's some distance between you and him and Ann."

Gloria sighed. "Oh, we talk, but not the way I'm talking to you."

"Why?"

"Because."

"Okay, look," Megan moved forth in her chair, as if the main reason for coming there was to straighten Gloria out, not herself. "What are the biggest most important things in each of your lives right now? And are *they* the things you really try to share with one another?"

Gloria thought about it. The difficult realization made her shake her head no.

Megan continued, "Ann, for instance."

"Oh, I've tried and tried to talk to her about her divorce, if that's what you mean."

"But about the *reason*? The honest to goodness reason? She didn't get divorced just to upset you, you know, Gloria. *She's* the one who's hurting the most over it. But she can't make *you* understand that. Of all the people in the world, she needs her mother to understand it and comfort her. Leon's been good for her, but he's not her mother."

"Leon...where does she expect to get with *Leon?*"

"He's a very special guy, Gloria."

Gloria listened, trying to revise her judgments.

"And Will..." Megan continued, "the biggest thing in his life is his music. And...and, Gloria, you only seem to treat it as some silly hobby. But it's not, it's far more. In turning your back on that, you're also turning it on him."

"Well, I...I have gotten to like and understand this music thing of his more lately."

"Good. That's good. It's a beginning. Because Will needs you on his side."

Tears began to sting in Gloria's eyes.

But there was yet more to come from Megan. "And you—have you tried sharing your deepest, recent feelings with your kids? Like this restlessness? And Joe?"

"No," Gloria scoffed at the idea.

"They need to know."

"I told you...I can't talk to them."

"You can't *not* talk to them. If you want to stay close to

Ann and Will there has to be some three-way sharing going on. You have to give and take a whole lot more than you have been. I really think that's the answer. But—" Megan withdrew from her words, her enthusiasm, and sank back against her chair as if with a sudden block of uncertainty, "Maybe I shouldn't be talking to you this way, Gloria. Who am I to be giving all this advice? I don't have a mother. I haven't had one since I was eight years old. What do I know about what's good for you?"

Gloria left her own chair to go around the table, bent down to Megan and gave her a big motherly hug. "You know a lot, my dear."

"I can only speak from the heart."

"I don't know of a better place."

Megan gave her a look that was half laughing, half crying. "I'm glad we ran into each other the way we did."

"Me, too." Gloria straightened up with a good new feeling. "Okay now, you come on upstairs and pick out a bedroom to settle into. Get your suitcase from the front hall and follow me."

"Are you really sure this is all right?"

"Like there's someone *else* around here to ask?" Gloria remarked.

The two of them laughed as they left the kitchen.

Megan chose Ann's room. It surprised Gloria, as she would have expected her to chose Will's. But maybe the feminine features of a pink bedspread, eyelit dust ruffle and puffy tie-back curtains won her favor.

As Megan walked further into the room that was to be hers, she viewed the figurine cat collection on a wall shelf and old family photographs displayed in a collage. Then the Boston rocker in the corner by the window seemed to beckon her to sit in it.

Gloria excused herself for a moment and left for her own room down the hall. She fetched her pair of big fuzzy slippers to lend Megan.

"Here," she said, returning and handing them over to the

girl. "Put these on. They're wonderful. Relax your feet and your mind will follow. You'll see."

"Okay," Megan said, immediately taking off her shoes in exchange for the slippers.

"Take a nap. Take a shower. Do whatever you like, dear. I want you to feel at home here."

"I do already, Gloria."

"Good."

"I'm not going to work tonight. I'll call Nick later and tell him it's a personal problem."

"He'll understand, I'm sure."

"Thanks for taking me in. For being so nice."

Gloria smiled. "You're welcome."

Megan stood up in the fuzzy slippers and tried them out by plodding happily around the room. It was obvious she'd never had anything like them on her feet before.

"I'll be downstairs," Gloria said, leaving. "We'll talk more later if you want to. Meanwhile, I'm going to start working on a very nice supper for the two of us for tonight."

• • •

Megan did not see or hear anything more from Will Sunday, Monday or Tuesday. But she knew she would run into him Wednesday night, when they both worked at the Rusty Door.

She'd no more arrived at the club and changed into her black skirt and blouse outfit than Nick summoned her into his office. "I want to know," he began in a swift cool tone, "if we're going to be having any more troubles tonight."

"I don't think so," was the best she could tell him.

He sat behind his desk, leaning back in his chair. Thinking. As if he had some troubles of his own, aside from any of hers. "You don't like me, do you?"

It was the last thing Megan would have expected to hear from him. It threw her, making her much more uncomfortable than getting yelled at about something might have.

"You always seem...well, sort of afraid of me," Nick said, studying her in a way that would make *anyone* uncomfortable.

She became brave. And told him, "Maybe it's just the way you seem to see women."

He cocked his head to one side with a slight grin. "The way I see women? Like I have a unique way or something?"

"Yes."

"How's that?"

"Nothing," she backed down.

But he wasn't about to let it pass. He straightened up. "You said I had this *way*. How? You said it, now explain it."

She wished they weren't having this conversation. She only wanted to be out there waiting tables with Pam. It was almost five and dinner people would be coming in. "You take advantage of your waitresses," she told him

Nick laughed, shook his head and leaned back again. "Cheryl. Of course you've got to be referring to Cheryl. Well, let me tell you, Megan, that what you've heard about her and me isn't true."

She wanted to die, for having gotten into this. It was *so* uncomfortable. Besides, she didn't know what to say. She shouldn't have even said what she had.

However Nick continued willingly. "The word is that I'm the father of her baby. But I'm not. I dated her a couple times, which was probably a big mistake on my part. People get the wrong idea about me. Somehow they just do, and it sticks."

"Somehow..." Though Megan repeated the word as verification, it came out more like a question, a doubt.

"I know I shouldn't date any of my waitresses. But I have. And I guess that looks wrong. Somehow...I don't know...it just does. It's given me this bad reputation. Which I don't think I deserve. I don't want *you* believing the smut it's been made into, Megan."

"What does it matter what I believe?"

"Because...it does. I don't like how you look at me most of the time."

She shifted uneasily, glancing away from him but immediately back. "Maybe it's not just you. Maybe I...I just kind of have this problem trusting men in general lately."

He looked both surprised and relieved. "I'm your boss, not your boyfriend."

"Either one seems a little scary to me right now."

"Don't label me, Megan. Just consider me a person—Nick, the *person*. No boss, no boyfriend."

She smiled half heartedly. "Okay, I'll try."

"I'm really not a bad person and I don't like seeing that accusing look in your eyes all the time."

"I'm sorry."

"No, I'm sorry if I've created it."

He seemed sincere enough for Megan to suppose she believed him. But she had to go. "I really should start working."

He nodded. "I know. I'm glad we had this talk. Okay, go ahead."

As she left Nick's office, a disturbed Pam took her aside. "He's not about to leave you alone, is he?"

"We just had a little talk."

"You two have a *lot* of little talks."

"He claims everyone's got the wrong impression of him."

"Come on—majority rules, don't you think?"

Megan hated the confusion. She'd had some very calm, relaxing days at Gloria's...only to come back to this. Gloria had worked days, leaving her alone to enjoy the house, the yard, and the peaceful privacy. Then evenings the two of them sat in the living room with munchy snacks and sodas and endless girl talk. It had been like a slowed down mini getaway vacation. Now she was back to life's hard fast realities.

Will came to the club early. He approached Megan with a long face and drooped shoulders.

"Hi," he said cautiously.

"Hi," she said back.

"Megan—" he started.

But she motioned that she had a table to take care of and took off right away.

As she went to turn her order in to the kitchen a couple minutes later, he followed her and tried again, "Megan, I'm sorry if I scared you away the other night."

She stopped to give him a minute. "Will, I need some freedom in my life right now."

"You're getting that at my *mom's*?"

"Yes. In the way that I need it."

He all but laughed. "She'll mother you to death, Megan."

"Maybe I *like* being mothered. Maybe I like being asked how I feel, what I think. Maybe I like wearing her fuzzy slippers and having her butter my toast."

Will stepped directly in her way when she tried walking off again. "I know I broke my word to you about the hands-off deal, but if you come back I'll—"

"I'm not coming back, Will." Surely the straight eye-to-eye she gave him had to prove her sincerity. It did. Because he gave up and was first to walk away this time. It was Megan's chance to feel what it was like being walked away from. Cold, deserted, empty.

Will didn't turn up again until nine o'clock, when he and the band positioned on stage and he announced, "Hi, everybody! We're the Sidetracks and ready to kick it loose!"

The music disbursed into a reveling instrumental led by Vince on guitar. Randy drummed the dynamic pace. Jeff played the pulsating bass. Will rhythm guitar, with an occasional switch to tambourine.

Megan felt a heavy aching in her heart. Will was bothering her far more than she wanted to admit. The turmoil was that she really liked him but wished she didn't. Her aching intensified as he stepped forward to his mike to begin vocal. Though the song was a fast rock, he sang as if there might be an ache going on in his heart as well,

"Magic in the road I'm taking
Leading me away like an eagle in flight
Can't look back, I don't want to
Knowing what I'm doing has to be right..."

"When you're not too busy," someone broke Megan's attention, "we'd like some drinks over here, miss."

It was Leon, at a near table with Ann. Megan welcomed the interruption and gladly went to their service.

"You were awfully wrapped up in the Sidetracks," Ann commented to her.

"Any certain one in particular?" Leon teased.

Megan skipped answering and merely asked what they wanted to drink. Then she took off to collect it from the bar.

"How's it going, Megan?" Joe asked as he got the two beers.

"I'm not sure," she said with a slight moan in her voice.

"Sounds complicated."

"It is."

"So's life, I guess."

"Guess where I'm living now, Joe"

"Radison penthouse?"

"No," she giggled. "Gloria's."

"*Gloria's*?" He set the beers onto her tray, looking interested.

"Will's mother. You remember."

"Yeah, I remember."

"You two made a nice couple that one night, Joe...slow dancing together."

"I was training a new bartender and wanted to give him some practice time alone at the bar."

"Sure, Joe."

"What's this *sure, Joe?*"

"Here—" She handed him a slip of paper.

"What's this?" He took it, unfolded it and read it.

"What's it look like?"

"A phone number."

She nodded. "It's Gloria's."

"Her idea?"

"No, mine. Call her, Joe."

"No. No, I don't call women."

She laughed. "You don't call women? Like it's a fixed rule of yours or something?"

"It is."

"Call her, Joe."

His eyebrows knitted together as he shook his head. "I'm a long-standing bachelor, Megan, and that's the way I prefer it."

"You like her, I know."

"She's a classy lady, I'm just a bartender."

"Call her, Joe," Megan coaxed.

"No way." He motioned her to go deliver her drinks.

Will avoided Megan on the band's first break, though surely he'd seen her standing there, off from her table section and momentarily not busy. And surely he knew that whatever was happening between them was just as confusing and upsetting to her as it was to him.

She watched him get a bottle of beer from the bar and head outside the back way. The painful distance wedging between them was as much her fault as his. They needed to talk. She followed him.

He was leaning against the front of his Mustang, swigging his beer, eyes holding on her coming toward him.

"Will," she began, "don't be mad at me."

He smiled softly. "I'm not."

"You act like it."

"I'm mad at myself."

"Yourself?"

"Yeah—for getting out of line with you. For starting to treat you like a girlfriend, which you specifically told me not to. And shit—I don't need that. It's like the *last* thing I need right now. I don't know what got into me the other night, Megan. But I'm sorry."

Crazy. This guy was truly driving her crazy. She leaned against the car, her right leg lightly touching against his left leg.

After a long pause of silence Will suddenly laughed outright. "But I just can't believe you left me to go stay with my mother."

Megan couldn't help laughing about it herself. "It was kind of funny how that happened. I just...just had this feeling like I needed to leave, but with no idea as to where, and then *she* appeared, out of nowhere."

For a moment the mood between them was light and frivolous. It turned heavy again when Will contradicted all he'd said by turning and stealing a fast kiss.

"What do you call that?" Megan drew back.

"A kiss. An apologetic kiss." He smiled.

"You apologize for kissing me by *kissing* me?"

"Sorry." He leaned back on the car again and took up his beer.

"You think that word is magic, don't you. Well, it's not. Saying you're sorry doesn't automatically make everything all right. I don't *want* this, Will. I don't *need* this."

He hung his head guiltily.

She continued at him, "I'm...I'm on the rebound here and—"

"You weren't even in love with Sheldon, so how does that make this a rebound?"

"The problem is I'm not sure I know what love is and—"

"Neither do I."

"And I'm sure not *looking* for it."

"I know," he exclaimed with as much drama. "Same for me. It's felt good to me, you know, just finally being free, with only myself to look out for for a change. Until you, Megan. All of a sudden there you were, in my life like...like some sort of sidetrack to what I—"

"Me? A *sidetrack*? No, Will...*You're* the Sidetrack, remember?"

It set them both bursting into new laughter.

When the humor settled, Will concluded, "Maybe we need a chance...the two of us. Just a chance to see if—"

"If I were to fall in love, why would it be with somebody like you? Who doesn't pay his bills, who doesn't know what a dust cloth is, who is addicted to gambling?"

Will turned on his infectious grin. "Maybe you like my music?"

She weakened, as only he could weaken her. "I *love* your music."

"I could work on my hang-ups."

"I don't want you to change for me."

"Okay, I *won't* work on my hang-ups."

"Your life is a *mess*, Will."

"I know. Don't you think I know that? I well knew that long before *you* ever came along. Megan, don't you think I want to make some changes in my life whether I do or don't have you?"

He was serious. He went back and forth from kidding to serious so fast it made her dizzy.

"Except..." he continued, "I think maybe the best chance of me straightening my life out would be *with* you."

"I don't know, I don't know," she said and yet *did* know. She looked at him knowing that the possibility of ignoring him was useless. "Oh, Will..." she gave in, "you just have this way of getting to a person."

He started grinning that grin of his again. "So you *do* care about me."

"I didn't want to." She threw up her hands as she started crying.

"I know. Neither of us planned on what's happened here."

"Then how could it happen?"

His expression turned soft, hopeful, his eyes as near tears as hers. He pulled her gently toward him. "Come here, sidetrack."

She smiled. "Okay, Sidetrack."

Later, back inside the club, with the band playing full force again, Megan went to see Joe at the bar. She stretched half way across the counter in talking to him. "Joe, do me a favor?"'

"Sure, Megan. Name it."

"Call Gloria and—"

"Whoa, now...I already told you how I feel about that."

"No, not for a date or anything. See, I'm really busy with tables and I want you to call and give her a message from me. That's all. She's expecting me to come there after work tonight, but tell her I'll be going to Will's instead."

Before Joe could protest, Megan hurried off to her customers.

• • •

Gloria couldn't imagine who would be calling her as late as ten o'clock. The phone ringing that time of night was frightening. She'd been in her nightgown watching TV for the past hour and ran out to the kitchen to grab the phone by ring four. "Hello?"

"Gloria, it's Joe."

A million thoughts went racing through her mind. "Did something happen to Will or Ann?"

"No, they're fine."

It was a relief hearing Will's voice singing in the background.

"What? What is it then?"

"Megan gave me your number and asked me to call you. She wanted me to let you know that she won't be coming there after work tonight because she's going to Will's instead. I think maybe they have something special going on between them." There was a certain amount of amusement in Joe's voice.

"No...no, I don't think so," Gloria said. "Neither of them are prepared for a relationship at this time."

Joe laughed. "Well, maybe they're not prepared, but I don't think it's stopping them."

Gloria felt completely thrown by everything Megan had led her to believe in the last few days. She gave it up with, "I guess it's their lives."

"What about yours?" Joe asked.

"Mine?"

"Your life. How's *your* life, Gloria?"

Why was he asking that? What did he mean by it?

"Fine," she answered, "just fine. How's yours?"

"Fine."

Gloria started to loosen up, and laughed at the sound of their conversation. "Actually, Joe, I'd have to say my life is a little drab."

It was nice hearing him laugh, too, as he said, "Same here. So when are you coming to the Rusty Door again?"

It was a question over all other questions. It threw her far more than the matter of Will and Megan. "I don't know," she had to say.

"How about now?"

"Now?" She wriggled her bare toes in the scatter rug beneath her feet. That nervous sixteen-year-old feeling was coming over her again.

"It's Wednesday and quiet," Joe urged, "and maybe the Sidetracks will play a few slow songs."

"Are you asking me to dance again?" she heard herself ask almost flirtatiously.

"Yeah, I guess I am."

"Well..." She held herself back from responding as eagerly as she was feeling. "I...I suppose I could come by for a while. But I have to work tomorrow and can't stay too late."

"See you soon then?"

"Soon." She hung up the phone, let out an excited girlish scream and rushed upstairs to get herself ready.

• • •

It was raining hard as Megan and Will drove home from the Rusty Door late that night. She sat snuggled close to him in the Mustang. The windshield wipers swished back and forth, back and forth.

They parked in the apartment building lot, left the car, dashed through the wet weather holding hands, and took the inside stairs two at a time to third floor.

They kissed the moment they entered the living room. Not bothering with lights, they undressed each other on their way to the bedroom. Will's western shirt was easy enough to undo, with its row of snap buttons down the front. However Megan's sweater was a little more difficult, as it got tangled in her neck chain and ended up stuck over her head for a few anxious moments.

The bed squeaked as they went down on it together. The blinds were up and the rain streaming down the window made long squiggly shadows against the walls.

"Megan...Megan..." Will breathed her name between kisses. "I want you so much."

She wanted him, too. They held, touched and fondled each other with equal desire.

Still...just when he was about to lay himself fully atop her, she pushed at him, saying, "Could you maybe put some music on the stereo first? It'd be nice having some music, Will."

"Oh, Megan..." he moaned at the delay.

"Please?" she added.

"Yeah, sure." He got up to find a cassette.

Click, click. Something country western began to play lowly.

"And a condom," she added. "Don't forget a condom."

"Right." He pulled out a dresser drawer.

"And a Coke," she said before he could get back into bed.

"A Coke?" He was a confused man, standing there nude.

Lightning flashed through the window, followed by a crash of thunder.

Will was about to crawl back into bed, as if she were only joking. "Megan, I don't think you—"

"Please, Will," she used her most convincing voice. "I...I need to relax more. A Coke would help. There's some in the refrigerator, I know. Let's just take this slower, okay?"

"Slower..." He nodded and went.

As soon as he'd left the room she jumped out of bed and into her clothes as fast as she could. Her underwear was near. Her jeans, sweater and shoes were in the other room, but she grabbed different ones from the closet. Luckily she had extra time because Will stubbed his toe somewhere in the dark, let out a yelp and stopped to rub it before continuing his errand.

This was wrong, so wrong, Megan had decided about their being together this way. And just in time. She had to leave, get away.

Will was carrying two cans of Coke back through the dark living room as she went tearing on past him and out of the apartment.

"Hey!" he shouted. "What are you *doing?* Megan!"

She fled down the stairs and outside into the thunder and lightning and rain. It was really something, preferring a storm to him. But that had been close, too close, what had just about happened back there. Will was too misleading. She wasn't sure about *half* the things she did with him, let alone this. She needed to be more responsible for her actions. She didn't need another mistake. After so many bad relationships in her life she needed to be sure, *had* to be sure. Right now she was feeling horribly *unsure*. About him, about everything.

The the lightning was harsh, thunder fierce, and the rain stinging cold. Megan hated that she was running away again. Hated all her uncertainties. She didn't *want* Will to be a mistake. But he was probably just another guy who would be. And it made her scared enough to flee.

As she reached the edge of the parking lot she heard his voice shouting at her. She looked back.

He was coming after her in only his jeans. His chest and feet were bare. "Megan! Megan, stop! This is crazy! What's wrong?"

Though she was running her fastest, he was soon gaining on her. He was definitely a much faster runner than Lewis. "Megan!" he kept yelling. "Megan!"

A glare of lightning came brightly, instantly followed by the loudest ka-boom of thunder yet, causing Megan to scream and almost run blindly into a tree.

By the time she got to the end of the block Will had caught up to her.

"Megan!" He grabbed her and stopped her and pulled her around toward himself.

She didn't want to look at him. She didn't want to see his face or feel his persuasion. With her eyes downward, she started to cry.

"Megan..." he said more softly, though still keeping a firm hold on her arms.

They stood there on the corner, unshielded and drenched from the wretched storm. Megan no longer felt it to be a safe trade-off for the apartment.

"Why did you run out like that?" Will demanded. "I thought we'd come to an understanding."

"I don't understand *any* of this." She chanced a direct look at him now, eyes blinking rapidly against the rain.

More lightning, more thunder—violent, frightening.

"And I don't understand why you're always running away!" his voice rose to somewhere between anger and panic.

"Which proves we *haven't* reached an understanding," she argued.

"Come on. This is ridiculous. We have to get out of this storm."

As he started walking her back toward the apartment building, she flared up all over again. She fought him, yelling, "I don't have to do *anything!* You have no control over me! Go away! Leave me alone!" She broke away from him.

He stopped in dismay. "You think I'm trying to *control* you?"

"Yes."

"You think all this has been one-sided?"

"Yes."

"You haven't felt *anything*?"

"Well..."

"Okay, fine! Then you just run your way and I'll run mine." He left her and started down the sidewalk alone.

Megan stood there hurting to a whole new depth. There seemed to be no easy way with Will, no easy way with herself. It was like two wrongs trying to make a right. Why did this relationship have to be so difficult? So different from any she'd ever known?

In another moment she was running after him, shouting his name, "Will! Will!"

He stopped, turned, waited. His arms caught her. She clung to him. Maybe difficult and different were good signs. For whatever their relationship had developed into, it was definitely very serious. "What if it doesn't work out?" she needed to ask.

"What if it does?" he asked her back, smiling.

"I'm scared, Will."

"Don't be scared, Megan. Don't be scared." He kissed her wet forehead. "Megan...oh, Megan, I've never felt this way about anyone else ever before."

"I've never felt this way about anyone either." A new sense of trust and tranquillity came over her.

Will kept his arm protectively around her as they scurried back to the apartment building through the storm.

Eleven

"It's time I started managing my life without the horses," Will stated the next morning. "At least I'm going to *try* managing without them. Guess it won't be easy." He sat at the kitchen table, finishing his second cup of coffee.

Megan, in scruffy clothes, with her hair pinned up and wearing no make-up, stood just a ways over from him washing the living room window. "It's not like you're managing *with* them has been so good."

"I know. Don't think I haven't known that for a long time. But it's taken you, Megan, to make me really, really care about quitting, about taking charge of my life." He left the table to come give her a hug and a kiss. "Thanks."

Distracted from window washing, she smiled in the

warmth of his arms and said, "You're welcome." Then as he went back to pour himself more coffee, she added, "But I'm not out to change you, Will."

He laughed. "Influence. How about influence?"

"That's almost the same thing."

"No...no, Megan. You're the influence over my...*my* deciding to quit gambling. You haven't pushed me or forced me. You've only influenced. I want to, need to, do this. It's time. The time just had to come, you know."

"Will, can't you make ends meet from your band earnings?"

"No. We make good money, but there are four of us to divide it among."

"So how do the other guys get by?"

"Second jobs."

"Is that what you're going to do then?"

His laugh held a twinge of pain. "Playing the horses *was* my second job."

Megan sprayed more Windex in the upper right corner of the window where it still looked streaked, then rubbed over it hard with the paper towel.

"Was...I said *was*," he assured her. "I don't know where my head's been. I've got a lot of debts to clear up. Including to you, for that ring."

She didn't feel owed for the ring. Not at all. It had served its purpose as far as she was concerned. She thought she'd made that perfectly clear to him. Except...what he *didn't* know was that Lewis was demanding it back. She turned to give Will another look. If she was going to support his giving up gambling, she certainly couldn't reveal the trouble she was in about the ring. She would have to handle it on her own somehow. "You don't owe me for the ring, Will. It's a done deal. Just forget about it." She sprayed another squirt of Windex on the window and rubbed the paper towel around some more.

"I don't think I can do that," he said.

"A done deal," she repeated.

"Megan, *why are you washing that window*?" It was as if he'd only just then come aware of what she was doing.

"Because it's dirty."

"Oh."

"Next," she told him, "I'm going to straighten your kitchen cupboard and—"

"Megan, you don't have to do all this stuff."

"I want to."

"Did you clean *Lewis's* apartment?"

"No. He had maid service."

"Of course. But then he probably wasn't a slob like me either."

"No," she said again. "Actually he was neat. Very neat. Which can really be worse. There's a lot more comfort and coziness here than there ever was at his place."

"Really?" Will came toward her again, brimming with satisfaction.

"Yes," she laughed.

"Like the comfort and coziness we had last night?" He was hugging her again and nuzzling her for another kiss. "After we got dried off from the rain, that is."

"Yes," she said, giving in to his affection.

"So what can I do?" he murmured sexily.

"Do?" she asked.

He slid his face against her hair. "Yeah...I mean, maybe I should be helping with the cleaning."

"You *are* a sidetrack, aren't you," she too spoke in a warm, sensuous murmur. "Weren't you...going to go job hunting?"

"*Was* I?"

They kissed again. And again.

"Yeah...okay," Will eventually responded. "I guess I was."

After he'd showered and left the apartment, Megan broke from her cleaning to conduct a search. She started by going through Will's dresser drawers. Guilty as it made her feel, she was determined to find what she wanted, needed, somewhere in his belongings. A telephone number.

After an unsuccessful bedroom search she scanned the living roam, taking special note of the scribblings on the telephone book cover and scraps of paper lying on the end table. However nothing turned out to be a phone number.

She worked her way to the kitchen and carefully inspected the cupboard, drawers and counter. Her adrenaline spurted when she spied two phone numbers written on the wall right next to the phone. An obvious place. Of course. Why hadn't she looked there first? Why hadn't she remembered seeing them there before?

Standing with the phone in her hand, it took her a few minutes to work up the courage to actually dial one of the numbers. When she did, it rang several times.

A girl's voice answered, "Hello?"

"Is Henry there?" Megan asked.

"Who?"

"Henry?"

"There's no one here by that name."

"How about Stan?" she asked.

"No Stan either. You've got the wrong number."

"Who is this?" Megan felt driven to ask.

"Julie. Who's this?"

"Uh...nobody."

The Julie person said smartly, "Well, why don't you recheck your number, *nobody,* and redial correctly."

Embarrassed by the response she'd gotten from the first number, and feeling certain that the second one would be Chris, Megan was more apprehensive than ever about dialing. But she had to. And did. And it rang.

"Hello?" It was a male voice. Good.

"Hello," Megan spoke carefully, "is this Henry?"

"No. Who's this?"

"Uh..." Megan was close to hanging up.

But the party she'd reached said, "It's Stan. Henry's not here right now. Anything I can help you with?"

She had the right number. She couldn't believe it. Relief

and fear both hit at the same time.

"Stan, hi...this is Megan...Will's friend. I'm not sure if you remember me, but—"

"Megan, yeah. Hi, honey, how ya doin'?"

"I need to talk to you and Henry."

"Okay, so talk."

"In person."

"All the better."

They set a time for late afternoon. That was good, she could finish doing all the housework she'd planned to do first, then go directly to her job at the Door following the loan shark meeting.

She was given an address and instructions on how to get there. It took her a bus ride and a walk of several blocks. The location turned out to be a tan stucco house in a fairly nice neighborhood.

Going up the front steps, her legs turned to rubber and her feet to lead. She pressed the doorbell.

A familiar looking pair came to the door together.

"Welcome," Henry said eagerly.

"Come on in," Stan held the door for her.

Megan entered cautiously.

"Well, well..." Henry said in his sneering way, "you've got us mighty curious here, Megan. You want to make a little loan, do you?"

"Or a *big* one?" Stan added laughingly.

She came to a stiff, frozen stance in the middle of the living room. The window drapes were drawn and no lights were on. Only a dim sort of haziness filtered through.

"Which?" Henry asked.

Megan forced her bravery. "I...I was just wondering...if you still had the ring."

"Will's last payoff?" Henry asked with surprise.

"Yes. I need it back."

Henry and Stan looked at one another, laughing as if this was fun.

"I'm serious," she told them, wringing her hands together, wishing the drapes were open.

"Did Will send you?" Stan asked.

"No. And please don't tell him about this either. It's private, my needing the ring back."

"It was yours?"

"A friend's of mine."

"A friend gave you his ring to give to Will to pay off his debt?"

"Not exactly."

Henry was first to get it. "The ring is *hot*?"

Megan nodded.

"Damn," he said.

"You stole it from a friend?" Stan questioned.

She nodded again.

"You sure don't seem to be the type." Henry paced around the room as if trying to decide whether to believe her.

She grew impatient, afraid she'd lose what nerve she had if she didn't keep moving. "Look, if you still have the ring I'd like it back. I'll make it up to you somehow."

"Somehow...?" Stan's interest perked.

Henry stopped pacing to give her new consideration. Megan could pretty well read the type of terms that were gathering in the sharks' minds. She was embarrassed at the misunderstanding, scared of the outcome. "It's a business deal, that's all. I'd make payments to you."

"Payments...?" Stan said, as if still taking it to mean what he wanted it to mean.

"*Money* payments," she clarified. "Do you have the ring or don't you?"

Henry stopped drooling over her to go to a side table, pull out a drawer and take out the gold ring with the diamond lightning bolt. "You mean this?"

The ring had never looked so wonderful to her. "Yes—please let me buy it back from you."

Stan clasped an arm around her and pulled her close to him. "We could talk about it."

"Not like that," she said, quickly pushing away from him.

"So why isn't Westin taking care of this?" Henry wanted to know.

She was nervous, so nervous. More over Will's finding out about what she was doing than anything. "I told you—leave him out of it."

"Gladly..." Stan slithered his arm back around her again.

Megan realized now that she should never have come here, that the possibility of getting Lewis's ring back was totally unrealistic, or at least beyond her willing means. "Maybe I'd better forget the whole thing." She started edging away from Stan and toward the front door.

Henry moved with her. "I'm not sure that *we* can forget it, Megan. Now that you've gotten us all hot and bothered."

She grabbed the doorknob. "Keep the ring. I've got to go."

Stan pulled her hand off the doorknob.

Henry took her by the waist, saying, "You're not going anywhere, honey, till we settle this."

Horrid thoughts rushed into Megan's mind—like what exactly these two might demand from her, like if she'd ever see the outside world again. She felt so sorry, so dumb for thinking she could just waltz in here, make a clear deal with them, and waltz right out again.

"There's nothing to settle," she said. "I...I changed my mind. Let me go. *Please* let me go. I don't want the ring after all. It's yours, keep it."

Stan forced her further back into the dim room and Henry tried to kiss her. She knew they were taking advantage of her because she'd said she didn't want Will to know anything about this. She struggled against both sharks and kept turning her face away. Finally, she kicked Stan in the shins and punched Henry in the chest. She worked herself free and ran out of the house without looking back. And without Lewis's ring.

She made it to the Rusty Door by four-forty. Ten minutes late wasn't bad for what she'd just gone through. She made a breathlessly fast change into her skirt and blouse uniform then started helping Pam take chairs off tabletops before Nick ever noticed her lateness.

When her eyes began tearing up and the chairs were down, Megan took some time out to go sit on a stool at the bar.

"What's wrong, Megan?" Joe asked.

"Wrong?" It showed. She hated that it showed.

"Yeah. You look down and out."

Leon. She needed to talk to Leon. "Can I borrow a quarter, Joe?"

She went to use the pay phone in the back hall. She dialed his number.

Ann answered, "Hello?"

"Hi, it's Megan. Is Leon there? I need to talk to him."

When Leon's voice said hello over the line it caused Megan to break emotionally. She started crying through trembling words, "Leon, I…I just needed to…to…"

"Meggie, what's wrong? Where are you? Are you all right?"

"I'm in trouble, Leon."

"You're *pregnant*?" he exclaimed.

"No."

"So what do you mean, trouble?"

"I need to talk to you. But not on the phone."

"Okay, sure. Are you at the Door? Should I come there?"

"I started working, but no…not here. I'll get away. I'll meet you somewhere else."

"Okay. Name it."

She went to tell Pam that there was an emergency and she would have to leave for a while.

It was almost six when she met Leon at Trevor Park. He was there ahead of her, sitting in a swing. She sat on the swing next to him. He said nothing, but kept looking steadily at her, concerned, anxious for her to talk.

"It's a money problem," she finally said.

He laughed. "How much do you want this time?"

"Twelve hundred."

"*What?*"

"Twelve hundred."

"That's what I thought you said."

"I'm not asking you for the money, Leon, I'm just telling you the type of money problem I have."

"To pay for your appendix surgery?"

"No. I can't tell you what it's for. Just that it turned up after my living with Lewis." She pushed her feet against the ground, setting her swing into a gentle back and forth motion. Ever since she'd been a child she'd loved swinging. Had never outgrown it. And needed it now as a pacifier. She pushed harder, upping her speed until the wind tousled her hair and her stomach rose and fell and she did indeed feel years younger and freer.

With his own swing moving more slowly beside hers, Leon reached his own conclusion. "I'm getting it...this money thing has to do with Will and his gambling, right?"

"Yes—no—anyway that's not really the point."

Leon left his swing to go sit on a bench across from Megan, shaking his head and muttering to himself.

She kept swinging. Back and forth, back and forth...a comfort she wasn't ready to give up yet. Despite the fact that watching Leon sitting over there made her realize how frustrated *he* probably was now. Because of her. And because she'd put him through so many frustrations so many times before.

Leon was so sweet. As was the friendship they'd always had. Always. And she had to wonder now what it might have been like if they had chosen to cross the line, from friends to lovers, way back when. Maybe they would have been married now, with a house and a couple of kids. Maybe her life wouldn't have gotten so crazy if she'd have chosen to make more out of her closeness with him. Maybe...though certainly not guaranteed. Where *were* the guarantees? She'd wasted so much time looking for them.

She smiled over at this special friend, glad at least for what they had always had and maintained between them. He gave her a wave and a smile. He could be so patient sometimes. She loved his patience more than anything else about him. Not wanting to take advantage of that, she didn't swing too much longer before jumping off and going to sit with him on the bench.

As though sensing that this was something extremely difficult for her to open up about, he slipped an arm around her and held her.

It took a few more minutes for her to begin. "When I left Lewis, I took his ring."

"Yeah," he said, nodding, knowing.

"And then these guys were after Will for the money he owed."

"Yeah," he said, with another knowing nod.

She sighed. "Lewis wants his ring back."

"Tell him to go to hell."

"I've got to get it back for him, Leon."

"No, you don't."

"It's important."

"He doesn't deserve anything important."

"Maybe it's important to *me* to get it back to him."

"Let Willie worry about getting it back."

"I can't."

"Why?"

"Because he's got enough other stress to handle right now."

Leon laughed. But he quickly became serious again. "Meggie, Meggie…what have you gone and gotten yourself into here?"

"Will wants to give up gambling. It's a difficult thing for him to do. He needs my support. If I tell him he has to get the money to get the ring back now it might force him right back into playing the horses again. He's taken a big step and I can't spoil that. I can't involve him in this, Leon. I *won't.*"

"Meggie, Meggie…" Leon shook his head at her.

"I went to see Henry and Stan on my own today and—"

"You *what*?" He took his arm from around her and turned to see her face directly.

"They gave me a bad time and I didn't get the ring. They do still have it though. I saw it. Hopefully they'll sell it back to me if I get the money."

"Meggie, I don't have that kind of money to lend you."

"No, I didn't expect you would. I only thought maybe you could help me figure out what to do."

"I told you—let Willie handle it."

"No."

"Have you fallen for this guy or what?"

She lowered her look to the ground.

Leon took it for a yes. "I don't believe this."

"I didn't *want* to. Leon."

"Right."

"I *didn't*. After Lewis I didn't ever want to get involved again."

"Until Willie happened."

"Give me a solution, Leon."

"Like I'm made of them." The dear person that he was put his arm back around her. "I don't know. Meggie, I just don't know. Unless..."

"Unless what?"

"What about Nickie? Maybe he could advance you some money from your wages or make you a loan."

"No way. No. I could never ask Nick."

It was seven-thirty when Leon dropped Megan off at the Rusty Door. As she got out of his car, he told her that he and Ann would be by later and they'd see her then.

She walked into the club, feeling chilled to the bone from the time she'd spent sitting in the park. The dinner crowd had built to a good size and Pam was rushing around trying to cover both sections of tables by herself.

Nick, with his eagle eyes, saw Megan come in and made a signal for her to come straight to his office.

She went, knowing this meeting could either mean she was fired or that she might lower herself to an even greater risk by asking him for a loan.

Twelve

Megan stepped into Nick's office, perfectly willing to apologize. "Before you say anything—"

"No!" He pointed a finger at her. "Before *you* say anything let me tell you you're skating on very thin ice here."

"I know. I realize it. I'm sorry."

"You seemed very sincere about this job less than three weeks ago, when you came in asking for it. And I bought that. Megan, you *know* how fast I bought that. But you've been a constant insult to my judgment ever since, because so far it's been nothing but old boyfriend problems, new boyfriend problems, lateness problems..."

"I know. I'm really sorry."

"A good club can't run on sorry."

"I've just had all these problems and—

"So have I, you know. You're *one* of them. Megan, you were three hours late tonight. *Three hours.*"

"I was here on time but then left again."

He grinned, more amazed than amused. "Like that really makes it all right. Pam was going crazy trying to cover for you."

"It was an emergency."

"If you really had to leave you should have at least come and asked me."

"I should have," she agreed.

Nick lit a cigarette and sat on the front edge of his desk to stare at her. "What am I going to do about you, Megan?"

"I don't know."

"I'm your employer. I'm directly affected by whatever it is that's bugging the hell out of you."

She focused her gaze straight into his and tried to work up her courage. There was no way out. This was it. "I need twelve hundred dollars."

He stood on his feet again. "That's a pretty big problem."

"Nick, could you lend me that much?"

He laughed. "Talk about being directly affected."

"I don't know where else to get it."

"Want to tell me what this money is for?"

"No. I can't."

"No, of course not. Just gimme the money, huh?"

"Please," she added.

He thought it over. It didn't take him long. "Okay, Megan...I suppose I could. But not without some interest."

"Interest? How much interest?"

"Interest in going out with me."

She should have seen that coming. God, she felt stupid. She spun away from him and started for the door. "Just forget it."

"Wait a minute, wait a minute—" He hurried to get in front of her. "Nothing raunchy here. Just a nice casual date, like maybe a movie on your night off."

She paused, feeling suspicious but forced to consider.

He explained further, "Maybe it'd solve one of my problems too, you know. You could let me prove that I'm a nice guy and not what people have made me out to be. Maybe that's as important to me as the money seems to be to you."

"That's it? You'll loan me the money if I go out on a date with you? A *casual* date?"

"That's it." He went behind his desk and unlocked a drawer. From it he took a metal box, opened it up and counted out twelve one-hundred dollar bills. Just like that.

Megan couldn't believe it. The sight of it made Nick's conditions seem worthwhile.

"What night, Megan?" he wanted to know.

"W-what...?" Her trance broke.

"Name the night and I'll give you the loan at that time."

"Doesn't that belong to the Rusty Door owner?"

"Yeah, but you're going to pay it back, right?"

With her eyes staring steadily at the money, she replied, "My first night off is Monday."

"Okay, Monday. I'll come pick you up about—"

"No, I'll meet you here."

"Fine."

Before leaving his office, Megan paused to ask, "Can I also borrow a quarter? Right now?"

He dug into a pocket, came up with a coin, then held it out to her, making her walk back across the office to take it out of his hand. "This may cost you a drink after the movie," he said teasingly.

She went to the pay phone in the back hall and dialed the number that was still etched in her memory.

Henry answered, "Yeah?"

"It's me, Megan."

"Oh, me-Megan..." he said in his sneering manner. "What can I do for you, honey?"

"I'll have the money for the ring Tuesday."

He laughed. "What ring?"

"The *ring*. I want to buy it back from you."

"So exactly what time on Tuesday can we expect you?"

"No, not there." She was wise enough to avoid going to their house trap again. But she wasn't prepared with an alternative. She thought under the pressure of his waiting. Where? Where? Somewhere open and safe. She hurriedly came up with, "Markway's Supermarket."

"A supermarket?" he exclaimed.

"Markway's—you know where it is?"

"Yeah, but—"

"The frozen food aisle, two o'clock Tuesday."

"AM or PM?"

"Afternoon."

Henry moaned, disliking the plan. "Okay…I suppose my next question should be—this ain't a set-up, is it?"

"What do you mean, set-up?"

"Are you for real, girl?"

"You make this sound illegal. " She went up on her toes and down again, taking a nervous look over her shoulder. "I'm only buying my ring back, that's all."

"It's just that this supermarket bit is—"

"Please. It's not a set-up or anything. It's just me alone. It's my way of handling this. I have to be comfortable."

"Right. Comfortable. But *Markway's*?"

"Deal or no deal?"

"You're not real used to this, are you?"

She was going crazy, needing a settlement. "Please…please just meet me there Tuesday and let's get this done."

"Don't cry. All right. Tuesday at two P.M. Markway's. Frozen foods."

When Megan hung up and turned around, Leon was there. She hoped he hadn't overheard anything. She asked him outright, "Eavesdropping?"

"The ring thing?" He guessed. He only guessed.

She was so nervous. But she smiled and bounced on her toes, pretending not to be. "It's okay. Everything is cool."

"Cool? No, I don't think so." Leon was serious. "See, I've

been thinking, Meggie, and—"

"Excuse me, dear friend, I've got tables to wait." She tried getting past him but couldn't.

He stayed in her way and held both her arms. "Meggie, I've been reconsidering that advice I gave you earlier. And I'm retracting it. I really don't think you should hit Nickie for a loan."

It felt like a gigantic tidal wave surging through her. "What? Why?"

Leon shrugged, still holding her. "Well, because the guy's got quite a reputation with girls, you know…and…well, I wouldn't want you putting yourself in a position he could take advantage of. Asking him for twelve hundred might do that."

"Maybe everyone has the wrong picture of Nick. Maybe he's not the bad guy they've made him out to be."

Leon let go of her. "Maybe some of us have known him a little longer than you have. Trust me here, okay. Just don't give the guy the opportunity to make you his next victim."

She forced a smile. "Okay."

"Anyway—I think if you really try you can get Lewie to forget about that ring. If not, I'd be glad to make him do so."

Megan nodded, pretending to agree.

"That *was* him you were just talking to, right?"

"You can be so intrusive sometimes, Leon." She managed to get around him and headed out to her tables.

He followed, talking to her as they went, "Intrusive? A little while ago you were desperate for my help. So don't call me intrusive, Meggie. Anyway, I'll never stop trying to look out for you, you know that. Hey, if you'd have listened to me about Lewie in the first place, you could have—"

Megan stopped. Leon stopped abruptly behind her. It seemed like a good time then and there to ask him. "Leon, what about Will?"

He stood wondering what she meant.

What she meant was, "What kind of advice do you have about *him*?"

He squinted at her, as if wondering if she was being serious or smart. "I like Willie, sure."

"That makes him the first guy you've ever liked that I've gotten involved with."

"Well, yeah...except that you and he just happened so fast."

"Like you and Ann weren't fast?"

"Annie and I—"

"*What*?" Ann herself asked, walking onto the scene right at that moment, hearing her name mentioned.

Megan smiled at her timely appearance. "Hi, Ann. I've got to hustle my tables. Leon will explain. Bye."

The Sidetracks wore their checked western shirts that night. Their music, throbbing, driving, rocking through the Rusty Door, entered Megan more deeply than it ever had before. As she waited on her tables, she glanced frequently at the stage, especially at the lead singer. Will's voice was vibrant and affecting, his body moving to the beat. Megan felt mesmerized.

• • •

Will didn't forget that his audience appreciated occasional slower, softer songs. He simmered the band down to one midway through the second set. He was still damp with perspiration, still slightly breathless and drained from the previous fast pace as he began,

"My feelings are running me over
Don't know what I'm doing these days
Just going with notions and strange motions
And living my life in a haze..."

He really didn't mind the quieter songs. Especially having someone special to direct them to. Vince, Jeff and Randy all knew it was Megan and easily backed up whatever he wanted to do. No one jostled him about it, except for maybe a now and then reminder about his falling over a chair that first night he'd seen her.

His first break of the night had been hectic, and over in no time. But on his second one he went to get Megan and take her outside. He walked her into the cool dark parking lot, bursting with smiles.

"What?" She laughed at him. "What's up? Something's up."

He gave her a quick kiss before telling her, "I got a job."

She thought he was joking. "Will, you only started looking today."

"Pretty fast, huh?" He hardly believed it himself. Nevertheless it was true and he felt very proud.

"Where? What kind of job?"

"Shipping."

"Boats?"

"No," he laughed, "warehouse. Loading and unloading trucks."

She scrunched her face. "Heavy stuff?"

"Hey, come on—just because I'm a singer doesn't mean I don't have a few muscles."

"I hope I didn't *push* you. You seemed to have really rushed into this."

"You didn't push me, Megan. It was something I had to do eventually. Come on, be happy about it." He put his hand beneath her chin and raised it until she was looking back into his eyes again. "Because *I'm* happy. I feel like a brand new person."

"I kind of liked the old one."

"Never fear. Plenty of him left, too." He put his arms around her and gave her a much bigger kiss than before. She responded warmly. And he felt her acceptance of whichever person, past or present, he was.

• • •

Megan saw Lewis come into the club later. Instead of waiting for him to hunt her down, she went straight over to him.

He smiled at being treated so nicely. "Hello, Megan."

But she was only there to ask, "Where's Dana? If you're supposedly getting back with her why are you always doing so much running around on the side?"

"You *know* what I'm after, Megan."

"Wednesday," she said. "You'll get your ring Wednesday."

"Fine."

"During the day," she told him.

"Why don't we make it lunch?"

"No lunch, Lewis. Two o'clock on the river path behind Sheldon Electronics."

He nodded. "Two o'clock. Wednesday. River path."

She started away.

Lewis grabbed her arm. "Megan—"

"No, don't," she warned, "I'm in enough trouble around here."

"I just want to ask…if you're okay?"

He seemed to mean it. Still, she was far beyond ever trusting him again. "I'm fine." She pulled free and hurried away.

• • •

Just as Gloria was entering the Rusty Door, a familiar distinguished-looking man with sunglasses was exiting it. They bumped into one another. Both laughed, for having run together in that very same place once before.

"We've got to stop meeting like this," Gloria flaunted a quick joke to the occasion.

"Oh, I'd hate to think that," he said, lowering his dark glasses to smile over the top of them at her.

"Excuse me." She turned, embarrassed and ready to retry her way through the doorway.

"Wait," the man stalled her. "Let me buy you a drink."

Kidding around was one thing, being serious another. "Oh, I…I…"

"Because surely this is something meant to be, don't you agree? My name is Lewis. What's yours?"

"Gloria," she gave way to him.

"One drink?" he coaxed.

She guessed she was intrigued and flattered enough to say yes. One drink, what was the harm? Passing the bar, she made a subtle little wave at Joe.

The tall handsome Lewis, by fate, led her to a table on Pam's side. She wished it had been on Megan's side, but didn't suggest changing. He held the chair out for her.

They sat across from one another and ordered from Pam. Gloria couldn't believe she'd been so swept up by this person. And yet, this wasn't just any person, any man. He was so dashing and well-dressed and mannerly that *any* woman would certainly have wanted to follow up and see what he was all about.

He smiled steadily at her as they waited for their drinks. "So tell me, what's a nice girl like you doing in a place like this?"

Gloria laughed. "Girl? I'm not exactly a girl, but if I were I wouldn't be trying to pick up *boys*, that's for sure. And what, may I ask, has been your purpose here?"

"Oh, I've had some business meetings here lately and...well, I can't believe how you and I have run into each other twice in the same place. I really figure that to mean something. Don't you?"

Their drinks came. He lifted his Scotch, and she her wine. They clinked their glasses together.

"To the crossbuck door where we met," he said.

"So you're a businessman," she said.

He took off his sunglasses. Gloria was glad. He had such nice eyes—very intense, serious, honest. "What business are you in?"

"Sheldon Electronics. I own it, run it."

She knew the place and nodded. "Blue building on the Mississippi River near Russell Bridge."

"That's it."

She was impressed. He seemed so young to own a business. Well, younger than *she*, but maybe not so very young. He did make *her* feel young, she knew that. And giddy. She laughed, simply over sitting there with him.

"You've got a nice laugh," he told her.

"Thank you." She looked around, finding that Joe, from the bar, was keeping close track of her. He was no doubt wondering what on earth she was doing. She guessed she wondered the same. But looking back at Lewis, she felt so caught up with…something.

"What's wrong?" he asked her.

"Nothing." She sipped some more of her wine.

"So, do you come here often, Gloria?"

"No, not often. You?"

"No. But I could be persuaded." He laid his hand over hers.

Gloria glanced nervously away from him. As she did she caught sight of Megan standing off near the back hallway. The girl was watching her, even more intently than Joe was. And in catching Gloria's attention, she began making a sneaky type of signal for her to come over.

What could she want right then like an emergency. "Please excuse me for just a minute?" Gloria said politely to Lewis as she rose from her chair.

"Certainly," he allowed her. "But *only* for a minute."

She went to meet Megan in the back hall, to find out what in the world she wanted.

Megan could hardly stand still with her anxiety. "Gloria, what are you doing with that guy?"

"What is this?" Gloria exclaimed. "You're beginning to sound like my kids."

"Do you know who he is?"

"Yes. We introduced ourselves."

Megan moaned and leaned against the wall. "Oh, Gloria…he's the guy I just broke up with."

Gloria leaned against the opposite wall. "You're kidding."

"The one I lived with for three months then found out he's married."

"That's him? The one you told me about?"

"Yes."

"Oh, Megan…you told me about him, yes, but you never told me his name or where he worked or—"

"I never thought I had to be that specific."

"Well, now you know that you *should* have."

"Gloria, what on earth are you doing with him?"

"Well, I didn't know that he was who he was, of course. We...we just ran into each other in the doorway, for the second time, and it got to be funny, and we spoke, and he thought that happening called for a drink together."

"Gloria, watch out."

"A drink, just a friendly drink."

"I thought you liked Joe."

"Relax, Megan. I haven't exactly promised my life to Joe, you know. And I'm not about to do so to Lewis either. We're just having a drink together. A *drink*."

Megan took a deep breath, going up and down on her toes and flapping her hands about nervously. "Gloria, will you do something for me?"

"What?"

"Check something out?"

Gloria was hesitant. "Like what?"

"Play up to Lewis and—"

"*What?*" That was going from one extreme to the far other. Gloria didn't like it, couldn't agree to it. She shook her head to the audacity.

"*You* know," Megan prompted, "flirt, play up to him, try getting him to—"

"No! Are you crazy?"

"—ask you out," Megan finished.

"Look, didn't you just warn me to watch out?"

"He told me he was going back with Dana. He even told me I helped him come to that decision. Now here he is, flirting around with *you*. I think we should put him to the test and call him on it."

"Test?" Gloria questioned.

"Here's the plan—" Megan began.

By the time Gloria returned to Lewis, she was totally committed to Megan's revenge. She'd sprayed herself with fresh perfume, smiled more than ever, and this time laid *her* hand lightly over *his*.

His interest flared. "Would you like another drink, Gloria?"

"Not yet," she said in a very soft, toying voice. "You're not trying to rush this moment, are you?"

His dark glasses were on again, as though he might be playing a mystery of his own against hers. "Gloria, why don't we get out of here? Together."

"Out of here?" *Yes*, the plan was working. Scary as it was. It hadn't taken long, just as Megan had predicted. "Why leave?" she asked, making him believe she was content right there.

Lewis motioned to the stage. "It's so noisy here. The music is as horrid as it is loud."

Gloria turned to see the Sidetracks. She'd really come to like their music and now resented anyone's putting it down. But her agreement with Megan made her excuse Lewis's remark. She had a game to play with him. A test. She smiled and cooed, "What did you have in mind?"

"My place."

"Y-your place?" The game seemed to be going too far, too fast.

"I've got a great apartment."

"You do?"

"Gloria, don't fight this fascination between us."

"No...no, I'm not." She swallowed the lump in her throat. "But isn't this kind of fast?"

"Fast is where it's at these days."

"Where *what* is?"

He wriggled a finger, coaxing her to lean forth toward him across the table so that he could whisper into her ear, "Hungry hearts, fulfilling moments." He took her hand and squeezed it.

She felt awkward and lost as to what to say or do next.

"Come on, Gloria." Lewis smiled as though he only took her stalling to be teasing and cute. "Our running together, twice as we have, has to mean something. I think it means we could make beautiful music of our own together."

Gloria eyed her son on stage again, thankful that he

wasn't aware of her sitting there with this guy who was coming on to her. Then she looked off the other way, seeing Megan over in her table section, still watching, watching. Back to Lewis, she asked, "Music? As in *making love*?"

He slipped his dark glasses down just enough to peer over them and signify a silent *yes*.

"You and me?" she asked. "At your apartment?"

"Yes," he said aloud this time.

"Well…I…I have my own car. Why don't you give me your address and I'll meet you there."

"Leave your car here, Gloria. I'll drive."

"No, I don't want to do that."

"Then follow me."

"No…no, just go ahead, Lewis, and I'll meet you there. There's something I need to take care of first. I'll be along soon, real soon."

"Promise?"

"Yes."

"Every minute counts." He wrote his home address on the back of one of his business cards for her.

• • •

Megan saw that Lewis was leaving. She purposely rushed herself over to catch him just as he got to the door. "Who was that woman you were with?"

He laughed that she should ask, care. "A casual business acquaintance I happened to run into as I was leaving earlier, if it makes any difference to you. I stayed to buy her a drink and discuss a couple of accounts."

"It didn't *look* like business."

"Well, I don't think it's any of your business."

"It's not," she said smugly.

He left, seeming hurried and preoccupied. Of course. The *jerk.*

Megan couldn't wait to get back to Gloria. "Well? How'd it go? What happened?"

While Gloria was notably upset, she also was eager to say, "You were right, Megan. As soon as I loosened up some, he came on strong. We have a date to make music in his apartment."

Megan cheered the success. "Yes! I knew it! I mean, I didn't know it but suspected it."

"So he's a real womanizer."

Megan nodded. "And you just helped prove his true colors. "Thanks."

"You're welcome."

"Gloria, are you okay?"

"I guess so."

"You're shaking."

"It's just that it isn't easy playing a slut."

"Come on..." Megan took her by the hand and delivered her to Joe.

Joe welcomed the chance to ask, "What's going on?"

"Why do you think anything's going on?" Gloria took a stool before him.

"A bartender sees."

"Just buy her a drink and be nice to her," Megan advised him. "Gloria, I'll talk to you some more later. Meanwhile, you just sit right there and relax. Your job is done. You did good."

Gloria nodded, Joe served her a white wine, and Megan returned to her tables. The Sidetracks were playing "Roadway Run."

Thirteen

Megan had supper waiting Monday night when Will got home from work. He moped in the door and plopped wearily onto the couch.

"How did day one of shipping go?" she asked, stirring a pan of green beans on the stove.

"Wonderful..." he moaned. "Don't I *look* wonderful?"

"You look beat."

"More than a Henry-Stan workover, I'll tell you."

She winced at the mention of their names. How ironic that Will should decide to rid himself of them only as she'd taken up with them.

"Something sure smells good," he said, lying there with his eyes closed, one arm across his face, the other arm dangling to the floor.

"Chicken and rice casserole. I got the recipe from your mother. She said it used to be your favorite."

Will sprung up like a delighted child. "I haven't had that in years."

She smiled and with potholders carefully lifted the Pyrex dish out of the oven. "Well, now you will."

He got off the couch and wandered out to her. "Is this a ploy to make me feel guilty?"

"Guilty?"

"For not being nicer to my mom."

"No. I just wanted to have something special for you when you came home from your first day on your new job. So...get washed up and we'll eat."

"You even *sound* a little like her," he said, though went willingly to wash at the sink.

Later into the evening, after they'd done the dishes together and cleaned up the kitchen area, Will returned to the couch and Megan went to spend some time in the bathroom and bedroom.

It was difficult for her to walk back out in front of Will, changed into a dress and collecting her sweater and purse. Difficult for her to have to tell him, "I'm going out for a while."

"Out?" He looked both puzzled and hurt.

"Yes." She tried not to care one way or the other about his reaction. "I've got something to do. I'll see you later."

"How can you go out when I practically just got home?" He straightened up, not about to let her off so easily.

She stopped at the door. "Cut it out, Will. We're not married."

"I didn't say we were."

"You act like it."

"I'm not *acting*."

"No strings here, remember?"

He left the couch to come put his arms around her. "Oh...I think we do have some strings now." He kissed her.

Yes, okay, there were strings. Knowing it made Megan's getaway even more difficult. "Will, I...it's something private. Trust me. Can you please just trust me?"

He studied her, still with that hurt look in his eyes.

"Please?" she asked.

"You're asking a lot here."

"Please?" she asked again.

As though he had no choice, he gave in with a slow reluctant nod.

"Thanks," she said and left.

During her bus ride to the Rusty Door, she felt no enthusiasm whatsoever for meeting Nick. There was only a sick ache in the pit of her stomach, caused by doubts about whether this was the right or the wrong thing to do.

She wore her beige cardigan over her green-print cotton dress. How she wished she'd have worn jeans instead. A dress made her feel as if this were a date. A date...yes...she guessed it was. A date that was going to earn her twelve hundred dollars. No, *loan*. It was a loan. This was business. She had to keep the right perspective. She only hoped Nick would.

By the time she got there the sun was almost down, with the west sky blurry in tones of purple and pink. She entered the Rusty Door and headed for the manager's office. It wasn't Joe behind bar, but rather his new young trainee, managing on his own. Megan gave him a wave and he waved back. The place was different, so quiet and empty now compared to the nights she and the band worked. The jukebox was playing something mild and just a few people were seated here and there, talking softly.

Megan knocked on Nick's door and he called for her to come in. He was doing some paperwork at his desk, a cigarette in his left hand, a pen in his right. He looked up, and smiled his cocky smile. "Hi."

"Hi," she said, feeling more nervous and unsure of what to expect now than she had that first time she'd come in there to apply for the waitress job.

"I'll just be a minute," he said. He finished writing something in a ledger, shuffled some papers about, then eventually stuck everything into a file drawer.

Megan wished she was back home with Will and didn't need to go through this.

Nick crushed out his cigarette and came around the desk to where she stood waiting. "You look beautiful, Megan."

"Do you have the money?" she asked.

"Yes."

"Can I see it?"

He returned to his desk, unlocked the top middle drawer and took out a thick envelope. "Twelve hundred."

"Okay, let's go," she said. But when he started putting the money back into the drawer, she added, "Aren't you bringing it?"

"Carry that much cash around all evening? No. We'll stop back for it later."

Megan tensed at the idea.

Nick noticed and laughed. "Will you relax?"

"Sorry."

He opened the door for her. "Let's go."

They went to a comedy movie starring Steve Martin. Megan was surprised to find that Nick could care about or enjoy anything funny. But he turned into a different person in the theater than he'd ever been at the club. He laughed so loosely through out the movie that Megan wound up being almost more amused by him than by the movie itself. She was also surprised that he was a perfect gentleman as they sat there together for two hours in the dark. He never once tried putting his arm around her or whispering intimate things into her ear.

After the movie they stopped in at a coffee shop for coffee and pie. They discussed Steve Martin, which started them laughing all over again.

When they finally wound down, Megan truthfully concluded, "I'm having a good time, Nick."

"You didn't think you *would*?"

"Well..."

"It's okay. I know you had your reservations about me, certainly about going *out* with me." He sat there not looking like the stern boss he usually was, but rather just a regular guy.

"I'm glad I was wrong."

"I'm having a good time, too," he told her, with the warmest smile she'd ever seen from him.

"From what I'd heard about you, I have to admit I was uneasy about going out with you."

He nodded. "I have a reputation."

"Yes, I guess you do."

He stroked his mustache. "Megan, I work awfully hard for the Door, for the *owner* of the Door. I'm a damn good manager. A few years ago the place was nothing. Then I took over and put it back on its feet."

"The band is the drawing point, wouldn't you say?"

"Definitely. They're great. I don't even think *they* know how great they are. You know, a lot of bands came and went from the Door, but when the Sidetracks came, that was it. *They* were it. They had something special. I kept them. Didn't let them go. I paid them well and made them stay. They fit the place. Just as I did."

"I don't think they'll stay *forever*."

"Nor will I."

"Meaning?" Megan felt a rising interest and intrigue in this man. "That you might want to do something other than manage the Door some day?"

"Possibly. I have thoughts. Thoughts that there just might be something a lot more challenging...and new...and fun."

"Sounds exciting."

"We'll see."

"Nick, tell me about the waitresses."

"Yeah, right...the waitresses." He was less happy with that subject.

"I'd like to know, to understand," she said.

He lit a cigarette. "Yeah, well...seeing how most of my life is spent at the club and I never get much of a chance to meet women elsewhere, I *have* dated lots of them."

"But you're not the father of Cheryl's baby."

"No. For sure no. How could I be...if I never even made it with her?"

Megan laughed and shook her head. "Why have you been so badly labeled?"

He drew deeply on his cigarette, exhaled slowly. "I'll tell you if you won't jump on me for it."

"Okay." She laughed again.

"True, I've dated a lot of our waitresses. Unfortunately, followed by a lot of stories. The thing is...most of the girls have been down-right bitches." He paused, as if waiting for Megan to break her word and jump on him anyway for saying such a thing. But she didn't.

So he continued, "We'd go out a few times. On very casual, nice dates. Then they'd go making up stories to one another, and to my other employees, that I'd nearly torn their clothes off, that we'd had wild sex, that I threatened their jobs if they wouldn't do things with me."

"Why?" It angered Megan. "*Why?* I don't understand. Why would they make up stuff like that?"

"I don't know. I guess because they were *bitches*. And because I was pretty much of a boring let-down from what they'd really expected of me. Maybe that added to their low salaries. They just always felt they had to get back at me somehow. And they did."

"It's dumb."

"Very dumb. I'd begun to think there were no nice girls left."

Megan didn't mind that he put his hand over hers.

"I guess it became some sort of an out-of-hand game to them," Nick added. His look became deep and appreciative of her. "So when someone nice does come along, like you, it's a little hard to prove my real self."

"You *have* seemed flirtatious sometimes at the club."

"Flirtatious, yes. Wild animal, no."

"What about Pam?"

Nick lifted his hand off hers and tipped it in the air. "She isn't quite sure about me."

"You never went out with her?"

"She's engaged. To a nice guy. *She's* nice. Not one of the usual bitches. Although I have to say that rush times have been known to push her limit some. Mostly she and I leave each other alone."

"Maybe your bad reputation will change. Because I won't be saying anything bad about you, Nick."

He laughed. "This is really weird, isn't it? A guy and a girl out together and it's the guy who's worried about his reputation."

"Nick, I won't say anything or make up anything if—"

"Here it comes. The threat. The blackmail."

"—if you don't say anything to Will about our date or the money," she requested.

"This money thing—it's *because* of him, right?"

Megan lowered her eyes, saying nothing.

But Nick was sure. "Well, it's no secret he's a gambler and it's became pretty obvious you've become his girl."

"Don't try to understand it," she said. "Just don't say anything to him, please."

"Our secret," he promised.

She smiled thankfully.

"So we honestly had fun tonight?" he asked.

"Yes."

"Enough to change your opinion of me?"

"Yes."

"Then it's worth twelve hundred dollars."

"Nick, it's a loan—not a bribe."

"Yeah…that's right. Come on." He stood up. "Let's go get your money from my office, maybe have a quick drink, then I'll take you home."

• • •

Gloria brought a tray of coffee and cookies into the living room and set them on the coffee table. Joe leaned forward from the plaid chair and helped himself.

"It must feel strange having Monday and Tuesday for your days off," she said to him. "Your *weekend*."

"You get used to it, to being out of sync with most of the rest of the world."

He had called her earlier, when she'd just gotten home from work, and wanted to take her out. She'd been surprised, and taken off guard, Monday having been a hard day at the office for her. When she said she was really tired, he asked if she had a VCR and if it would be okay, instead of going out, if he rented a movie and brought it over for them to watch at her place. She wasn't sure her acceptance had made the situation better or worse—she was far more scared of dating than she was tired.

But he came and they watched the movie, separate chairs apart from one another. It hardly gave them the opportunity to talk much, but it did feel nice being together. Gloria was finding out, more and more, what a comfortable person Joe was.

By the time the movie ended, she was actually looking forward to some conversation with him. Except then the phone rang, an untimely interruption. She got it in the kitchen.

It was Will. "Hi, Mom. I know it's late, I hope you weren't in bed."

"No..." She glanced back through the dining room and into the living room where Joe was waiting for her. "Will, what is it? What's wrong?"

"Megan went out hours ago and hasn't returned yet."

Gloria sighed. "What is going on with you two?'"

"Nothing."

"Then why do you worry so about her every time she's out of your sight?"

"I'm not worried. I just wondered if she was there."

"She's not here. And you sound *very* worried."

"It's late."

"Will, relax. She'll be home soon, I'm sure."

"Where the hell can she be?"

"I don't know."

"Maybe I should go out looking for her."

"You have to wait. That's all you can do."

"Yeah, I'll just sit back and wait. Like it's nothing. Thanks a lot, Mom."

"Will—Will—" Gloria said quickly before he hung up. "It *is* something...but there's just nothing you can do."

She returned to Joe in the other room, her good mood tinged with concern. "I'm sorry. That was Will. Seems Megan went out and hasn't come home yet and he's getting worried. And now, it seems, I guess *I'm* worried also."

"How do you feel about the two of them? Their living together?"

"I like Megan. I've gotten to know her and really do like her. I'm just not sure it's good timing for her and Will to become involved right now."

Joe took what was probably his third cookie off the tray. "What's so wrong with the timing?"

"Megan is just out of a broken relationship. And Will...oh, Joe, I haven't even wanted to see this for what it is until lately, but I think Will is into some very serious gambling."

Joe nodded all too easily. "I *know* he is."

His knowing scared her more. "You do?"

"I also happen to know, Gloria, that you've been one of his main supporters."

She sat down across from her guest, the bartender, and lifted her coffee cup off the table. She took a drink, as if it was a soothing wine. "W-well...I...I help him out with a little money now and then, but certainly not for his gambling. What I give him has strictly been for rent or a past due bill or something."

Joe was giving her a knowing look. "Gloria...wake up, dear. Unfortunately, I'm afraid that money too often gets put on the horses first. And when he loses...well, the money never gets to the bills."

Gloria sipped some more coffee then bent forward to set her cup back onto the coffee table. She stared at her guest, a bartender who seemed to know her son far better than she did. "You're making me feel really guilty here, Joe."

"Guilty? I sure don't mean to do that. Look, Will's having such a gambling problem was something I myself had to face not long ago."

Gloria tried to read into what he was saying. "You mean…?"

He nodded. "Yeah. I used to feed Will's addiction, too. Every couple weeks or so he'd hit me with a sad story and a desperate plea and I'd give him a loan. Then he'd pay it back. Then he'd borrow again. Back and forth, back and forth. Until the borrowing began to get way out of line from the paying back and I said *no more, Will,* no more."

So much had been going on without her knowing. "Oh, Joe…I had no idea. I'm embarrassed. And sorry. Ashamed of my son's doing this to you. I don't blame you for cutting him off."

"I cut him off, Gloria, because I *care* about him and finally realized it would help him more by saying no to the borrowing than saying yes."

"I…I guess that's what I'll have to do."

"It may be too late."

"What?" She felt beaten before she'd begun.

Joe shook his head. "No…I mean in a good way. I mean, I think maybe he's already sworn off gambling. Seems Megan has gotten through to him like nobody else ever could. He's taken a second job in addition to the band and seems determined to square up all his debts."

"Really? Oh, Joe, that's good. I'm relieved."

"Yeah, me too. Will's a pretty special guy."

"Yes, I certainly think so."

"His mother is pretty special too," Joe studied her intently.

"No, I'm not so special," she claimed, shaking her head with a whole new sense of embarrassment. "Go ahead, ask my kids. They'll tell you I'm not."

"Why would they tell me that?"

"Because. Because things haven't exactly been so good between them and me for some time now."

"Why?"

"I guess because maybe I've tried mothering them too much. Which has only turned them away. I guess they've gotten too old and too busy to need a mother."

"Oh, Gloria...no, I don't believe that. I'm sure they love you and need you very much."

"No, Joe—I'm not so sure."

"Maybe you just expect too much. Sometimes parents tend to expect too much of their grown-up kids."

She shrugged. "Maybe that's it."

"Maybe you need more of a life of your own. Maybe...you need to spend more time with me."

She met Joe's sincerity with that of her own. "You're a nice person, Joe. I'm glad I met you."

"I don't want you to think I pick up with every woman who walks into the Rusty Door."

"No. No, I wouldn't think that."

"Basically, I'm a loner. Except...you kind of had this effect on me that I couldn't resist."

Gloria stood up, suddenly finding that the nervous sixteen-year old within her was completely gone, and that she was openly and honestly only herself. It felt good. "Joe, I don't want you to think I pick up with every bartender I meet either."

He laughed. "No, of course not." He also stood, checking his watch and saying, "I'd better leave so you can get some sleep. Not everybody has bartender hours."

"Thanks for the movie, Joe." She took the tape out of the VCR, put it into its case and handed it to him. "I had a very nice evening."

"Me, too," he said.

She walked him to the front door. "You're not only a nice person to watch a movie with but to talk with as well. You offer good advice, Joe."

"Comes from years of bartendering."

They both laughed. Joe paused before opening the door, wrapped his free arm around her, drew her close and kissed her. "I'll see you again…real soon."

It'd been a long time since Gloria had been kissed like that. She liked it. After watching Joe drive away, she closed the front door, returned to the living roam, sank down into the plaid chair he'd sat in, and took another cookie. It'd been a long time since she'd felt this way. It was *wonderful.*

• • •

It was almost one A.M. when Nick dropped Megan off at the apartment. She left his car, entered the building, hurried up the stairs and down the hall. She unlocked 316 to a dark room. Before she could turn on a light, she saw Will's silhouette by the window.

"Nick?" he asked. "You were out with Nick?"

She had never expected to be checked up on this way and questioned. The thing was, she couldn't explain it without telling him the truth. And she couldn't tell him about the loan, she just couldn't. She stood there, a few feet away from him, saying nothing.

"I thought we were a couple now," he said. "I thought you and I were—"

"Yes, I was out with Nick." She went toward him, admitting as much. "But not like you think. It was business."

"Business," he repeated doubtfully.

"Yes."

"Come on, do you really expect me to believe that?"

"That's why I didn't tell you in the first place. Because you wouldn't believe it. Nick had some important work-related stuff he needed to discuss with me and…and there's never time during my regular work shift and…and I agreed to see him about it on an off night."

"With his reputation?" Will was not soothed.

"Mostly it was *about* his reputation."

"I'll bet."

"He's not the father of Cheryl's baby and—"

"And you believe him?"

"Nick is a nice guy."

"Fine. Then go live with him."

"Can't you *listen* to me? Do you always have to jump to the wrong conclusions?"

Will became quiet. Still stubborn, though possibly considering.

Megan stood close to him and lowered her voice gently. "I'm sorry I didn't tell you I was meeting with Nick tonight. I'm sorry it upset you. I'm sorry you don't know how I feel about you. She put her arms around him and kissed him.

He liked the kiss and was soon holding her and kissing her too. "I'm not sure I understand or like your being with Nick...but if you say it was business, okay, I guess I believe you."

"Will..." she whispered, "let's go to bed."

Fourteen

"I don't want to go to work..." Will moaned in bed Tuesday morning. The alarm had gone off ten minutes before and he had reached to turn it off then snuggled back down with Megan.

"You're stiff and sore from your first day on the job yesterday right?" She lightly massaged his arms that were about her.

He sighed. And moaned again, "No, that's not it. I just don't want to leave you." He kissed her bare shoulder, then her neck, her ear.

She giggled and struggled playfully. "Come on, Will...you'll be late for your second day."

"But hey—I'd walk in with a smile on my face."

"No." She worked her way out of bed, then stood shifting her nightshirt back in place.

He jumped out after her, catching her in his arms again. They kissed long enough and well enough to make it last for the day.

After Will left for work, Megan showered and dressed and tidied up the apartment. She was starting to feel more and more confident about their relationship. It was turning out much better than she would have thought. If only it weren't for the ring thing hanging over her. But soon now that would be settled. She couldn't wait.

The morning went fast, but from noon on the time seemed to drag. Carrying the twelve hundred dollars in her hand, Megan paced around and around the apartment, anxiously awaiting her meeting with Henry and Stan.

The time finally came to leave. She walked to Markway's Supermarket and arrived there at five before two. Crossing the parking lot, she felt a fluttery sensation in her stomach and weakness to her legs. Why was she doing this? She didn't have to do this, she didn't have to. Yes, she did.

Suddenly her ankle turned out and she stumbled and fell. How could that have happened? She was more mad than hurt. As she maneuvered from sitting to kneeling, she looked for the cause of her accident. There was a rough and crumbly portion of blacktop. That was it. She hadn't seen it and had stepped in it. Now she was really mad.

She got up physically okay, but feeling stupid and embarrassed. Looking around, she realized no one had even noticed her or what had happened. She brushed off her pants legs, collected her purse and the few things that had spilled out of it, and proceeded bravely into the market.

Henry and Stan were not in the frozen food aisle as per plan. Where were they? Megan started looking around some, but then decided it was best to stay put in just one spot and let them find her. She leaned against the edge of the frozen vegetable bin.

The store seemed extremely busy for a weekday afternoon. There were a lot of elderly people—stooped frail bodies taking careful tiny steps, pushing carts and looking everything over as if it were a museum rather than a grocery store.

A little old woman, in a housedress and sweater, paused noticing Megan's fixed position, and asked, "Can I help you find something, dear?"

Megan smiled uneasily. "Oh, no thank you. I...I'm just waiting for someone."

The woman reached down into the bin for a package of frozen peas. Then she dropped it in her basket and started pushing away again. "Have a good day," she said, leaving.

"You, too," Megan told her.

Before the woman got more than a few steps, another elderly woman, coming from the opposite direction, met her with some sharp words, "Better move it, Aggie. The bus leaves in fifteen minutes and we've got the check-out line yet."

The woman who had just gotten peas near Megan maintained an unhurried walk. "He'll wait, he always does."

"It's always you who makes him wait," the friend spluttered.

The woman named Aggie looked back at Megan. "I've had enough rushing all my life. Shouldn't have to buy groceries like it was some kind of race. Bus will wait. Always does."

Megan nodded approvingly and smiled. Then she noticed the big sign at the end of the aisle, SENIOR DAY—TUESDAY. Yes, of course, that was it, what was going on. That explained why there had been several buses parked out in the lot.

A man of eighty-something, with a cane hooked over his cart handle, came down the frozen food aisle with a curious look at Megan. She guessed she should have taken a cart so as to have at least looked like a shopper. She felt more and more conspicuous every minute. Where were those loan sharks?

Will would have a fit if he knew what she was doing. They were just starting their relationship and already had this big secret between them. But she had to get Lewis's ring back for him or it would only lead to more trouble. And she couldn't talk about money problems to Will now that he'd given up gambling. Which brought it down to her having to deal with the loan sharks on her own. Yes. But where were they?

Finally the two familiar figures came around the corner and toward her, one with the slid-back hairline and the other with the muscular build.

Henry reached her first, anxiously blurting out, "Why today? Why on Senior's Day?"

Megan shrugged. "I didn't know that till I got here."

He was not at all happy. "We had to stop and help one old lady get a certain particular box of cereal off a mile-high shelf, and another one restack a soup can display she'd accidentally rammed into and we helped an old man to find the bathroom."

Megan could only feel amused. "I didn't know you guys were so service-oriented."

Stan was first to rise above all the inconveniences for the real matter at hand, "Okay, girl, where's our fifteen hundred?"

Henry jabbed him. "Not so loud."

"*Fifteen* hundred?" Megan said, even louder than Stan had.

"Shuu…" Henry told her, as another shopper came inching down their way.

"You said twelve hundred," Megan whispered angrily.

"You never considered interest?" Henry said.

"You never told me."

"It's assumable. Like it's been a while since we took it as a twelve hundred dollar payment, and value doesn't sit still, you know, Missy."

"Megan," she corrected him.

"Megan."

She held out her hand. "I want the ring."

Stan held out his hand. "Fifteen hundred."

"You can't do this."

"We can," he nodded.

"This is crazy."

"Take it or leave it."

"I've only got twelve."

"We'll give you a time extension on the three hundred."

She hesitated, hating that she'd ever gotten into this. "With more interest?"

"Depends on the length of extension," Henry said. "I don't believe Westin hasn't explained to you about our interest terms."

"I told you," Megan shot back at him, "he doesn't know about this and I don't want him to."

Henry looked both directions over his shoulders before taking the lightning-bolt ring out of his pocket and flickering it before her eyes. "You sure this ain't a set-up now?"

She made an impulsive grab for it. Henry lunged back, bumping into Stan, which caused the ring to fly out of his hand and over and down into the icy cold bin of frozen vegetables. All three of them made a dive to retrieve it.

A woman shopper, just then coming along, stopped, looking curiously at the action. "Is there a good special in there?"

Henry swooped up a bag of broccoli for her. "Yeah—here."

Megan figured the ring must have gone clear down between the vegetable packages to the very bottom of the bin, as neither she nor Henry nor Stan could find it with their rooting. Her fingers were soon aching from the cold and her back straining from the stretch.

"How could you drop it like that?" Stan grumbled at Henry.

Henry raised himself out of the bin like the devil from hell. "Because I bumped into you, you jerk! You're always in the way!"

Stan straightened up out of the bin to face him. "You don't

think that maybe you're just clumsy?"

"I couldn't have bumped into you if you hadn't been in the way."

While the sharks stood there arguing, Megan kept searching the frozen vegetables. Moving this package, moving that package. She only hoped the store manager wouldn't come along. Finally...there. She spied the ring and made her furthest reach yet, down between the carrots and the green beans.

Henry and Stan stopped bickering the instant she came up with a tightly-closed hand.

"You got it?" Stan exclaimed. "You really found it?"

"Yes." The numbness of her hands and arms didn't matter so much anymore."

"Gives us the money and it's yours," Henry told her.

She opened her purse. "Twelve hundred, that's it. That's all I've got."

"With an extension on three," Henry reminded her.

She rooted through her purse. At least it was warmer rooting through there than rooting through frozen packages. But where was the money? The envelope? Though she had it out and held it and walked around the apartment with it earlier, she knew she'd specifically stuck it back into her purse before leaving. Except it wasn't there *now*. Her heart sank. She felt sick.

Henry read the look on her face. "You don't have it, do you? You don't have *any* of the money. What the hell is this?"

"A hoax," Stan suspected, reading her as well. "You thought you would come hoax us in a supermarket where we couldn't do you any harm, right?"

"No," she pleaded, wanting more than anything for them to believe her. "I *had* the money, I really did. But now I don't. It's gone. I don't know where. I can't imagine what happened. I—"

"Friday." Henry pointed his finger at her as though it were a gun. "You just keep the ring, Missy, but have that fifteen hundred Friday night at the Rusty Door or we break bones on both you and your friend."

"Friend?" she winced. "Which friend?"

"Westin, of course."

"I told you, he has no part in this."

"He does now." Henry reached to clasp his hand around the back of her neck. He squeezed it hard. "See you soon. Hopefully with fifteen hundred...cause I don't think black and blue are your best colors, are they, hon? Westin's, maybe, but not yours."

The sharks left. Megan wanted to look at the ring again, but her hand was so tightly clamped over it she wasn't sure she would even be able to open it. She was glad to have the ring, but the money...what happened to the money?"

Two more women customers came down the aisle. "Where's the broccoli? Someone told us there's an awfully good broccoli special in this aisle."

Megan motioned to the bin behind her, the one in the sorry looking state of upheaval.

She left the store. The sunshine outside felt warm and soothing to her chilled skin. She headed through the lot. Okay, she had the ring, Lewis's ring, and that was at least something. Only now she had to come up with fifteen hundred dollars for Henry and Stan as well as the twelve hundred to pay back Nick.

Her head was down and laden with worry. She looked for bad spots in the blacktop as she walked. Until a noisy commotion just ahead of her made her stop and look up. A group of elderlies were standing about laughing and cheering. Something was going on. Nearing them, Megan saw that one man had an envelope. It looked like—

"Hey!" she shouted. "That's mine. You have my—"

"Found it!" he said, holding it possessively against himself. "It's mine! I found twelve hundred here on the ground and I have never before had a stitch of luck in my entire life."

The gathering around him cheered louder.

The amount—why did he have to say the *amount*? Now she would have no way of proving that it was hers. Except,

"Hundreds!" She tried wedging her way into the group. "There are twelve one hundred dollar bills and—"

Nobody was paying the slightest bit of attention to her. Everyone was focused on the man with the money. "Way I figure it," he was telling them, "a man is richer with friends than with money. There were twelve of us on the bus together today...and I want to share my sudden fortune with all of you."

There was a lot of clapping and praising as he began passing out a hundred dollar bill to each of them.

Megan gave up. There was nothing that she could do. Nothing. She was not about to take on a dozen senior citizens in Markway's parking lot. She reached the sidewalk and headed back home.

After supper that evening, she sat cuddled against Will on the couch watching TV. Though she had a heavy sweater on, she was still shivering.

"How come you're so cold?" he wondered, with his arms as snug about her as they could be.

"I...I don't know." Her teeth chattered.

"Maybe you're coming down with something."

"I feel fine. I...I'm j-just cold."

"How about a hot shower? Or bath? *Together.*"

"No."

"Oh, Megan..." he drawled. "I just want to make you feel better."

"I f-feel...fine."

"Yeah, right. You're shaking like crazy."

"Just hold me."

"It doesn't seem to be enough."

"I'll be okay," she said.

"What's wrong? What's really wrong, Megan?"

She felt like bursting into tears and telling him, but she couldn't. She had to keep it in. "I've...just got some things on my mind."

"What things?"

"Things I can't discuss with you."

"Thanks," he said, moving away from her. "I'm glad you think so much of me."

"Don't get mad."

"I'm not mad. I'm concerned. Maybe a little rejected."

"I'd tell you if I could, but I can't."

"Sounds pretty mysterious, Megan."

"Hold me, Will. Please, just hold me."

He moved back, rewrapped his arms around her, and asked no further questions. They continued cuddling and watching TV.

Wednesday afternoon Megan waited out behind Sheldon Electronics along the grassy bank of the Mississippi River. It was two fifteen. Lewis was late for their meeting.

She paced back and forth on the walk path. She watched a barge going down the river. The Mississippi was so beautiful—wide, deep, free flowing, edged with trees and brush and scatterings of houses and businesses. She turned again to gaze at the blue building that had, on this back side as well as on the front side, a sign with a lightning-bolt insignia plus the big letters of SHELDON ELECTRONICS. She opened her hand to look at the lightning-bolt ring she was holding.

She wished the other office workers had told her Lewis was married, way back when she had first started getting involved with him. Why hadn't they? If it was because they'd assumed she'd known, then why...*why* wouldn't it have at least come up in some way at some time or another? She felt betrayed by all of them. What she ought to do was march on in to her ex-office and tell everybody off.

But then Lewis came from the building, cutting across the lawn and over onto the blacktop path before her, looking as sharp as ever in a gray pinstripe, straight posture and sunglasses.

"You're late," Megan told him.

"I know. I'm sorry. Last minute phone call from a New York distributor."

"I know how that goes," she said coolly.

"You look great."

"I don't feel great."

"Megan...don't let what happened between us have an everlasting effect on you."

She shook her head. "No, it was actually a worthwhile, valuable learning experience for me."

A half grin came over his face. "Good."

"I've learned that you can't judge a book by its cover."

His grin turned into curiosity.

"Because I thought you were a respectable guy to start out with," she explained.

"I still am."

"You lied and took advantage of me."

"I never lied to you about Dana."

"You never *told* me about her—same thing. You could have told me about her, Lewis. You *should* have."

He stared at the river, as if for help in contemplating his next words. "Megan, would you have had anything to do with me then, if I had said I was married, but separated?"

"I don't know what my choice would have been, whether I'd have gone ahead and gotten involved with you or whether I wouldn't have. But I deserved a choice based on truth, don't you think?"

"Yes, okay. You're right. I'm sorry. Now, if you've got my ring, Megan, I'm kind of pressed for time."

She was still holding it but was not ready to give it to him. "So, are you getting back with Dana now?"

"Yeah, sure. We're working on arrangements. She and the kids and—"

"You have *kids?"* Megan gasped.

"Only two."

"I'm learning more about you *since* our break up than all the time we lived together."

Lewis checked his watch, glanced at the river again, and then back at her. "Megan, I was under a lot of pressure when you came into my life. You...you were a very refreshing change of pace for me. A distraction that I hadn't expected, wasn't really looking for, but turned out to be so right. I thank you for being so special to me."

"And now Dana is the special one?"

"Yes."

"You're going from me back to her with no further doubts or—"

"What *is* this, Megan?" he asked impatiently.

"I want to know if you're going to be sincere with Dana."

"Yes."

"Really?"

"Yes. So what is this? What are you—"

"It's about trusting and believing. It's about...something in the bushes."

"Huh?" He removed his sunglasses and swung them nervously in his hand.

"I have something for you in the bushes."

"You put my ring in the bushes?"

"Is that all you can think about? That ring? You don't seem to care as much about people and what you do or don't do to them as much as you care about that ring."

"Megan, I said I was sorry. You said you've learned a lot from our relationship. Well, me too. So let's let it go at that."

"But you really do love Dana now?"

He sighed, looking away from her and then back again. "Yes."

"Then what about..." She signaled toward the hedge of nearby bushes and Gloria stepped out of them.

Lewis was shocked. Definitely caught in another lie.

Gloria came toward him, saying nothing. She didn't need to. Just her being there said it all.

Megan, however, had more words. "Fine. Okay. So you decided to go from me back to your wife. You said you loved Dana all along. And missed her. I was really ready to accept that and try to understand that...but then Gloria happened."

Lewis's face drooped sheepishly. "I bought her a drink, one drink at the Rusty Door."

"Along with an invitation to go back to your place with you...and do things," Gloria reminded him.

"To which you never showed up," he said, like an allowance to it all. He looked from Gloria to Megan, back and forth. "You two know each other and this was a set up."

"How many others?" Megan drilled him. "Were there others while you and I were together? There probably were. I'm sure there were."

"No, damn it. No, Megan!" Without his sunglasses on, his eyes turned glassy. Either the sun was too bright for him, or he was almost believably sad. "I was a lonely man. You happened to be someone very special who came when I was at a very susceptible time. And you were the *only* one then, Megan, the only one."

"With a wife in the background."

"Except for her, yes. And as for her, at that time I never thought Dana and I would get back together. Not until she phoned me one day and wanted to meet with me."

"And you don't think you could have met somewhere else besides the park right across from the Halloren Towers? You *knew* I spent a lot of time in that park."

"A mistake, yes."

"And Gloria was another mistake?"

Lewis looked at Gloria, then at Megan. "You want the truth?"

"That would be nice," Megan said.

"Yes," Gloria agreed.

Though he put his shades back on, it somehow failed to return him to his previously cool image. "Truth is…" he stopped, sighed and began again, "Dana doesn't want me back."

This was something far removed from anything Megan had expected. As was her feeling sorry for him now. "But you said—"

"Wishful thinking. Guess I had myself believing it for a while there, with her wanting to see me like that. But from our second meeting, it turned out she only wanted to tell me she was starting divorce and child custody proceedings. I'm not good at this, I'll tell you. Me, a high-paced business person who should be tough and strong and smart, much smarter than this. Only it's taken me down, really down. Made me look for cover."

"Cover?" Megan asked.

"Yeah. You know—things like sunglasses...extra long working hours...someone to be with. Gloria seemed like a possibility the other night. But no, I guess I'm losing my touch there, too."

Megan gave him his lightning-bolt ring. "Maybe what you need, Lewis, is to get more in touch with truth and reality. Because that's where everything has to start in order to continue. I know it's sometimes pretty difficult and painful, but you can't go on trying to build any kind of life for yourself without it."

He stood staring at the ring in his hand. "You know why I wanted this ring back so much?"

She thought she did. And she nodded. "Because it's a symbol of your success with Sheldon Electronics?"

"Two reasons," he claimed. "First, yes, it's a big reminder of my achievements and I cherish it. Second, I didn't want you to have lowered yourself to thievery because of how our relationship turned out."

"Revenge," she said. "It was revenge."

He nodded. "Which I drove you to. And I couldn't let you walk away with that kind of attitude. It's not you, Megan. I couldn't see you lowering your integrity because of me. I didn't want this ring, or me, to be responsible for doing that to you."

She stood with a whole new insight into Lewis. A glimpse of what was going on beneath that shrewd exterior of his.

"Yeah, this is a reminder to me, all right," he went on about his ring again. "A reminder that building up Sheldon Electronics was how I lost my family in the first place. My head and my heart and every bit of my time went into my business. That's how it was, how it had to be. I guess it impressed me in one sense, disgusted me in another. Then one day I realized that my business achievements completely overshadowed all my family achievements. I guess maybe…for some time…I didn't think I cared so much. I guess maybe now that I do, it's too late."

Megan and Gloria exchanged solemn looks.

"So…" Lewis stepped off the walk path and headed toward the edge of the river bank, "hopefully, Megan, I've cleared you of the ring hex…and I guess now it's time that I cleared myself of it, too." He drew his arm back, then shot it forth as hard as he could, throwing his ring into the Mississippi.

"Lewis!" Megan rushed to his side, startled at what he'd just done.

But he turned with a smile of relief on his face. She guessed she understood.

Fifteen

"Here…I hope this makes you feel better." Will brought a bowl of vegetable soup in to Megan on the couch that night.

"Thank you." She was cold and tired and sat with a blanket wrapped about her legs.

When Will had come home from work he'd found her just that way—sitting, staring, doing nothing. "You're worrying me lately, Megan. You were like this last night and now again tonight. Maybe you should get a check-up or something."

"I'm fine," she said.

"You're not fine. I can see you're not fine."

"Okay, I'm not, but I will be." The soup was good. It was hot and nourishing and seemed to help. She paused between spoonfuls to give the concerned Will a slight smile. "I'm just a little worn out lately. Aren't you eating?"

"Yeah." He went to get himself a bowl.

"I called in sick to work," she told him. "Nick didn't like it, but I'm sure Pam can cover since it's only a Wednesday."

"I'm sure she can," Will agreed.

"How was shipping today?" she asked.

He came back, trying to eat his soup as he walked. He took the chair across from her. "It was okay. Physical—as in lift, carry, put it here, put it there. Rough—but nowhere near as rough as being on stage."

"Come on…you have *fun* on stage."

"It *looks* that way." A quick grin flashed over his face.

"So you'll probably be glad when some day you can give up the shipping," she assumed.

"Yeah. Someday. When all my debts are paid off. Some day when I'm singing in a place bigger and better than the Rusty Door…as my mother says."

"How about recordings?"

Will laughed. "A dream beyond dreams."

"You could do it. Make a demo, get an agent."

"What's *your* dream, Megan?"

She gave it some thought while finishing her soup. Then she set her empty bowl on the end table and said, "To be a waitress in a place bigger and better than the Rusty Door." She laughed, causing Will to laugh, also. More seriously, she added, "To become my own person, to believe in myself more and not be such a follower."

Will ate the rest of his soup, then took both his and her empty bowls to the kitchen sink and washed up the few dirty dishes and pans that were there.

Megan snuggled further down on the couch and felt herself begin to drift in and out of a comfortable doze, a welcome escape.

Later, after Will had showered and changed clothes for the Door, he came to stoop down beside her. "How you doing?"

She opened her eyes to his closeness. He looked and

smelled wonderful. She felt sad that he would be leaving. "I'll miss your music tonight."

"That's why I thought I'd play something special just for you before I go."

He had his acoustic guitar from the bedroom. He backed over to the chair and sat down with it. His fingers moved gently over the strings, creating a very soft, affecting melody. One Megan had never heard before. One that was even more soothing than the bowl of soup had been.

She listened, with the blanket drawn up to her chin and her eyes heavily falling closed again.

Thursday night Megan was back on her waitressing job.

She was rested, though not entirely over thinking about the twenty seven hundred dollars...like where she could get it and how much longer she could keep this mess from Will.

Leon took her aside on one of her frequent trips to the kitchen. "Meggie, Willie said you were sick last night."

"Yes, I was."

"Annie and I missed you."

"Thanks."

"What was wrong?"

"Everything. Only everything."

"Sorry. Sounds bad. Want to talk about it?"

She stopped walking and turned face to face with him. She wanted to tell him, of all people. She started to...except Ann came along right then.

"Hi, guys—" she intruded flippantly. "Why the long faces?"

Leon gave her a quick kiss and hug. "Hi, hon."

Amidst Leon's affection, Ann maintained a curious fixed look upon Megan. "Aren't you over whatever you had last night? You look kind of puny."

Megan exploded, "Ann, why don't you go phone your mother!"

"Huh...?" Ann blinked her eyes.

There were other problems. So many other problems, Megan thought, besides just those of her financial debts.

Ones she could maybe actually do something about. Like, for instance, Ann and Gloria. "She's a wonderful person. She loves you very much, don't you know that? She doesn't deserve to be treated like crap. I think...I think you'd just better learn to appreciate her and be thankful you have her."

"What is this?" Ann balked. "Why are you attacking me about my mother?"

"Because I like her and don't like how you treat her."

"Oh, really. Well, maybe I have my reasons. Maybe I—"

"There are no reasons, Ann. No reasons at all for the way you treat her."

"Oh, yeah? What about her being too domineering and—"

"She's your *mother.* Of *course* she wants to be involved with your life. It's not because she's interfering or domineering, it's because she's loving and caring. Give her a chance, Ann. Just give her a chance. Maybe *you'll* be a mother someday."

Ann's mouth dropped wordlessly.

"You do love her, don't you?" Megan persisted.

"Well, yeah..." Ann said, "but—"

"She needs you. And I think if you can be really honest with yourself you'll admit that you need her too."

Ann looked at Leon, then back at Megan. It all seemed to finally be getting through to her. Enough so that her disposition soon sweetened. "Okay, okay—I'll go call her." She headed off to the back hall phone.

Leon laughed and shook his head at Megan. "You have an amazing affect on people, you know?"

She nodded, but was more somber about it than he. "I must have. Because I got a twelve hundred dollar loan out of Nick, and Lewis's ring back from the loan sharks."

"So you did borrow from Nick after all?"

"Yes. And he was nice about it."

Leon shrugged. "Hey—okay then—mission accomplished. Why so gloomy?"

"Because—"

"What, Meggie? What?" His concern heightened.

"Because I'm also very stupid."

Pam brushed past the two of them on her way to the kitchen, warning Megan, "Nick is watching, and your customers are growing restless."

Leon clasped Megan's arm before she could get away. "I want the whole thing here and now, Meggie."

"I have to wait on customers."

"Not until you tell me what's wrong."

She felt the resolve within her break. "I *lost* the twelve hundred Nick lent me and I couldn't pay Henry and Stan after all."

"*What*?" Leon gasped.

"Lost. Like dropped and someone else found it."

"God, Megan!"

"They'd upped the twelve hundred to fifteen hundred, so it wouldn't have been enough anyway. They're giving me till tomorrow night. Now I owe them *and* Nick. Nothing's solved. Only worse."

Leon's eyes were large with rage. He still had a tight grip on her arm.

She continued with the most important part. "Leon, I can't tell Will, so don't *you* go telling him because he's just now gotten himself away from gambling and I don't want him forced back to it. And forget any ideas of hassling Lewis any more because I…I'm actually kind of feeling sorry for him now."

Leon gave a sigh. "*Sorry* for him? Geez, Meggie…you *have* been sick."

"Yeah, sick." She moaned, looking beyond him. "Oh-oh—Nick is coming this way. I've got to get back to my tables."

Megan's customers, as though making up for lost time, were at her right and left for drinks. She covered them quickly, jotting their orders onto her note pad.

The Sidetracks were playing exceptionally loud and well. All four of the guys were completely submerged in their music. Megan wished she felt half as spirited as they did. But the pressures and worries in her mind failed to lighten.

When Will caught her pausing from her own work to watch him, he acknowledged her with a quick smile and nod. She waved to him, but was much closer to tears than to smiling.

Will switched from guitar to tambourine. He slapped it against his thigh, then to the heel of his hand, then into the air. Slap, slap, slap—shake, shake. Slap, slap, slap—shake, shake. He and Vince broke into their ever affecting harmony,

"I hear the night calling, calling
I hasten to a place I've never been
I feel myself falling, falling
Only you can save me, my friend..."

Megan's night at the Door had been long and tiring. It felt good finally getting home to the apartment at one-thirty A.M. Will had stopped on the way for a take-out pizza and they sat on the living room floor to eat it. A burning candle glowed from the end table near them and made for a peaceful, cozy setting.

"I love pepperoni," Megan said, surprised that she had any appetite at all.

"Me, too." Will finished off his third slice to her one.

"Your music was great tonight."

"I thought it was great *every* night," he teased.

"It is." She smiled her first smile in some time.

"Megan..." He pulled a rolled-up paper out of his hip pocket, "you know that second stop I made on the way home tonight?"

"I wasn't paying much attention. Just that you ran in and out of some place very quickly. Yeah, I remember that much. Why?"

"It was to get this." He spread open a small newspaper on the floor next to the pizza box.

It was a Racing Form, and she was not at all happy about recognizing it. "Oh, Will...no."

His look was set with determination. "One last time, Megan."

She rose quickly to her feet. This was the last straw in her difficult day. "Why, Will, why? You said you were through gambling. You—"

"It's not for me." He stood up closely beside her. "This one last time is for you, Megan."

The picture cleared. Suddenly she *hated* Leon. "He told you! I told him not to and he went ahead and did it anyway!"

"Hey, Leon's *my* friend too, you know. I'm glad he did."

"Well, I'm not." She went to the window to stare blankly out at the darkness.

Will came over beside her. "Looks like you've been trying to solve a very big problem way over your pretty little head all by yourself."

"It's not going to help any, putting it over *your* head as well."

"Megan, you shouldn't have thought you had to handle all this all alone without telling me."

"It's my problem, Will. *Mine.*"

"You gave the ring to *me* to pay off Henry and Stan—that makes it *my* problem too."

"It was me who *took* the ring from Lewis, so that makes it more *my* problem."

"I can't believe you borrowed money from Nick to buy the ring back from Henry and Stan."

Her anger swelled as she decided to tell him the worst of it. "Try believing I *lost* the money and now owe the sharks *plus* Nick."

"Yeah...yeah, Leon told me everything."

"Great, just great," she moaned.

"Don't you think I want to know everything that's going on with you and help?"

"You just gave up gambling. Why should I expose you to big money problems that might drive you right back to it. And see...you did exactly what I was afraid of. You turned to the horses."

"Megan, it's the only way I know how to even *try* helping here."

"Aren't you listening? I don't *want* you to help." She walked away from the window, from him. She paced the limited space of the small apartment.

Will followed her, waving the Racing Form. "You're in this because of me, and it's up to me now to help you out of it. Just accept that."

"No."

He kept after her. "Megan..."

"No."

"Megan, be realistic."

She stopped. "Okay, if I'm in it because of you, it's because of your *gambling*. Do you think it's a good way to try getting *out* of it by the same means you got *into* it?"

"Yeah," he laughed. "Yeah."

She herself weakened into a helpless laugh. "You're crazy! You know that? Crazy!"

He took her by the arm and made her sit down with him on the couch. "Totally Mine is racing tomorrow. My horse, Megan, he's my horse."

"He didn't win last time."

"I know. But he's good. And he wins *most* of the time. He'll do it for me this time, I know. For *us*."

"It takes money to make money, remember. How are you going to win money if you've none to bet?"

He took a wad of bills out of his shirt pocket. "Seven hundred. Two from Randy, two from Vince, one each from Jeff, Joe and Leon. They all invested...because they know the situation and believe in my saying that this is a one last time...for you, Megan."

She shook her head disbelievingly. "They all...they..."

"Look, they've known exactly what I've been going through with this gambling stuff for a long time now. They don't want me starting up again, that's for sure. But they know about the mess you're in because of me and they agree I should give it one more shot. For you. They all know how I feel about you, Megan." An endearing look came over him that seemed far more meaningful than the point of their arguing. "Don't *you* know by now?"

"I...I do..." She stood, leaving him and the couch. "That's what I'm the most afraid of here, Will." She returned to the window.

He followed her there. "Don't be afraid, Megan."

She looked at him, at his face that was so soft and sincere in the candle light. "I'm tired of being disillusioned. I'm...I'm just so tired..."

"I won't let you down, Megan."

"This wasn't suppose to happen. Us, everything."

"That doesn't mean we can deny it."

She walked away from him again. "This was only supposed to be a financial arrangement, Will. A *financial arrangement*."

He held up the money to her, grinning in that way of his. "Financial it is, wouldn't you say?"

He made her laugh again. As always. Yet she said, "I didn't want to get this involved."

"Neither did I."

"I'm not sure of anything I'm doing anymore."

"I know. Me neither."

"I'm so confused."

"We'll be confused together, okay?"

She could no longer resist him. She went to lay her head against his chest. "I can't fight you, Will."

"Good." He put his arms around her.

"I'm scared."

"Me, too."

"I've had some bad relationships."

"Hey, me, too."

"I don't want to get hurt again."

"I won't hurt you, Megan."

"Do you have a guarantee?"

"I have seven hundred dollars in my pocket. Plus this." He kissed her.

"Do you think Totally Mine will win tomorrow?" she asked.

"Yeah." He kissed her again.

Sixteen

Will called in sick to his new job Friday morning, then spent the next several hours preparing for the track.

"You're enjoying this too much," Megan said of his deep enthrallment with the Racing Form.

"Would it be better if I tried to hate it?" He made a fake frown at her.

"It would be better if you didn't need to do this at all anymore."

"One last time, Megan," he reminded her. "One last time to clear up this big problem of ours. *Ours*," he stressed. He handed her his empty mug. "Would you mind getting me some more coffee, please?"

She went for his refill. No matter what he said, she still felt guilty for turning him back to gambling. "What if Totally Mine doesn't win?" she worried. "Then in addition to owing twenty-seven hundred we'll owe seven hundred besides. Oh, Will...I don't know, I don't know."

He had some lines highlighted in yellow on the form before him. "Total looks better this time. Plus he's going a mile rather than six furlongs and is getting Howard."

Megan took him his coffee and settled herself into the chair across from him. "I don't know what any of that means, and I'm still feeling very insecure."

"What it means is that Totally Mine does better with distance, and Bret Howard is Canterbury's top jockey. It means we've got it made, Megan."

"But what if we don't?"

He shook his head, grinning at her. "Well, what if we *do*? Come on, Megan, think positive."

"I'm scared. I'm just so scared."

"Megan, it's going to work. We'll get this problem out of the way and then maybe we can start concentrating more on each other."

"Maybe that scares me too."

He sprang to his feet, dropping the Racing Form along with his good mood. "Hell, life *alone* is scary! Don't you know that? Haven't you ever known that before now?"

"Don't get mad."

"I'm not mad."

"You *sound* mad."

"I'm...I'm just *scared*."

Together they broke into a hearty release of laughter, which was precisely what they needed.

They got out to the racetrack early and roamed the grounds in an anxious wait for the mutual windows to open. Totally Mine wasn't listed until the third race, but Will wanted to make a couple of minor bets on the first and second.

They ate junk food and eventually took seats on the outside benches. Megan kept her eye on the weather. "Will, it looks like rain."

He, too, checked the sky, though with less concern. "That's okay. We can go inside and watch through the glass."

"The horses. What about the horses?"

"They won't melt."

"They'll still run if it rains? But won't that alter the odds?"

He laughed fondly at her. "Hey, you're really getting into this, aren't you? Okay, yeah...it would throw things off some if it rained. But not necessarily for the worse. Totally Mine happens to be a pretty good mud-runner. So if it wants to rain, let it rain."

He'd no more than said it when a few scattered drops began to fall. They sat it out through the first race. Will had twenty to place on Blue Jack. The horse came in first and Will cut himself down for not having bet to win. Anyway, he cleared twenty-five dollars. It wasn't bad, though was hardly a drop in the bucket to what they needed.

"This calls for another hot dog." He took Megan by the hand and started toward a concession. They stayed inside the grandstand for the second race. They watched through the big glass windows and also on the TV monitors.

It was bad news. The horse Will chose to win came in *sixth*. To console himself he bought a pretzel. Megan was full and didn't want anything more. The only thing she did want was to get the mounting tension of race three over with.

Will placed their whopper of a bet on Totally Mine then kept the ticket tightly grasped in his hand. "If he does it for us, Megan, we'll be able to make a complete payoff. Do you realize that? *Complete*."

"What if he doesn't?"

"Let's stay positive."

She forced a smile.

"A kiss for luck?" he asked.

They drew together for a warm good-luck kiss. Then they went outside, preferring to watch this race close up. A misty rain was falling, but they didn't mind. They went down to the track fence. There were six minutes left till post time.

Totally Mine paraded back and forth in his final pre-race showing. His reddish-brown coat shone as much from the wetness as it would have from the sun. And his grace and pride seemed uninhibited by the sloppy track. Bret Howard rode him with the confidence of winning.

Megan and Will left the fence and walked back to the bench area. The horses soon entered the starting gate. Will grasped Megan's hand tightly. The bell. The announcer shouting, "They're off!"

Totally Mine was in the lead right from the start. But he had the entire length of the track ahead of him to hold. His long slender legs sliced through the air, hoofs kicking back spats of mud.

Megan and Will jumped up and down beside one another, screaming and yelling and cheering their horse, as if his ability to win lay strictly in them.

Totally Mine seemed destined for winning. There seemed to be no doubt. Until the home stretch. Where things often had the tendency for quick change. Where a gray horse called Winkler passed him at the last moment like a shot from a cannon. Totally Mine crossed the finish line in second place.

Megan and Will sank down onto the bench together. They let go of hands. Megan's was nearly numb from the squeezing Will had given it. The hand holding, the cheering, the mega-buck bet…nothing made the race come through for them. Their one chance to meet their huge financial debt was gone. Gone.

Will tore his ticket to shreds and threw the pieces to the wind. Then he walked down ahead of the benches to the track fence. Megan stayed in place, watching him, feeling far more sad for him than for herself. He stood there waiting for Totally Mine to come back down the track past him toward the stables.

Eventually the horse came, slowing to a trot, head high, eyes blinking against the rain. Bret Howard was stroking his mane, as if consoling him that second place was okay.

As they passed along the fence, Megan heard Will call

out, "You're a great horse, Total! I love you anyway!"

He left the fence and lagged back to her. "I'd still bet on him anytime," he said.

She gave him a hug. "Will, we tried."

"I really thought he would make it."

"I know. Me too."

"Yeah...well...that's the way it goes." He put his arm around her waist. "Let's go home."

The two of them were quiet on the ride back to Minneapolis, and even more quiet at the apartment. Neither wanted any supper. Will slumped down onto the couch while Megan showered and got ready for work.

He offered to drive her to the Rusty Door, but she said it was okay, that she'd catch a bus. "I don't *mind* taking the bus," she assured him. "I like buses, I really do. Besides, the rain has stopped and the clean fresh air will do me good."

She paused beside him before leaving. "Are you going to be all right, Will?"

He gave her his ever wonderful grin. "Why wouldn't I be? I'm more used to losing than winning."

"Maybe Henry and Stan will let us work something out."

"Yeah, they *love* working things out."

"I'll see you later. Okay?"

"Right."

Neither the fresh air nor the bus ride lifted Megan's mood as she'd hoped. She couldn't stop worrying about how she, or as Will would put it, *they,* were going to pay all that money back. Payments would take forever. And as for Henry and Stan, she rather doubted that they would take them at all, not to mention their outrageous interest. She also worried about having left Will there alone back at the apartment in the low mood *he* was in. She could only hope that time would ease him out of it before he came to the club to sing.

"What's wrong?" It didn't take Nick long to notice and ask her soon after she'd arrived at her job.

"Nothing," she answered.

"It doesn't *look* like nothing," he insisted.

"I said nothing."

"You're not smiling."

"Look," her anxiety surfaced to a quick temper, "I'm here on time, I'm going about my work, and I'm not causing any scenes. Isn't that enough?"

"I'm concerned about you, that's all."

"I'm fine." Realizing how needlessly short she'd been with him, Megan got a hold of herself, took a deep breath and managed to at least say in a much softer tone, "I'm fine, Nick. Thanks. But if you'll excuse me, a new customer just sat down." She hurried off, leaving her boss standing there.

At nine o'clock on the dot the Sidetracks, in their western shirts and jeans, took the stage. Will announced, "Hi! We're the Sidetracks and ready to kick it loose!"

It was a welcomed lift, finally having lively music shaking the place. At least Megan, more than anyone, needed it. She took time from her busy waitressing to listen and watch. Will seemed okay now, in much better spirits than he'd been at the apartment. His body rocked, bent and twitched in time to the loud fast rock number as he sang into the mike,

"Breakin' down to twenty
Twenty more minutes till I see you
Closin' in on fifteen
Fifteen more miles down the road..."

"Can we get some service over here?" a gruff voice interrupted Megan's concentration on the music.

She turned to see the table in need. It was Henry and Stan, sitting down in her section. Her heart skipped a beat. She started toward them.

"May I take your order?" she asked coolly.

"Yeah," Henry sneered, "we'll have fifteen hundred dollars, please."

Megan looked around, hoping that nobody heard him. But everyone nearby seemed only attentive to the band.

Stan grabbed Megan's wrist. "You got it, Missy?"

"Megan," she corrected him.

"Megan," he said, eyes glaring, grasp like a vice.

"You're hurting me," she said.

"It could get worse," he warned, "if you don't pay us the money.

"I...I..." She couldn't think of anything to say.

Henry guessed. "You wouldn't be trying to say that you still don't have it, would you?"

"I...I..." Her wrist had no more circulation. "Let me go."

When Stan released her, she rubbed the red mark he'd left.

"So you need another extension?" Henry guessed again.

"Yes," she said, so desperately that she hoped they'd go for it.

"You want to pay us later?" Henry verified.

"Yes."

He began to nod, all too willingly. "Okay...later it is. Like how about nine forty-five? The time of your boyfriend's first break. That late enough?"

"*No.*" She'd hoped to obtain days, or weeks, not just minutes.

"More time than you deserve," Henry stated. "Both of you meet us in the parking lot at nine forty-five and we'll see if we can't get this resolved...somehow."

The loan sharks got up and left, heading toward the back exit. They were going out there to take their stand and wait. And nine forty-five was bound to come all too soon.

Megan returned to watching Will sing. He seemed unaware of Henry and Stan's presence. The club was so crowded he probably hadn't caught sight of them at all. That was good. For now.

It was her last chance to think. Think. Of what? She saw Nick over by the bar. But no, she couldn't go to him for more money. And there was Joe behind the bar, but she couldn't ask him. And Leon...he'd just walked in with Ann. Even Leon, as good a friend as he'd always been to her, wouldn't be able to help her out of this one. She was sorry, so sorry about everything.

• • •

Rocking…strumming…singing…Will was feeling high. High on music, high on hope, high on knowing that everything was going to be all right. There was passion in his voice and in his heart. He'd definitely come alive again since earlier at the apartment.

Randy's drums pounded the pace. Jeff's bass delivered the soul. Vince's guitar the melody. Will stood forth in the middle front, strumming rhythm. Singing lead. Tapping his foot. Loving his place, his life, Megan.

• • •

When Will came looking for Megan later, she was so tense she hadn't even noticed that the music had stopped. That the Sidetracks were on break.

"Where are they?" he asked.

She gave him a dazed look. "Who? Oh, you mean Henry and Stan?"

"Haven't they showed up yet?" He fleetingly looked through the crowd.

She nodded.

"You've seen them? Talked to them?"

She nodded again.

"So where are they now?" he asked. "In the lot? Come on—" He pulled her by the hand.

She tried holding back. "No, Will, no! We can't go out there!"

"It's okay," he laughed, still pulling her along. "I took care of things. Don't worry."

"But we don't have the money."

He didn't seem concerned. How could he not be concerned? Megan didn't understand. She followed his lead through the club. He kept her hand, making sure that she did.

They went out the back door. It was quiet and the air had that nice clean-washed smell from the earlier rain. It was indeed a nice night, except for what was about to happen. She cringed at the sight of the sharks

"Hey, Missy—" Henry called out before she and Will got all the way to them, "bring your bodyguard along?"

"That's right!" Will responded for her. "I'm it."

"Heard you took a dive at the track this afternoon," Stan said, as though it was to his pleasure.

Will didn't seem to mind.

Megan minded. "Will, I didn't tell him about that. I don't know *how* he knew."

"We have our sources," Henry sneered.

"Well, I, too, have my sources," Will said mysteriously. "Sources *beyond* the track."

"Oh, yeah?" Stan tested. "Like another hot ring or something?"

"No." A wide confident grin came over Will's face. "Like...you might say another sort of horse."

What did *that* mean? Megan wondered. She thought he'd said sources *other* than the track. Now he was talking horses again.

Henry also looked confused. "So you *did* get in a lucky bet after all."

"No. No bet," Will said. He let go of Megan's hand so that he could reach into his pocket. He withdrew a wad of money and handed it over to Henry. "Fifteen hundred. Go ahead and count it."

Henry took it and thumbed through the edges.

"Will," Megan whispered closely at him, "where did you get it?"

"I got it this afternoon after you left the apartment," was his strange and incomplete explanation.

"It's all here," Henry verified. "Okay, Westin...guess we're square. You're off the hook till next time."

"There won't be a next time," Will assured him.

"Yeah..." Stan honored him. "Well, what the hell...you two hardly seem right for this sort of stuff anyway." He offered a handshake to Will.

Will refused it, in a way that indicated he'd already gone his limit.

"Sorry we had to get rough that one night," Stan made a surprising apology.

Will said nothing.

Henry had a last word for Megan before he and Stan left for their car, "You know, I'll always think of you when I eat broccoli."

She broke a quick smile.

"What did he mean by that?" Will asked her as they stood watching the loan sharks go down the aisle.

She giggled. "Just another part of this whole crazy thing I might tell you about some day. But tell me first, what about the money? Where did you ever get it? You said from *some other kind of horse.*"

He grinned. "That's right. An old Mustang that was still in good running shape."

"Your *car?* You sold your car?" No…no. How could he do that? It'd meant so much to him.

He nodded, acting proud but surely feeling some pain. "I put a lot of good care into that car over the years. Guess it paid off, probably better than any race ever had."

"Fifteen hundred? You got fifteen hundred for it?"

"Yeah."

"Who bought it? Who would pay that much and on such short notice?"

"Nick."

"*Nick*?" she exclaimed. "I don't believe it."

"Believe it, Megan."

"You went to *Nick*? But you *hate* Nick."

"No, I never said I hated him. Actually, he's not so bad. We had this talk. Besides the car. He says he's tired of managing the Door, and guess what—he wants to discuss with me and the band his interest in managing the Sidetracks."

"Really?" Megan's excitement surged as high as Will's.

"He feels he can take us a lot farther in our career than where we are right now. So what do you think of that?"

She went up and down on her toes. "Wow—Nick really wants to manage the Sidetracks? Who would have ever thought?"

"Yeah. How about that. Good idea though, don't you think? It's probably our missing link."

"It's...well, I just can't believe it, that's all."

"I know."

"But Will, *your car.* What about your car? You loved it. How can you get along without your car?"

"I can. I will. Megan...it's *you* I just don't think I could ever get along without. I love you."

They kissed. Then started back to the club.

"But I still owe Nick twelve hundred," she reminded him.

"I know. He said we'd work something out, not to worry."

"'And the guys...the seven hundred you owe the guys?"

"They said they'd wait. As long as I don't try getting it back for them by way of the track."

In a dazed sort of way, Megan was relieved with how well everything seemed to be working out. "I can't believe this, *any* of this. Especially about Nick."

Will shook his head. "You never know about people, do you? You just never know. I did know that he always really liked our music. And that he'd always done a good job managing the Door. I just never knew he was thinking of putting *our music* and *his managing ability* together. Anyway...I guess we'll see how it goes."

"It will go *fine*, Will, I know it will." She had never felt so positive in her whole life. She smiled and snuggled up to him for another kiss.

The Sidetracks resumed playing, strong, loud, their usual perfection, while Nick sat at a table, with a drink, watching them with a whole new perspective.

When Gloria came to the Door later and sat at the bar to spend some time with Joe, Ann surprisingly went over to greet her and join her for a while.

Megan jumped at the chance to have Leon to herself for a moment. "Thanks for being such a brat," she blurted out to him.

"Excuse me?" he questioned her attack.

"For going ahead and telling Will about my money

problem even after I'd specifically told you not to."

"You're *thanking* me?"

"Yes—because amazingly it all turned out for the best."

"Well, you see, Meggie, honesty is always the best policy, isn't it?" he rubbed it in.

"I do honestly know what a good friend you are, *Leony*." She threw her arms around him and hugged him dearly before going back to her waitressing.

At one o'clock, when the Rusty Door started closing, Will eagerly came to collect Megan. "Hi...ready to go?"

"Yes," she said, tired but happy.

"Will..." Gloria called to her son before he got away.

He stopped at the bar, with something to say to her as well. "Mom, I'm going to be paying you back every cent I ever borrowed. I've got this second job now and—"

"I know, I know..." She shooed it off as though it wasn't the most important thing to her right then. "That's good, dear, very good...but I just wanted to tell you—"

"Tell me what?" He looked at her curiously.

She smiled and touched his arm. "That I think Megan's hair is perfectly beautiful. *And* trustable."

Megan had no idea what that meant. Obviously something between the two of them, which now left her the curious one.

Will laughed and gave his mom a hug. "Thanks. That means a lot to me. Got to go now. Good-night."

"Hey—" the bartender was next to detain him. "I heard about the car sale. You two need a lift home? Gloria and I can drop you off."

"No thanks, Joe," Will told him. "We're going to take the bus."

"Bus?"

"Yeah, we'd kind of like to be alone."

"On a bus?" Joe laughed.

Will's attention was completely drawn back to Megan. In fact, there seemed to be little stars twinkling in his eyes, for which she felt entirely responsible. However, looking more at her than where he was actually walking, he bumped hard into a chair and fell partly over it. "You're *doing* it to me again," he teasingly blamed her for the distraction that she was.

Megan giggled and took his hand to lead him safely through the rest of the club.

They left the Rusty Door and started across the side parking lot. They strolled past the black Mustang that now belonged to Nick. Will gave the TRACK license plate a fond last stroke. Then putting his arm around Megan, they headed for the bus stop.